CRIMEUCOPIA

WE'LL BE RIGHT BACK - AFTER THIS!

A Murderous Ink Press Anthology

****

CRIMEUCOPIA
WE'LL BE RIGHT BACK - AFTER THIS!

First published by Murderous-Ink Press

Crowland

LINCOLNSHIRE

England

www.murderousinkpress.co.uk

Paperback Edition ISBN: 9781909498426

eBook Edition ISBN: 9781909498433

Acknowledgements

To those writers and artists who helped make this anthology what it is, I can only say a heartfelt Thank You!

Additional thanks must go to Jim Guigli for his assistance.

And to Den, as always.

Contents

Rock and a Hard Place Magazine Issue 7 includes Jim Guigli's short story *Looking for Mishka.*

The cat and the tattooist and the old lady and the missing man.

Paperback 9798985290431
$12.99
eBook/Kindle
9798985290448
$2.99

Approaching his sixth-floor office in the Cahuenga Building, Marlowe —
No. That's not it.
The pulsing red neon sign on Sunset outside his hallway window painted the frosted glass panel in Lew Archer's office door.
No. That's not it.
The day-dreaming Bart Lasiter was in Sacramento, not Los Angeles. He'd been trying on the personae of his favorite fictional private detectives as he approached his own office door.
Still, there really was a pulsing red light. It was behind the frosted glass panel in the top half of his office door. With each pulse the painted letters on the glass glowed: *Lasiter Investigations*
One hand holding a warm, aluminum-foil-wrapped super burrito, his other turning the key in the lock, Bart entered and moved straight to the answering machine.

Don't Touch That Dial!

(An Editorial of Sorts)

So has it really been a nine-month hibernation? It's been a bit of a rollercoaster, but it looks like things are getting back to the usual CRIMEUCOPIA chaos once more – thus proving that publishing short crime fiction is either an addiction or a genetic compulsion.

Does that mean we will actually be keeping to our original plan of 4 anthologies a year? I doubt it, but that's just another part of the chaos after all.

This is the first of several 'Free 4 All' collections that were supposed to be themeless. However, with the number of submissions that came in, it seems that this could be called an *Angels & Devils* collection, mixing PI & Police alongside tales from the bad guys. Mind you, that's not to say that all the PIs & Police are Good Guys – though hopefully this collection is not too NOIR for some.

Jim Guigli opens this collection with a *Bart Lasiter* outing in **Blood on the Stairs**, and Glen Bush gives it to us totally stone cold in **Cold Eyes, Cold Blood**.

Under the Table sees the humorous return of Edward Lodi, and Cate Moyle makes her Crimeucopian debut with **A Jeweled Anniversary**, before I present the initial 'origin' story in the *Tomaso Memindip* series of short stories. This is Memindip's second MIP appearance – his first was in the *Murderous Ink Press Sampler*, **Criminal Intent**, with the second in the series, *Memindip and the Persian Poet*.

From there, another new Crimeucopian, Bob Ritchie, gives us an English lesson with his **Learning Vocabulary with the Jence Brothers**, while Michele Bazan Reed takes us back in time and introduces us to **The Devil's Accountant**.

Cruel as the Grave sees Eve Fisher raise a smile, and the word count, before we get into the slightly more darker humour of Michael Wiley's *All That Glitters*.

Joan Hall Hovey returns with *A Long Dark Road*, before our third and final new Crimeucopian takes centre stage, and J. T. Seate explains about the perils of a *Deadly Sideshow*.

And to close out this anthology we have the equally darkly humorous Madeleine McDonald with her *Watching Over You*.

This time around has not only seen a move to a larger paperback format size, but also in regard to the length of the fiction, as well. Followers of the somewhat bent and twisted Crimeucopia path will know that although we don't deal with flash fiction as a rule, it is a rule that we have sometimes broken. And let's face it, if you cannot break your own rules now and again, whose rules can you break?

Oh, wait, isn't that the basis of the crime fiction genre?

Oh dear....

As with all of these anthologies, we hope you'll find something that you immediately like, as well as something that takes you out of your comfort zone – and puts you into a completely new one.

In other words, in the spirit of the Murderous Ink Press motto:

You never know what you like until you read it.

Blood on the Stairs

(A Bart Lasiter Mystery)

Jim Guigli

A shout down in the entrance lobby cut into Bart Lasiter's quiet morning and ritual study of *The Sacramento Bee*. His live-in office was up on the third floor, but the thin walls of his Old Town historic building held back no sound above a whisper. He thought he'd heard a sharp single word, "No!" Then a muffled shriek of pain?

He set the newspaper down on his desk and listened. Was it nothing? Confrontation? Violence? Maybe, maybe not. Then he heard the lobby door slam, followed by the sound of someone outside running down the wooden sidewalk. After a few seconds, it was quiet again. Bart sighed and returned to his newspaper. Probably nothing.

Soon the quiet was again interrupted, now by a slow beat pulsing through his building. Someone was climbing the wooden stairs from the lobby. From his desk, Bart could usually identify each of his neighbors by the signature of their individual stair-climbing rhythm. But this new music, step by strange step, was foreign to him. This someone was not a neighbor. Bart thought this was a big person, or someone with heavy shoes, maybe both.

After pausing a few seconds on the second-floor landing, the visitor started up again. The steady slapping of foot to tread became louder as the pace became slower and unsteady.

Of course, it could be just an out-of-breath senior citizen here to see one of Bart's neighbors in another third-floor office. A new customer for the tax accountant?

Sitting at his desk, master of his domain, *Lasiter Investigations*, Bart didn't think so. He had a feeling. He observed his cat had a feeling, too.

Agamemnon, or Aggie, as the cat preferred, a fixed-male orange tabby, sat on his favorite corner of Bart's desk, closest to their office door. With his right ear cocked toward the hallway outside the office, Aggie's only movement was a tail twitch following each footfall. Guard cat.

Bart knew, and surely Aggie knew: The visitor had to be one of *those people*.

*****

Since that mystery writers' conference, *Crime Happens 2012*, had started earlier in the week, *those people* had been knocking on Bart's door. The first day it was just two during the morning, and then three after lunch. The next day there were dozens, starting at eight in the morning.

"You're a real detective?" a man asked, not sure, looking around Bart's tiny one-room office. "I didn't see your name in *PI Magazine*." Noticing Bart's single bed and mini-fridge behind a screen, he said, "This is really your office?"

At first, Bart hoped they might be new clients.

An older woman said, "No, Mr. Lasiter. I don't want to hire you. I just want to learn what I can about private detectives. For my stories. What was your biggest case?"

They all had questions.

"Ever shot anyone?" asked a young woman who avoided eye contact. "What *wouldn't* you do for a client?"

"URL?" a man asked.

"Earl?" Bart said.

"Uniform Resource Locater — your website address. You have a website, don't you? Blog? Twitter?"

"Blog? Twitter?"

Another woman said, "Glock? Use a Glock? Nineteen-eleven? Nine-mil or forty-five? Thirty-eight Super? Shoulder holster?" She must have been eighty.

Two women who said they were sisters asked, "How much do you charge? Do you take PayPal?" They told him they were in town, "For the Conference. At the New Coloma Hotel. All week."

Aggie hated the interruptions in his daily routine. After the first day, he stayed away from the office, prowling Old Town while he waited for *those people* to disappear.

One night, a group of five showed up late, near ten. Bart was already in his *Maltese Falcon* polka-dot pajamas, safe in bed reading. His pajamas were loud, but not as loud as the five mystery fans climbing his stairs. Their laughing echoed throughout the nearly empty building as they approached his office.

Aggie folded back his ears and hissed. He answered their pounding on Bart's office door with a low growl. Guard cat.

Bart jumped out of bed and rushed to open the door before they broke the glass. When he saw their faces, he detected they had just come from the conference hotel bar. When they saw his pajamas, they checked each other and grinned. A young woman stepped forward and spoke for the group. "Sorry Mr., uh" — she looked at a booklet in her hand, and then at his name on the glass in his door — "Lasiter, but we just heard about the list. Could we each, please, have one of your business cards?"

"Okay, okay. Wait here."

On the way to his desk for the cards, Bart heard some snorts and guffaws outside his door. He stifled his temptation to tell these people to get lost, adhering to his golden rule: Never annoy someone who might pay your bills.

"Here you go. Try to hold down the noise on your way out."

"Thank you!" They skipped down the stairs, laughing all the way.

Bart locked his door. Back in bed, he thought this was like last Halloween. Only in his mid-forties, he was beginning to feel old.

The next morning, a visitor explained. "The list? Here, in the Conference Program," she said, waving a booklet, its pages folded back. "They listed all the Sacramento private detectives and their addresses. You're the closest. I walked from the hotel. There's a free-book offer for registered Conference attendees who visit at least three of the private detectives on the list. Like a treasure hunt. You have a business card? I have to prove I was here."

"Your friends have taken all my cards — I'm all out. Sorry."

"Maybe you could write a note or something?"

"Wait." He reached across his desk for a mug full of yellow pencils. "How about this?" He gave her one of his *Lasiter Investigations* promotional pencils. Like his card, it carried his promise:

— I'm ready to help —

After spinning the pencil between her fingers to read all the printing on it, she smiled. "Cool. Thanks."

She must have told the others. After her, they all wanted pencils.

*****

A grunt followed by a heavy thud snapped Bart back to the present. The music from the stairs had ended abruptly with a blow that shook the floor and rattled the glass in his door.

Yikes. He had a feeling. He had a bad feeling.

He opened his door and peeked into the narrow hallway leading from his office at one end to the stairwell at the other end. He saw the morning sun through the hallway windows fall on an arm reaching up from the stairs and across the brown linoleum floor. A woman's hand and wrist, encircled with blue, yellow, and red plastic hoops, extended from a green satin jacket sleeve. The hand was open and cupped, like one from the spare-change people down on the street — tired, but hopeful, ready for donations. Please? Like she wanted a pencil. But there was no gesturing, no tambourine, no sound, no movement at all.

Bart approached the staircase. The hand belonged to, he guessed, a two-hundred-pound six-footer. She'd landed stretched out and twisted onto her left side, looking up and back toward him. Her round face, surrounded by short, purple-streaked brown hair, still had some color, but no smile. The look of sudden and final surprise in her wide-open eyes said he was too late to help her.

Bart bent down and felt for a pulse, but the blood in her veins was still.

He found a black cloth pouch attached to a cord around her neck. In the pouch's center, a clear plastic window covered a 3 x 5 white card:

Writers-Love-Readers, Inc.

Crime Happens 2012

Sacramento

The bottom of the card said she was — had been — Karen Wilcox, from Fox River Grove, Illinois.

One of *those people.* Bart had no sympathy for her. No pencil for you, Karen Wilcox. She'd wasted her last breath trying to reach his office. Must have really wanted to win that free book.

Aggie arrived and looked. Pleased that the stair thumping had stopped, he showed the same lack of concern he'd have for a rat he'd just beheaded. After a few seconds, with a subtle flash of his yellow-green eyes, that bored look returned to his orange face, and he padded back to Bart's office.

Aggie's disdain reflected Bart's attitude. Bart felt guilty. He didn't know this woman, but fortyish was too young to die. For a pencil. Okay, that might be why she came, but why was she dead?

Bart switched from witness to detective. Overdose? She didn't look like a user. Heart attack? Stroke? Could be. He saw her shoes, the percussion instruments of the stair-thumping music. Large and stylish, to Bart they were fashionable speed-laced evening-wear combat boots with gum-rubber cleats and a hint of Italian park ranger. But what did Bart know about shoes? Until a woman recently corrected him, he thought a Blahnik was a Croatian pastry.

Then, beyond the shoes, he saw it.

Blood on the stairs.

Fresh, stomach-turning-red blood traced a thin, wandering line of drips and splashes from around the corner on the second-floor landing, up the stairs until it disappeared beneath the woman. The woman's right arm and her leather purse rested behind her back. Bart carefully lifted her arm and moved the purse, which popped open. He saw a matching leather wallet, fat with cash. Not a robbery. Beneath the purse he found the blood trail's source, a stab wound in the back of her green jacket.

A murder victim, twenty feet from Bart's office door. Did this ever happen to Jim Rockford, a body outside his trailer door? This was bad news.

But the really bad news was the stabbing instrument. It stood up straight like a miniature yellow foul-line pole set in the grass-green outfield of her back. Bart looked closer — and froze.

The foul-line pole was a smooth, round, school-bus-yellow pencil. He didn't have to be a detective to know it was a number two. The eraser-end portion visible above the wet, red hole in her jacket read:

— I'm ready to help —

*****

The patrol officer diverted to Bart's building by the Sac-PD Dispatch was in her late twenties and athletic. Stepping carefully around the blood trail, she climbed the stairs, looking up toward Bart and Karen Wilcox. She stopped at Karen's feet. "Nice shoes." She reached up with her left hand to check for a pulse, while her right hand rested on the grip of her holstered pistol. "You called this in, Sir?"

"Yes. I'm Bart Lasiter. I found her here and called. My office is up here."

"I'm Schaefer. Officer Schaefer. Anyone else up there? In your office?"

"Just my cat."

"You didn't see anyone attack this woman?"

"No. I heard her coming up the stairs and fall here."

"All right, Mr. Laster. I want you to back up and lean against the windows behind you for a few minutes. Rest up. Do that for me."

"It's Las-*i*-ter, with one S." He began to spell it. "L-a-s-*EYE*-t —"

But she'd already turned from him to talk toward her shoulder and the microphone clipped to her dark blue uniform shirt. She talked and listened, but her eyes kept returning to Bart, like he was a coiled snake pretending to sleep. When she'd finished her call, her hand still rested on her pistol.

"Okay, Mr. Laster. Help is on the way."

Bart did as he was told. He leaned back against the street-side windows of the narrow hallway. He turned away from the young officer and bloody Karen Wilcox to look through the windows down onto Second Street.

While Bart waited, his mind sorted through possible suspects. He had no clue. It could have been one of *those people,* or it could have been a stranger who chose Bart's building at random and attacked the woman because she was there. That could happen in Old Town, just like almost anywhere in Sacramento.

But not with his pencil. Unless it was one he handed out months or years ago. But it looked fresh, not used. And why did Karen Wilcox, seriously wounded, climb the stairs? Was she in shock — total zombie mode?

The paramedics Bart had suggested in his call, just in case, pulled up, double-parked their ambulance, grabbed their equipment, and rushed into the building. They hustled up the stairs to Karen Wilcox. After a quick exam, they turned to Schaefer and shook their heads. "She belongs to the coroner now — we've got another call." Back down the stairs they went, slamming the lobby door on their way out.

An unmarked sedan arrived and double-parked across the street. A familiar muscular man forced into a business suit got out and stood looking up at Bart's building, staring at Bart in the window. "Help" had arrived.

Again, Bart had a bad feeling.

The lobby door slammed. Bart heard footfalls on the stairs again, but this time they sounded measured and strong. The man from the sedan appeared on the second-floor landing, looking down and following the blood trail. When he looked up, he saw the patrol officer, the body, and Bart. He shook his blond crewcut head.

"Okay, Schaefer. I've got it now. You go down to the street and wait for forensics."

"Yes, Sir. This is Mr. Laster. He called —"

"It's Las-*I*-ter. What did you screw up this time, Lasiter?"

"Good to see you, too, McGill."

★★★★★

McGill filled Bart's client chair, his accusing chin tucked into his neck, making his thick neck look even thicker.

"Is this your work, Lasiter? She didn't want to pay for your services, so you chased her and caught her in the lobby and stabbed her with your pencil? 'I'm ready to stab.' Yes?"

"Of course not."

"Why not?"

"I wasn't working for her, and I've never seen her before. And why stab her with my pencil? I could have *shot* her if I'd wanted. I've got a gun. Two, if you count my Wells Fargo," said Bart, now sitting behind his desk.

McGill unbuttoned his suit jacket and smiled.

"Maybe you're just too emotional and not decisive. The poet detective. Wait. Wells Fargo and Black Bart Lasiter — I remember that. Let's *see* those guns."

"Well, I *could* have shot her. If my guns weren't in the pawnshop."

"Where?"

"Capitol Pawn on K Street," Bart said in a strong, confident voice. "But...."

Bart didn't like the way this was going.

"Okay. I'll get them tested. Even if you didn't shoot her, I'd like to have the ballistics on record, in case you shoot anyone else."

"But I haven't shot anyone...lately."

"You wouldn't ob-*ject*, would you?"

"No...I guess."

"Pencils — give me your pencils."

"All of them?"

"Of course."

Bart opened his desk's center drawer and offered McGill his last five promotional pencils.

"This is it? Come on."

"That's all I've got left. In oh-seven I bought a case of them — five hundred. After five years I was down to a mug of them — maybe fifty — before the Crime-Happens people started taking them for their book contest, after they'd taken the last of my business cards. I was hiding those last five pencils."

McGill bagged the pencils and slipped them into a coat pocket. "You'll get your pencils back. Later. Maybe. I'll be down at the writers' convention. We want to go through her hotel room and interview anyone who knew her."

McGill stood and looked around Bart's office. His lower lip curled. "We'll talk. Don't go anywhere."

"*Conference*, not convention," said Bart.

"Whatever."

*****

When the forensics people and coroner had finished, Bart locked his office and left the building. He had to maneuver around a reporter and cameraman who were in the staircase filming the blood trail.

"Sir, did you see what happened here?"

"No. Didn't see anything."

"Wait. Do you have an office here? We want to ask you a few questions."

"No, no. Don't know anything. I was just getting my taxes done," Bart said, without turning back.

After a burrito down the street, and killing some time walking through Old Town, Bart checked to be sure all the TV people were gone. Coast clear, he returned to his office by the back stairs and fed Aggie. He went to bed early, hoping for sleep and peace. His sleep was sporadic, interrupted by slamming car doors down in the street. His address was temporarily interesting, if not infamous.

*****

Early next morning, Bart was at his desk, dressed and waiting for his coffee to perk, when his office door opened.

"Mr. Lasiter? My name is Pat...Patricia Callahan."

"Hello, Ms. Callahan. How can I help you?" He pointed at the Italian aluminum coffee pot shaking on his hotplate.

"Want some? Pop Tart?"

"Please, just Pat, and no, but thank you. I've already had some breakfast this morning, at the hotel."

"Okay. Please sit down."

She sat in his client chair and spent a minute settling herself before she looked up and said, "I want to hire you, Mr. Lasiter. I want you to find out who killed my friend, Karen Wilcox."

"Hmm. I'm not sure I can help you. Why me? You know the police are on this, and they have great resources. More than I have."

"See, I'm a mystery writer. Mystery writers — unless you're writing police procedurals — well, we know the police can't solve many cases. They're just not very good. And this happened right here, in your building. You're the closest. And not part of the police."

"True. I mean, it did happen here. You say she was your friend?"

"Yes, from back in Illinois. We traveled together to attend Crime Happens. People back home will want to know what happened."

While she talked, Bart sized her up. Like her friend, Karen, she was fortyish — but short and slight. Her sandy hair was thin and cut close, her features unremarkable, and her clothes like those a thousand others wore. What he really noticed was Pat reaching into her purse.

"What do you need to start?"

Bart thought, *finally,* he might receive some compensation for all his Crime Happens troubles. At least he needed money to replace the business cards and pencils they took.

"I like to start with a $500 retainer, against expenses — itemized, of course — and a hundred dollars a day."

Pat's face turned red, like a heat lamp over a rotisserie chicken. Her lips didn't move.

"$200?" he said.

She sucked in air like it was her last breath.

"$50?" he said.

"PayPal?"

"No. Cash or check."

She dug deep into her cloth purse and counted out fifty dollars in tens. Counted it twice.

Bart pulled a blank contract from a desk drawer and held it out to her.

"Oh. Can't we just do this on a handshake?"

"Okay, if that's what you want."

Bart put the blank form back into his desk and politely pressed Pat for details of Karen's history and enemies, and Pat and Karen's relationship. She was stingy with information.

"You're a smart detective. I trust you. You'll know where to look."

*****

Bart cleaned his coffee pot and mug, something he stuck to as routine, but the damage from the Pop Tart explosion in his microwave would have to wait. It was around 10:30 and he was just putting the pot back on its shelf when McGill shoved through his office door and sat down without a hello. Bart figured McGill had just finished his morning coffee, too, plus doughnuts and meetings.

"Did you learn anything from the Crime Happens people yesterday?" Bart didn't want to annoy McGill, but his curiosity wouldn't wait.

McGill rolled his eyes and looked up at Bart's ceiling. "Your fan work?"

"Most of the time."

"Too many people."

"Too many people?"

"Hundreds of them milling around the hotel. All ages, sizes, and shapes. Writers. Would-be writers. And writer groupies — they call them readers. And they're all obsessed with murder. Any murder. On a normal day, you'd suspect all of them. I had Billings and Jackson with me, but I could have used three more. Herding cats."

"At least they're interested."

"Not about this murder. Oh, a lot of them already heard about it, but only a few of them knew the victim and they weren't helpful. Except they gave me free bookmarks."

"Holding back?"

"I wish. It's more that *they* were interviewing *me* — no, *interrogating* me. They were critiquing my questions. They were *helping,* suggesting who did it. Maybe the Chief of Police, or the University President, or the mayor's son. They were telling me what books to read, mysteries where similar plots played out. Some were asking questions — *and* taking notes. *I'm* supposed to be the one taking notes. Nut jobs. I hated it."

"So, you didn't learn anything?"

"Besides a lot of them had your business card or pencil? No, I did learn something. Lasiter, do you know what a *cozy* is?

"A cozy? Something you put over a teapot?"

"Teapot? No, it's a book. A cozy is a kind of book."

"A book? What kind?"

"A mystery. A murder mystery, except sometimes it has recipes in the back."

"Recipes? What kind of murder mystery?"

"It's a story where an ordinary middle-aged divorced woman called the *Shero* — that's a she-hero — who's lived her whole life in a little town, or who has just returned after decades away from her little town, stumbles over a dead body. And that makes her 'deeply curious.' Always a homicide in the first chapter. The police focus on her or some friend of hers as the perp, while she races against the clock, stumbling and thrashing around, recklessly tempting danger, uncovering the town *secrets*, all while she romances her high school sweetheart, or some widower — he's expected to be *hunky* — and solves the crime herself...because the police are totally in-*ept, knuc-kle-dragging STUPID NEANDERTHALS!* You think we're stupid, too — don't you, Lasiter?"

"Troglodyte — I've heard a few say troglodyte. Not Neanderthal."

"What?"

"You know I don't think you're stupid, McGill. I was a cop, too. Remember?"

"A Berkeley cop. Separating angry mimes in People's Park doesn't count as police work."

"I just meant, did you learn anything about the murder, about Karen Wilcox?"

McGill's jaw tightened. "Lasiter, I always learn something. I'm getting to it. First, the coroner says, yeah, she bled out from the pencil-stabbing, but also the pencil nicked a lung, and then there was the fall at the top of your stairs. Hit her temple hard on your floor. Take your choice — your pencil or your floor."

"You make it sound like I did it."

"Why was she coming up here? Didn't she know she already had a pencil? In her back?"

"I don't know."

"Well, she was tough. Could use more women like her in police work."

"If you say so. What else?"

McGill smirked. "Then I got a rundown on several disagreements at the convention. About eight fights, but most of them were little tiffs about status. You can guess. Whose name gets top billing? Order of speakers at the Awards Banquet? They love dramatic conflict. Suspicions of vote-swapping in the award nominations. Tie votes on nominations and awards? Two authors had to be separated because they were each promised they would chair the *Quilts, Rubber Stamps, and Scrapbook* panel, and neither would concede to the other." McGill grinned. "They had to flip a coin."

Bart smiled. "Conflict Resolution 101."

"One fight was about names — the psychic-ESP people. Three different women claiming the same name, 'ParaNorma.' You'd think with ESP they'd be able to see the future and prevent conflict."

Bart was glad McGill was talking, but he wondered why he was also being, for him, so nice.

"Most of the convention people were from the west, but Wilcox was from Illinois. We got more background on her from her bio in their program than from asking questions. The people who said they knew her all had alibis or lacked motive. Some pointed to her writing partner, but when we interviewed her, she looked okay. People who knew her partner said she's not the violent type, and so far I have no reason to disagree. But we have a lead."

"A lead?"

"Lasiter, if you tell anyone this, your license is as dead as your pencil-seeking-writer."

"Tell what?"

"We lifted two good prints off the pencil in her back. As we told you, those were your prints —"

"And *I* told *you*, they're *my* pencils. I have to handle them when I give them away."

"Hold on to your spurs, Black Bart. I'm trying to tell you later we found a partial third print. *That's* what I don't want you to talk about. It's smaller than yours, maybe a woman's. We got it with the super-glue, but there were no hits with the FBI. SOL. Maybe she never got printed."

"Sorry. This whole thing about the pencil worries me. Was the pencil in her back sharpened, and how? Machine sharpened to a perfect point, or crudely whittled pen-knife style? All the ones I handed out were blunt, unsharpened."

McGill stood to leave. "Very sharp. Looked like from an electric sharpener."

"Hmm. Okay, let me know when you get something you can tell me."

*****

Bart thought about the Wilcox case while he consumed a burrito lunch and fed Aggie. Was he living in a cozy? If he'd walked into the hallway in the dark, he could have "stumbled over" Karen Wilcox. He certainly felt "deeply curious."

And he felt lost. It didn't feel right just sitting, paralyzed, waiting for something to happen. He owed himself and Pat Callahan some effort, pointless as it might be. He'd visit the people at the Conference. Maybe someone would say something useful.

*****

When he entered the Conference area of the New Coloma Hotel lobby, he quickly found he wouldn't be able to roam freely. A young woman stepped into his path. She was wearing a gold plastic badge announcing she was *Crime Happens* Staff.

"Sir, where's your entrance badge pouch? You're not registered? Sir, you can still register, just three-seventy-five. I'll take your credit card."

"Three dollars and —"

"Ha. You're making a joke, Sir, aren't you? Of course, it's three hundred and seventy-five dol —"

"Oh, I'm registered — for sure. I just misplaced my badge pouch."

"If you've lost your entrance badge, we can make a new one for you. Give me your registration receipt, or Social. I can look it up for you."

"Thanks, but later. I'm meeting someone now. In the bar."

Walking away before she could interfere with his plans, Bart noticed the street level public bar area of the hotel was full. Though the bar wasn't part of the Conference, he could easily identify the Crime Happens people by the little black pouches hanging from their necks.

Bart needed some cover. A Conference Program someone had left at the edge of a table caught his eye. He went to the table and, while looking away, sat on the program. After a moment, he stood with it in his hand. Turning pages, he stopped on Karen Wilcox's bio. People look better alive, even in a photo, than dead. He folded the booklet open to today's Panel Schedule. Now he belonged.

Next, to fill his other hand, he went to the *Prospectors Bar* to order a Classic Coke in a glass bottle. He had worked up a thirst on the walk over from his office.

Waiting for his Coke, Bart zeroed in on several groups of mostly women, all with black pouches, sitting on gray leather benches, chairs, and ottomans in the bar lounge area. The bartender, dressed in forty-niners' prospecting garb, handed Bart his Coke, and thumb-snapped one of his red suspender straps. Bart offered him a Pat Callahan ten and left a fifty-cent tip. Halfway to the lounge area, he counted his change and looked at the receipt for the Coke. Yikes.

An empty gray leather chair sat midway between two of the groups. Bart sank into the chair and relaxed. Tough day at the Conference. He sipped his coke and studied his Program while he listened. He listened, but had trouble sorting the wheat from chaff when both groups were talking at the same time:

"My agent is sooooo nice —"

"And I was all like, it ain't *happinin'*, and he was all like, oh *yeah* it is, and I was all like, uh-*uhh*."

"My agent is a creep."

"And like, I'd love a drink that actually has some alcohol in it."

"Wasn't the panel on forensics great?"

"I'll drink to that."

"Except for the moderator and her long, pedantic questions for the panelists. She even read them from a typed sheet."

"They should have a panel on drinks, *Mystery Drinks*."

"I almost forgot her. What a drone."

"Did you notice Mark and I were the only men out of — must've been fifty?"

Bart was ready to give up and move on when he heard something interesting from one group:

"So, did any of you know this Karen Wilcox, the murdered woman?"

"Wasn't she the one who wrote the Viet Nam thriller about the lesbian Rambo, Madison Steel? Or was Madison a SEAL? What was it? *Blond Hair, Dark Roots*?"

"No, that was another woman, Ellison Phillips, I think."

"Didn't Wilcox Chair the *Canine Crimes* panel? I think her latest hit was *Dogged Pursuit*, or was it *Doggone Murder*?"

"The Vic, she was the big gal in the green suit. I remember her from the first night, at the meet-and-greet. She was all bluster — life-of-the-party type. And she had some mousy writing partner."

"Yeah, Pat, Pat something."

"The little one. She's been strange since it happened, poor thing."

"Oh, her. The cops don't suspect *her*, do they? I'm Chairing the *Liars Panel*, and I'd trust her. She's not the type."

"But what *is* the type, except maybe someone who *isn't* the type?"

"I heard it was with a pencil. Someone stabbed her in the back with a pencil."

"That sounds like Mary Lazlo's book, *Crimson Holiday*."

"More like Becki Frankel's book, *School Teacher's Lesson*."

"No, *School Teacher's Revenge*."

"That Old Town PI's pencil, I heard. Stabbed with his pencil. Bart something. I got one from him. Guess the PI is too cheap to own a sharpener. Lived in his tiny office. The hotel has an electric sharpener in the room behind the check-in counter. When the desk clerk sharpened mine, he was doing a bunch of them. Must be worth more now than when I got it."

"Because it's sharpened?"

"No, because it's famous."

Yikes. Bart gave up on these people and took his Coke over to sit by an attractive woman he guessed was about his own age. She was sipping a tall vodka or gin drink with a lot of ice.

"Enjoying the Conference? I'm Bill." He'd almost said Bart.

"Yes, I always enjoy them. I'm Irene. This is my tenth *Crime Happens*."

"Irene, I'm thinking of going to this panel." He picked one at random and pointed to it in his Program: *Protagonists Overcoming Challenges*.

Swirling her drink, the ice cubes clinking, she said, "That's a good one. Used to be called *Handicapped Protagonists — Wheelchairs, Amputees, Dwarfs, and White Canes*. But then — well, you know how it is. Like last year, the Best First Mystery award went to an author whose protagonist was an ex-special-forces dwarf transgender amputee with PTSD. So, Bill, are you a writer?"

"No."

"Then you're a reader. What do you like to read?"

"I read some detective stories, PI stories. I love *The Maltese Falcon*. Read it at least twenty times."

"So old. Male private investigators — guy stuff. But if the PI is an ass-kicking woman, good. That's okay."

She dug into her Crime Happens book bag and pulled out a bookmark. When she handed it to Bart, he saw a book title and her name in gold script, Irene Kerrigan, printed over a soft-focus illustration of a tree-lined country path just before sunset.

"Here's what I like. *Country Secrets*. It's my latest, out next month."

"So, you're a writer, Irene. What's your new story about?"

She smiled. "It's a story of mystery, murder, secrets, and truth, betrayal, tradition, and romance."

"Wow. How does it go?"

"Well, it's a race-against-the-clock crime story where my Shero, a sensitive middle-aged divorced woman, has just left the big city behind to return to the country village of her youth. While reuniting with the recently widowed village doctor, who in high school was the star quarterback and her steady, she stumbles over a dead body, which makes her deeply curious. The chief of police suspects she —"

"Look everybody, look! It's the private dick with the killer pencils!" A woman at the far side of the bar area had recognized Bart, and she was racing her friends toward him. "I don't care about the free book — I want another killer pencil!"

*****

Back in his office, Bart faced a visitor, McGill.

"So, Lasiter, *private* detective, how are you doing on the Wilcox homicide? Free and unencumbered by bosses, you should have it solved by now."

"Sorry, McGill, but I'm not getting anywhere with this case. I couldn't get anything from the Conference people. While I was quietly interviewing at the hotel, some women recognized me. I hid in the men's room. And all my Old Town sources came up dry. I was hoping, if the stabber was someone not connected to the Conference, maybe someone in Old Town had seen or heard something."

"Well, you're not us, Lasiter, are you? I always suspect you — I hate peepers. But it doesn't look like you this time. Strangely, I believe you. We got nothing from the partial print. No suspects. I wish we could print everyone at the Conference, but rules, rules, rules. Karen Wilcox is now a cold case file. It's a murder, the file won't close, but we've done all we can until someone gives us a tip, a new lead, better — a confession. I got the feeling some of the Conference people we interviewed knew more than they said — but what? So, here."

McGill reached into his suit coat and brought out Bart's pencils. "We kept the murder weapon, the one with the print, but here are your others. If you hand out any of these, be careful about who's the lucky recipient. By now, every LEO in the county knows about this pencil. 'I'm ready to help.' Cute."

Bart took the pencils and held one out. "Want one?"

*****

The next morning, while Bart was cranking an old-school mechanical sharpener on his returned pencils, and Aggie napped on the desk, Pat

Callahan called to see if he would be in his office. Bart said he would wait for her.

She arrived soon after in a cheerful *Crime Happens — Sacramento 2012* T-shirt. But her demeanor didn't match the T-shirt.

She said hello and sat at his desk. Uncomfortable, fidgeting with her hands in her lap, she swiveled her chair. Her red eyes wouldn't settle on Bart for more than seconds before she'd turn back to her hands. Never would win any staring contests.

Pat looked up. "Mr. Lasiter, I can't stay in Sacramento any longer. It's time for me to go home, back to Illinois. Have you learned anything?" She looked away at a wall.

"Sorry, no. Not from my interviews, nor from my Old Town sources. But I'm in contact with the police. I know the detective in charge. He's competent, and he's keeping me informed. Sorry, Pat...sometimes these things take time."

"Oh, I should know, writing crime. Of course."

Bart sighed. "You never know when there'll be an answer. At this point, it depends on some new discovery, someone coming forward."

"I'm disappointed, but I can understand, Mr. Lasiter. Patience, right?" she said, as if she believed it.

She set an envelope down on his desk. "Here's what cash I can give you now. Please let me know if you learn anything, anything at all. My email, mailing address, and phone number are all in the envelope."

"All right." Bart let the envelope lay. "I'm sure this will cover what I've done so far. I'll let you know immediately if I learn anything new. If we find there is more work for me, then we'll decide what to do. I'm sorry I couldn't do more for you. I'm especially sorry your visit to my city was so sad."

"Thank you. It's not your fault. You've been good. And I like Sacramento. Small-town people, like back in Illinois. I'd like to come back some day."

She started to get up.

"Before you go, Pat, is there anything else you want to tell me about Karen? Some people at the Conference said you and Karen were a writing team."

"Yes. I didn't mention that before? We met at another Crime-Happens conference, in Chicago, five years ago. We were both writing similar things. We decided to team up. And we were good."

Bart leaned back in his swivel chair and said, "Tell me more."

"It was exciting at first, being a partner. Good not being alone. It can be lonely, even scary, writing by yourself. On the surface everyone — the other writers, agents — they're friendly, even helpful."

She sat down again. "But you always question yourself. Is it good? Is it terrible? Will someone like it? Will they hate it? There is a steady undercurrent of competition and self-doubt. The pressure never goes away. A lot of people quit before they get anywhere. Then, if you *are* published, when will that second book be finished? Will it be as good as the first? You never get to rest. It never ends."

She paused.

He watched her eyes.

"Having Karen with me offset that. I'm shy. Karen was always outgoing, the loudest voice in the room. She was my shield. It was natural that, at readings and signings, at conferences, she would talk for us both. She'd help when I got stuck. She would tell me my writing was good. 'Keep going, Pat,' she'd say. I needed that. That was special."

Bart, watching the way she looked around his office without appearing to focus on anything, thought she was viewing her own movie of the events she recalled.

She looked at Bart.

"I have to get back home to The Grove, to take care of the dogs. And then there's the funeral to —"

"Dogs?"

"Karen and I...we trained our Border Collies for agility competition. I don't drive. She did all the driving, to the events. Now I need to apply, get a license. We did a lot of things...together."

She continued to look around his office without focus. Her eyes became strange, pained, and appeared to grow larger.

Aggie looked at her face and backed up to Bart's corner of the desk.

Pat saw the sharpened pencils on his desk and picked one up. She looked at the point while turning the pencil in her hand.

"Have another one, Pat. It's okay."

"I lost mine, somewhere."

"It's okay."

Bart watched Pat tighten her grip on the pencil, like she wanted to squeeze words out of the pencil.

He let her talk.

"Mr. Lasiter...remember the afternoon when I first came to your office, and you gave me your pencil?"

Bart didn't remember. There were so many Crime-Happens visitors, and Pat was not the kind of person you would remember. He nodded to keep her talking.

"Karen was supposed to come with me then, but she said she wanted to see this writer, this other woman first, and she'd come here later. So, we came here together the next morning."

Bart felt a chill.

"We argued downstairs in the lobby. She...she and I, we were — she told me she was going to leave me. For that other woman. She said *they* were going to write together. She said I should forget about us and move forward. I said *no*, and she turned her back to me, like I didn't exist anymore."

Bart watched closely while she twisted the pencil in her hand. The point was digging into her palm. She didn't show any pain or notice her hand bleeding.

"Why did you hire me, Pat?"

"At first, if anyone suspected me, I thought they wouldn't believe I did it when they found out I'd hired you to find the killer. I guess I knew, after a while, someone would find out. And you were in trouble because of...us. You're a detective. You were nice to me. Better you get the credit than somcone not as nice."

"Do you want to tell me about it now? All about it?"

She stared at the pencil in her hand.

She was small, but so wiry, Bart thought, with thin, hard muscles, especially in her hands and forearms. If she changed her mind, it would only take a half-second for her to come over the desk to return his pencil.

Watching her, Bart slowly dragged his dial phone across the desk blotter to where he sat and brought the receiver up to his ear. It was an old AT&T classic, black and heavy. He could conk her with the receiver, if he had to.

She saw him with the phone. She looked at the blood oozing from her hand, sliding off the yellow pencil, red soaking into the green desk blotter.

"I...I didn't mean to, Mr. Lasiter."

He looked at the writer and dialed.

"I know, Pat."

Someone answered.

"McGill, please. It's Lasiter."

Cold Eyes, Cold Blood

Glen Bush

"You're apolitical, amoral, and asexual. You, Solomon Judge, are the most dangerous man I've ever known." I smiled at his description of me. The man speaking, Hollister Lodge, leaned a little forward in the mahogany and leather pub booth, stirred his Bombay martini with his pinky finger, the pinky's diamond ring flashing a sliver of light, and looked into my eyes, smiling. He wore a Milano pinstripe Brooks Brothers light gray suit, pale blue silk shirt, and a white silk tie. He was, and probably always will be, a man of money, of wealth. This suit was his casual go-to-the-Piggly-Wiggly suit. I knew his next words would be his offer, his business arrangement. He wanted me to do something that only a man of my character could and would do, unlike himself or one of his tennis partners would, but what?

"What is it you want me to do for you, Mr. Lodge?"

"I want you to kill a man for me." He was still leaning forward, but he had quit stirring his martini. I suppose this was his intense look, the one his underlings found intimidating. Interesting how cowards try so damn hard to be tough.

I didn't want to respond immediately. I wanted Hollister Lodge to wait. To ask himself a question or two about how our meeting was going. Maybe feel a tinge of aggravation that I didn't jump when he said "frog." Sipping my coffee, savoring the Blue Mountain aroma, I let my eyes rest casually on his. I realized that his pale blue eyes matched his pale blue silk shirt. Did he plan it that way? Was he that meticulous?

"Got a name, or will any male bystander fit your request?"

Lodge was not amused. Downing the remaining swallow of his martini, he set the glass between us and pushed it a little to the left. The muscles in his jaw tightened. He tried to drill those pale blue eyes into me. He failed, but he tried.

"It's worth fifty thousand dollars to me. Nothing ties it to me, but I want pictures of the body when you're finished. Make it painful. Real painful. Here's a cellphone for the pictures. Don't use it for anything else unless I instruct you to do so. I have a number in it for you to send the pictures. Destroy the phone when you're finished. No ties. Zilch. Do you want the job or not?"

I picked up the chrome coffee decanter the server had left and refilled my cup.

"Fifty thousand sounds good. You realize, Mr. Lodge, that you could get this job for somewhat less."

"I want you, and I want you to do it like I want it done. For that, I'll pay the fifty."

I'd done a lot worse for a lot less. I saw no reason to say "no" tonight.

"Deal." Simple as that, *deal.* It's so easy to take a man's life. Two men sit in a bar and have a casual conversation. At the end of the conversation a deal is struck. The third man, the main character in this little kabuki, never knows that he has just been nominated for a starring role. The first man gives the second man a stuffed business envelope. The second man picks it up, weighs its heft with his right hand, looks inside, and closes it again and slips it into the inside pocket of his Moroccan black leather coat.

"Twenty-five now. Twenty-five when I see the pictures."

"Who and where?"

"He'll be in New Orleans next Wednesday. He arrives on the three p.m. American flight. He's staying at the Royal Sonesta on Bourbon. You'll be registered as Cyphré Orez from Miami at the Napoleon on Royal Street. In the hotel safe there will be an envelope with an iPad. You'll get a text that afternoon on the phone I just gave you with a website and ID and password. You'll see the information you need then, not before then. On the website will be the rest of the instructions. Follow all the instructions exactly as they are stated. If you alter them in the least, your contract is terminated, immediately. After you send the pictures from your phone, destroy both the phone and the tablet. Any questions?"

Lodge leaned back in the booth and looked at me with an air of content. "By the way, you're flying on American as well, Monday afternoon, four-thirty. Your returning flight leaves Thursday at noon. You can pick up your rental car at Hertz. Please, travel light."

"I always do." At this moment, in this bar, Lodge was in his element. He was fond of giving orders and watching for the reactions to those orders. I had one last question, "You didn't say, do you prefer a particular way? Gun? Knife? Garrote?"

"Follow the instructions on the website. Remember, though, I want to see the excruciatingly painful, and preferably public death. I want certain people to see him die."

"You'll be in New Orleans next Wednesday? I collect from you?"

"Yes, I'll see you next Wednesday night. We can have a hurricane at Pat O's."

"I don't think so. Just give me the remaining payment, and we can call the arrangement complete."

We shook hands. Lodge left first. I finished my coffee and left ten minutes later.

*****

New Orleans is a fine city for murder. I knew a man on the West Bank who had certain connections. I'd called him the morning after I took the contract and given him a list of items I'd need Tuesday morning. Trusting Lodge's website completely was not something I was going to do. On Monday afternoon, I became a Miami businessman traveling to several cities for meetings before returning home to the pastels and art deco of South Beach. It was a great cover story. Maybe I should try making it real?

*****

I flipped the keys of the rental, a Mercedes S500, to the hotel valet. It was 8:00 pm, Monday night in the French Quarter. From my room I could see Brennan's and an antique store that sold firearms from the War of 1812, an important historical marker for folks in New Orleans. A bottle of chilled Moët was sitting in a bucket between the desk and recliner.

While sipping the bubbly, I opened the iPad and went to the designated website. I had to give it to Mr. Hollister Lodge, he knew how to treat his hired help.

My target was a French-Canadian businessman from Montreal. Pierre Gide. I had his picture, his hotel information, and his itinerary. He was scheduled to give a speech on EV technology and his proposal for an international business consortium. I'd heard of his EV ideas. A couple of those ideas could kick a few petrol fellas in the balls. My instructions were to complete the task before his scheduled speech at 9:00 pm Wednesday, and not worry about the petrol versus EV market. It was the next paragraph that caught my attention and made me set my champagne glass on the floor. I was to use poison. The poison was waiting for me at Barbeau's Vieux Carré Apothecary on Ursuline Street. If anyone asked any questions, no one would, I was to say the poison was for my father, a professor of biochemistry at Tulane. The poison was made from a plant in the northern South American rainforest. This was a few levels above my familiarity with cyanide and arsenic. I was to pour the one-ounce bottle into Gide's drink and then watch the commotion. All traces would be eliminated from his body naturally within fifteen minutes. I was to make sure he received no medical treatment during that time. Since Lodge wanted this done in public, that last item was going to take a little extra finesse.

I'd arranged to be on the West Bank to see my arms connection at 10 am Tuesday morning. For now, though, I decided to sample Brennan's gumbo and stuffed redfish.

*****

Driving across the bridge to the West Bank was a simple task. Gretna, the first town on the right across the river, is the safest city in Louisiana. The cops in Gretna are what some folks call "old school" while others recall the Biblical verse about "spare the rod, spoil the child." Gretna is also home to Johnny Pichon's Army Surplus Store. Johnny, a Marine vet from the Reagan Era, was a guy who remained pissed off at the government because he missed both the Vietnam War and both Iraqi Wars. If pressed, he admitted he was in Grenada.

In his back office, drinking a cup of New Orleans chicory, I watched as Johnny set a midsize duffle bag on the work bench. As if he were a jeweler offering an array of diamond rings, he carefully placed each of the three weapons in front of me.

"Here, Solomon, is the classic go-to MPA30SST, 9mm, with suppressor, thirty round magazine. Classic. It's been around for a while. I'm thinkin' you probably used it once or twice, right?" I looked at the MPA and nodded.

"Yep. Good little weapon. Always liked it."

"Next, we have this sweetheart. My little compact ten-round beauty, and believe me, sir, this baby can deliver. HK45 Compact Tactical. Great backup piece. Last is one that may come in handy if you need to work close range, quiet, and don't want any bullet traces. The .22 Smith & Wesson 43C, the rock n roll hitman special. Like 'em?"

As I went over each weapon, checking its weight and compatibility, Johnny asked the question he should have skipped, "You goin' to war, Solomon?"

Without looking at him or acknowledging his question, I reached into my pocket and pulled out a roll of hundreds. Johnny got the idea. The embarrassed look in his eyes let me know that he'd wished he hadn't asked the question. There're some things a man doesn't ask another man.

I slipped the HK45 into my waistband and tossed the bag with the other two pieces and several boxes of ammo into the trunk of the Mercedes.

*****

My next stop was the pharmacy on Ursuline Street. At this time of day, in this part of the Quarter, it's quiet. A few tourists walking around, taking pictures of the houses, a few residents doing errands, but, like I said, quiet. The man behind the counter looked as though he could have been a veteran from the War of 1812, still wearing the same faded white shirt, tweed waistcoat, and red bowtie. I told him my name was Orez and I was picking up a prescription. Looking at me over the top of his rimless spectacles, he nodded and walked softly to the back, and slipped behind the black curtain covering the doorway. A few minutes later, he returned with a small brown bottle with a black rubber eyedropper for the cap. It had already been paid for. Lodge again had taken care of that as well.

"Anything else, Mr. Orez?"

Looking around at the antique pharmaceuticals and paraphernalia, I shook my head "no," but then rethought my decision.

"On second thought, yes, I do have something else, or, at least, a question. Do you have an antidote for this?" I'd worked with poisons in the past, but not enough to be a hundred percent confident in their reactions and my response if something went wrong. An antidote would be my Plan B. Seldom has a Plan A proceeded without a glitch.

"Yes, we do, but that was not part of the request." Again, he showed little sign of caring one way or the other about the poison, its use, or the antidote. He was probably remembering his last drink with General Jackson and the pirate Lafitte.

"How much would I need to counter this prescription... you know, in case something goes wrong?"

"The same amount, one ounce, but you would only administer a half-ounce initially. That usually is enough to counter the effects of the poison. If something else has occurred, then the last half would be necessary. Would you care for the antidote? It's the same price. Should I bill Mr. Smith?"

Smith? I see I'm not the only one using a *nom de plume*.

"Yes, I would like it, but don't bother to send the bill, I'll take care of the charges myself. But, in case I drop this little gem, let me have a second bottle of the poison as well and a second antidote. Again, I removed my money clip and peeled off three Benjamins. I slipped the change into my pants pocket, the two small brown bottles, and two clear ones, into my inside jacket pocket, and left the apothecary to his potions and memories.

On the way back to the hotel, I began thinking about the coming event with Monsieur Gide from Montreal. EV technology? Interesting stuff.

*****

It was late Tuesday afternoon. I had time to take a lie down and think about Wednesday evening. The Quarter was beginning to get busy. Giving my car to the valet, I went up to my room, opened a Barq's, and stood on the balcony drinking it. The French Quarter is beautiful. Lot of history. It's a place where a man could get lost—if he wanted. Seventy-eight square blocks. Thirteen by six. For twenty-five dollars anybody can be whacked. That same twenty-five also can buy a decent cup of gumbo and a shrimp po'boy and glass of sweet tea. Either way, food for survival. It was too early for the hookers and hustlers to be roaming along St. Louis Street on their way to Bourbon and on to Rampart, but not too early for drunk tourists and street musicians to entertain the families walking along Royal window shopping. There's been plenty of twelve-year-old urchins who've gotten a glimpse of life that Mom and Dad and Preacher John didn't tell them about. Wonder how many came back ten years later to try it on for size?

My cold drink finished, I went back inside, took off my shoes, shirt, and pants, crawled beneath the cool cotton sheets, place the HK45 next to me, and watched the spinning ceiling fan until I fell asleep.

*****

It was a warm night. I wanted to meander toward Gide's hotel. I stopped on Conti Street for a frozen lemonade from a street vendor. At half past eight, I came to the Royal Sonesta, a fine French Quarter hotel. I used to stay there before the war. Since I had no particular interest in politics, the conversations that drifted in that direction were more abstract than substantive, and never personal, for me. I never understood, still don't, why people who sit around cocktail lounges slowly getting slouched spend their time working themselves up about the words of some politician or political policy. Nothing will come of their bantering. Politicians are never going to pay any attention to them, I can swear to that. I've known a few, and they are more than happy to pay a few bucks to ensure a political victory rather than work for some imaginary greater good. What a crock! Greater good? Sure.

Leaving the hotel, I made my way down to Dumaine Street. Heading toward a small, elegant restaurant on Dauphine, I walked up on three men beating the hell out of a guy on the ground. I was almost finished with my lemonade. The guy on the ground was really getting it. Curled up in the fetal position, he was bleeding, moaning, and crying. Looked like he was in his late teens. The three beating him looked about the same age. Street kids. The tall one, the one with the cowboy boots, was kicking the whiner in the ribs. His buddies, wearing work boots, probably steel-toed, followed up with a few more kicks to the back and ass. I stopped about ten or twelve feet from the beating, leaned against the lamppost and sucked up the last remnants of my lemonade. To me, this was a defense-offense exercise. What should the whiner on the ground be doing now? What should he be thinking? He was outnumbered and hurt. How bad was he hurt? As I licked the last drops of the frozen lemonade from the straw, the kid looked up at me and cried for my help.

"Please, mister, help me! I'll do anything, please, they're gonna kill me, please, help me."

The French Quarter, especially at night, can be a dangerous place. A guy needs to know what it is when he decides to go walking around, especially as he gets closer to Rampart.

I looked at the kid and said, "Yeah, that's what it looks like to me, too. I guess you better do something pretty damn quick."

Before he could say anything else to me, a cowboy boot struck his front teeth. More blood. It wasn't looking good for the kid. I dropped my lemonade cup in the trash can next to the lamppost and took another look at the ongoing beating. I knew I should be getting to the restaurant before I missed my reservation. As I stepped away from the lamppost, something unexplainable, nonsensical, happened.

"What the fuck ya lookin' at? Y'all want some of this, too?" The words came from the heavy-set guy with the work boots. I hadn't really cared too much one way or the other about them or the kid. It was just another street fight. Nothing more, nothing less. Tomorrow the sun would still come up and it would still be hot.

"Yeah, bitch, you heard him, keep movin' or you'll get the same, probably worse." Cowboy Boots had spoken.

"You know, boys, I was on my way to have some of Chef Maurice's crawfish etouffee, but since you're inviting me, in fact, just about insisting that I play, too, well, why the fuck not?"

The three now stopped beating the kid and squared around, staring at me. The whiner quickly crawled away from their boots and pulled himself up and started running down Dumaine toward Bourbon and the tourists.

I looked down at my custom-made black leather Italian shoes. I'd just had them shined at the hotel earlier in the afternoon. I love these shoes. They fit perfect. The three thugs were still watching me as I took off my beige sport coat and folded it neatly and placed it on top of the trash can lid. I try never to soil my clothes in a tussle.

"Look at this asshole! Who's he think he is…."

Before Cowboy Boots finished his sentence, I did what back in the neighborhood would have been described as, "That's not a fight, that's a massacre."

Two well-placed kicks, one slap, and two nicely, if I say so myself, delivered punches, and the three thugs were on the ground, unmoving.

The whiner was long gone. He never saw what happened to his tormenters. In a few more minutes I would be enjoying my crawfish etouffee.

It was a warm night. The streets were quiet.

*****

After dinner I walked back to my hotel to review some final arrangements before tomorrow. I decided to take a longer stroll back, one that took me down Dauphine to Iberville to Bourbon, down Bourbon to St. Louis and over to Royal and on to the hotel. The night creatures were beginning to come out. Mixing with the tourists, they sized up their victims and proceeded with their hustles. From the eight-year-old boys tap dancing for change to the he-she's hustling their wares to the hardened jailbirds perched and waiting for their prey, Bourbon Street was alive and well. At the hotel, I stopped at the gift shop and picked up several science and technology magazines and the Wall Street

Journal. I wanted a way to separate Gide from his associates so we could share a drink together. Knowledge of EV tech would be a good. And, if I came across anything on Lodge, that could also work. One never knows what will work in my line, but it is best to have as many options as doable.

While lying back in bed, I found three articles that discussed Gide's breakthrough technology. Two praised his work, one disparaged it. The author who did the disparaging discussed how Hollister Lodge's corporation were doing more practical advancement within the traditional petrol fields. Apparently, Lodge knew EV was the future, but he wanted to slow down the progression in that direction and insert his own petrol-EV alternatives. It didn't take too much to see billions were at stake. As I was getting ready to fold up the Wall Street Journal and slip it beneath the bed, my eye caught a glimpse of a short paragraph in the Lodge article that mentioned Lodge's cousin, Arthur Chester, a New York investor and ne'er-do-well, whose death had caused the Lodge family a certain amount of remorse. Chester and Lodge were related? I had killed Arthur Chester in Palm Beach eighteen months earlier. An *unfortunate* boating accident. At breakfast, I still couldn't shake the idea that Lodge and Chester were related, and that Lodge had hired me to kill Gide. Did he know I killed his cousin?

*****

"Gide, old sport, how the hell are you?" I tried to give it my best Jay Gatsby imitation, the Robert Redford version. Lunch had ended but happy hour hadn't started.

Pierre Gide stopped a few steps outside the elevator and looked at me, trying to place me. Luckily for me, one of the articles I had read on Gide mentioned his work on rebuilding the power grid in Haiti. Since I had been to Haiti on several occasions, I thought I could throw in enough references to convince him we had met there several years earlier, when he had first begun his work in Port-au-Prince. This was my moment. No rush. A drink in the lounge. A Pernod with black olives and brie. The article said it was his favorite afternoon aperitif. Thank you, Mademoiselle Chiraq.

In twenty minutes, I had convinced him of my interest in his EV technology and how it would definitely help my program bring energy self-sufficiency to several former French colonies in the Caribbean.

"Please, Pierre, we must continue this conversation tomorrow when I have more time."

"Certainly, tomorrow, before lunch. Let us finish our drinks so I can go to my early meeting, please. First, though, let me step away for a moment, nature calls, and when I return, we can finish our drinks and settle the time for our meeting tomorrow."

As soon as Gide stepped into the men's room, I removed the small brown bottle, poured its content into his Pernod, and leaned back in the Queen Anne chair and waited.

*****

The poison reacted as Lodge said, painfully. Gide was paralyzed. He could not speak. His facial muscles were twisted and hardened. His torso began to have a series of quick, violent contortions and tremors. As I watched Gide's eyes roll back in his head, I set my phone against the candle holder so the preset camera could record Gide's agony. This should satisfy Hollister Lodge. Gide's actions attracted the attention of several people. Cries of "Doctor" and "Help the poor man" spread through the beautiful lobby. As the crowd was gathering and I was leaning over the pain-stricken Gide, a vision of Chester Arthur stepping into his power boat filled my mind. *It's a set-up!*

That sleight-of-hand my father had taught me when I was twelve finally came in handy.

"Get back! Get back! Give the man air! Let the EMTs through," I yelled the commands as professionally as I could all the while slipping the clear bottle from my pocket, removing the cap, and pouring the full ounce into Gide's open mouth.

As the EMTs wheeled Gide toward the ambulance, I could see his body begin to quell. He was either dying or recovering. I just blew twenty-five thousand dollars! Or had I?

*****

"Thank you, waiter." I could hear Lodge paying the waiter for the extra drink while I was still fifty feet away.

This is something I try to avoid. Once the task is completed, I prefer having the remaining funds transferred to my Cayman account. My clients and I are not friends. This evening, though, a different delivery was going to be made.

Across the courtyard from the lighted fountain and a half-dozen tables from the nearest tourists, Hollister Lodge sat with his back to the brick wall, a banana tree behind him surrounded by tropical red and yellow flowers. He slid my drink to his right and continued sipping his exotic blue drink. The miniature red paper umbrella that had come with it lay next to the napkin.

"Thank you, Mr. Lodge."

Lodge slid a thick envelop toward me.

"Now, may I see the video? I hear it was quite dramatic."

Apparently, he hadn't heard anything about Gide after the EMTs took him away. I hadn't either. There was really nothing for me to do one way or the other about Gide. He would either live or die. Nothing other than what's in store for the rest of us.

I clicked the video icon on the phone and handed it to Lodge. He watched, smiling. When the short video ended, before the EMTs took Gide away, Lodge slapped the wrought iron table loudly and shouted with joy.

"Now, that is nice, Mr. Judge! Damn nice!"

Putting the envelop in my inside jacket pocket, I said, "Thank you, I'm glad you enjoyed it." Picking up my drink, I offered a toast to my employer.

As our glasses clinked, he said, "In fact, Judge, almost as smooth as that boating accident that killed poor Artie. You remember Artie, Arthur Chester, my cousin in Palm Beach, don't you, you *son-of-a-bitch*?" Those pale blue eyes now seemed to be a vivid red. Before I could respond, a terrible cutting and twisting started turning my guts into broken glass. The image of Pierre Gide twisting filled my mind. I fell to the brick courtyard, wringing with pain. Lodge stood over me, laughing, and then bent down and removed the envelop from my pocket.

"You won't need this, Judge. Enjoy your last fifteen minutes."

When I rolled back over, Hollister Lodge was gone, and three servers were running toward me. I knew I only had seconds before the poison completely paralyzed my whole body. Reaching into my pants pocket, I pulled the clear bottle out and struggled with the cap. The servers were kneeing around me.

"Help me. Antidote."

When I woke up, I was in a hospital bed.

*****

"Where am I?"

The nurse stopped writing things on her tablet and looked over at me. "Well, Mr. Orez, you had us scared. Seems like you got a hold of some bad seafood, probably those damn oysters. One of the EMTs said you had one of those servers at The Courtyard give you something from a little bottle you had with you. Were you anticipating this?"

"Where am I? Where's my clothes?" I felt agitated. I needed to get out of here and find that son of a bitch Lodge.

"Calm down, calm down. You're at Charity Hospital. You had food poisoning. I'll notify the doctor you're awake and feeling better. He can explain more about your condition." With that, she tapped me on the leg, smiled, and said she'd be right back.

I had no intention of waiting. All I needed was my clothes. I knew as soon as I pulled the tubes out of me, the machines would signal the front desk I was unhooked, causing them to come and check on me. I surveyed the room. In the corner, on the recliner, lay a plastic bag with clothes.

It was a smooth getaway. Nothing as dramatic as Hollywood, but smooth for my tired ass.

*****

Catching a taxi back to the Napoleon, I got my belonging out of the room and slipped out the side door. I had no idea how Lodge planned to handle the hotel and car rental, but I knew I couldn't take any chances. I still had part of the money from the first payment and the weapons. I ditched the duffle bag and suitcase in a dumpster a few doors down St. Louis and had the guns in my ankle holster and waistband. If my luck held out, Lodge would think I was dead. My case wasn't considered anything important enough for a news story, another case of a tourist with food poisoning skipping out on the hospital bill wouldn't be that uncommon in this city.

Where was Lodge?

My best bet was he headed home, and I was right behind him.

*****

It had been a little over a week of looking for and then of watching Lodge before I decided to make my move. During that week, I'd become judge and jury and, soon to be, executioner. The punishment needed to fit both the crime and criminal. By this time, Lodge had found out that Pierre Gide had survived the poison attack. He would try again. Gide was the reverse of Lodge. Their motives couldn't be further apart. Normally, I stayed out of these provincial disputes, but after reading the articles the night before the poisoning, and a little more since, I found Gide appealing. That, as well as Lodge trying to murder me, left me a little unsettled. I laid out my plan and made a few errands and by the end of the week, I was ready to go.

On Sunday night, while Lodge and his wife were out, I slipped into his house and planted several cameras. For the next three nights I studied his evening routine. People don't realize it, but everyone has a routine, some casual, others quite elaborate. Lodge was one of the elaborate fellows. His wife not so much. It was during these observations that I found the single routine I wanted to exploit. Every night at ten o'clock, before going upstairs to their bedroom, Hollister Lodge relaxed in his library with a cigar and cognac. This nightly ritual lasted thirty minutes. After disposing of the cigar butt in the outside bin on the deck, he returned the snifter to the shelf next to the cognac bottle. One snifter. One bottle of cognac. By ten thirty-three, he was upstairs. His wife, with the help of a vodka martini and two sleeping pills, invariably was already asleep when he came to bed. She never stirred.

*****

The library was dark with just enough light from the moon for me to see the leather Queen Anne chair in the corner furthest from the matching chair near the fireplace, Lodge's chair. The corner chair faced the French doors, away from the desk. A place to sit and contemplate the manicured lawn and garden.

I waited.

When Lodge turned the light on, I could hear him walk to the bookcase next to the fireplace and pour himself his snifter of cognac. Next, I could smell the aroma of the Cuban cigar. When I was sure he was seated comfortably and had begun to sip his cognac, I stood up, turned, and took a step toward the fireplace.

"Judge! I thought you were dead!" His surprise was quite real.

"Yes, I'm sure you did." Walking to the chair directly across from him, I sat down and scrutinized him watching me. I could see the wheels in his head turning rapidly, hamster wheels in a cage, turning, turning, turning. He took another taste of cognac, a longer one, one to savor.

"Well, Judge, what do you want? An apology? Money? Revenge? What?"

"Nothing. I have exactly what I want right now."

"What do you...." His voice stopped, the muscles in his jaw tightened. I could see him grip the snifter tighter, forcing it toward his open mouth.

"Mean? Is that what you were going to ask me? *What do you mean?*" I smiled as Lodge forced the last bit of cognac down, as though the alcohol would protect him from the inevitable. He tried to talk, but his muscles denied him that luxury.

"Hollister, you're going to die, and it's going to be a very painful, excoriating death, like the one you wanted Gide to experience. In fact, your death is going to be much more painful than Cousin Chester's death." Continuing to watch him struggle, I knew he would have a few more minutes left where he could speak, but they would be limited, very limited.

Finally, he asked, "What have you done to me? I can't...."

"You are not the only one who knows a little bit about poison. I have my own favorite poison. It's also from South America, the Amazon. I coated the inside of your snifter with it and let it dry. When you poured your cognac into the snifter, the poison was reawakened, and... well, you see now. You see, I thought you might try something when I read about Chester's relationship to you, so I obtained the antidote for your poison. I also have the antidote for the poison I gave you." Reaching into my jacket pocket, I produced another small bottle, this one blue. "This is your antidote. Do you want to ask me for it? Perhaps beg for it? Or *buy* it?" Watching him struggle to speak, his eyes flashing with fear and hatred, I could see the poison taking effect. Slumping forward, Lodge fell to the floor, his body growing stiff, his eyes wide open, still spewing fear and hatred.

"Unlike your poison, mine will kill you very slowly. It will take you ten, maybe twelve, hours to die. However, your heart rate will drop to thirty or less, your whole body will be paralyzed. You will appear dead. You won't be able to speak. Even your eyes will be paralyzed, staring contently upward at some devil. And this is the good part I think you will really appreciate, that is if it were Gide or me suffering, the inside of your body will be burning. The fire will be unquenchable." Then, kneeling next to the patriarch of the Lodge empire, I tapped my index finger on his forehead. "Well, Hollister, I must be going. You know, old sport, things to do, places to be, and all of that."

When I stood up, I was still holding the blue antidote bottle.

"Oh, by the way, the antidote. Here you go." I removed the cap and gently poured the antidote on his chest, letting it soak into his silk smoking jacket, and mix with his sweat that was seeping from his pores.

"Goodbye, Mr. Lodge."

Under the Table

Edward Lodi

Tony Atti awoke from a dream of tropical islands and scantily clad maidens to the hard reality of a man standing before his desk.

He yawned. "I see you found your way in."

The man looked at Tony as if he were a new species of primate. Maybe I am, Tony thought, his mind still fuzzy with sleep. He'd been called an ape any number of times, mostly by women he tried to pick up.

The man was taller than Tony, who was no shrimp, and skinnier—much skinnier. His other distinguishing features: a nose that started out broad but tapered to a sharp point, enough to make any woodpecker envious; gray eyes a tad too wide for the narrow face; and sandy-colored hair, the latter in need of combing and a trim. Tony pictured the man in a straw hat. If ever Tony needed an undercover operative disguised as a scarecrow he knew whom to call.

"Mr. Atti, I need your help."

"Have a seat." Tony nodded at the visitor's chair opposite his desk.

The man plunked himself down and leaned forward, like a Great Blue Heron eyeing a frog. Tony estimated his age at around forty. He was deeply tanned, his hands callused: a man who spent time outdoors. Not a laborer, though. Most likely a bog owner. Tony's father had owned a cranberry bog.

The man grabbed a handful of salted peanuts from the Depression-era glass dish Tony kept on his desk. You could learn a lot about a person by the way they treated the peanuts, whether they ignored them entirely, stared at them before eating a few to conceal anxiety, or whatever. The man studied the peanuts before popping several into his mouth. He chewed, swallowed, then said to Tony: "Like I said, I need your help."

Tony grunted. "Say it isn't so. I thought you came here to munch on stale peanuts." He nodded at the dish. "I keep 'em there for the mice. The peanuts distract the little critters from gnawing on the case records. Incidentally, you might want to look out for droppings. Mice aren't fastidious. They crap on their food even as they eat it."

The man's face took on a slightly green complexion. "Mr. Atti, I don't think I like you very much."

"Few people do," Tony conceded. "Now that my parents are dead I don't think anyone finds me particularly appealing. Saving for my cat, of course. He likes me. At least I think he does."

The man sighed. "They said you were eccentric."

"Who's they?"

The man shrugged. "I asked around."

Tony picked up a pencil from a glass tumbler on his desk and twirled it between his fingers. "They actually say 'eccentric'?"

The man gestured, as if shooing a fly. "'Wise guy' is what they said. A real pain in the ass."

"Ah, now that we've got the niceties over with we can get down to business, Mr....?"

"Saybrook. Edward Saybrook."

"As in *the* Saybrooks?"

Saybrook nodded. "Distant cousin"

The Saybrooks were an ancient Bay State family. They traced their ancestry to the Puritans in 1630 who joined John Winthrop in erecting his City on a Hill. Boston Brahmins. If Edward was representative of the clan, the dynasty was in serious trouble.

"What brings you here, Mr. Saybrook? Other than the peanuts, that is."

"My kid brother's gone missing, Mr. Atti. I need you to find him."

Tony leaned back in his chair. "Methinks I smell a rat, Mr. Saybrook." He made a wave of his hand that took in the shabby office, the worn linoleum, the cheap furniture bought at yard sales, the dust, the layers of embedded dirt, the frayed curtains, the flyspecked windows overlooking a salt marsh used by locals as an unofficial dump.

"Why me? Why choose a second-rate gumshoe with a reputation for, uh, eccentricity? Why not go to the police; surely the Saybrooks, even distant cousins, have clout. Or if you'd rather not involve the police, which I suspect is the case, why not hire one of the, uh, more elite agencies?"

Saybrook rubbed his nose between his thumb and forefinger, as if to quell an itch. "Besides being a pain in the ass, the word I hear is you're honest. Discreet. And let's be frank, Mr. Atti: you're not second-rate. Not from what I hear. All this"—he nodded at their surroundings—"the dinginess, the wisecracks, it's all a facade." He sat erect, as if to emphasize the sincerity of his remarks. It had, however, the opposite effect. Edward Saybrook reminded Tony of a praying mantis, about to clasp an insect in its gangly embrace. "You're good at what you do. And when you give your word you keep it. Which is why I came to you."

Tony leaned forward. "A hundred dollars a day plus expenses. Five hundred in advance—nonrefundable."

"A hundred a day? Bog workers don't earn that much in a week."

"Then hire a bog worker to locate your brother."

Saybrook heaved a sigh. "A check okay?"

✻✻✻✻✻

Saybrook lived with his wife and two young sons in Wareham, in a house overlooking his cranberry bog. The missing brother lived in an apartment built especially for him over the two-car garage adjacent to the house.

"James," *(the Saybrooks never used nicknames; to refer to James as Jim would, apparently, be as sacrilegious as referring to Jesus Christ as Jessie)* "is the black sheep of the family; he can't hold down a job. He studied agriculture in school; I'd gladly make him foreman—eventually a partner. But my brother doesn't like taking orders, especially from me."

According to Edward, the younger Saybrook was kicked out of college for unspecified reasons his second year. Since then he'd bummed around, sponging off his brother while getting into trouble with the law: reckless driving, public drunkenness, disturbing the peace. Two months ago, after a night spent in the county jail, he announced his intention to mend his ways and "grow up."

James took a job with a cranberry grower in Plymouth, a Finn named Bill Johnson. "Johnson's a crook; he pays my brother under the table. James is okay with that. He thinks he's beating the system. The damn fool doesn't take into consideration loss of potential benefits like Unemployment Compensation or Social Security."

A week ago Bill Johnson phoned Edward to complain that James hadn't shown for work two days in a row. It was late September; harvest would soon be under way. "Tell your brother he's fired!"

"All this time you didn't notice James's absence?" Tony asked.

Saybrook shrugged. "I assumed he was shacked up with some bimbo. He's done it before. In the end he always comes home. Broke, maybe with a dose of the clap. This time I'm worried. Eight days. He's never been gone that long." Saybrook stared at Tony. "Find my brother and haul his ass home."

*****

The first thing Tony did after Saybrook left was hoof it down to the bank to deposit the check. That accomplished, he climbed into his car and set out through the back roads to Plymouth.

It was mid afternoon when he left the paved road and turned onto a rutted track that snaked through a thicket of deciduous trees to Johnson's fifty-acre bog. The leaves on the trees had turned, the maples flaming red, the poplars pale yellow, the hornbeams somber orange. At autumn's end they would wither and drop to the forest floor. Tony thought of the withered leaves as messages from the dead, scribbled in haste, crinkled, left to drift in the wind.

As the wood ended the track forked, to make a loop around the property. Cranberry bogs, which must be flooded in winter to protect the vines from freezing, are laid out several feet below the surrounding soil. Laden with ripened berries, the carpet of ground-hugging vines stretched before him like an inland sea. On the far side, across from where he'd exited the wood, he could make out a rack truck and men working.

Tony drove to the screen house, the barn-like building where harvested berries were screened (ripe separated from green and rotten) before being packed for shipment.

He drew up between a mud-splattered pickup of ancient vintage and a spanking-new Chevrolet that made his own set of wheels look like the dilapidated wreck it was fast becoming. "Cranberries must be paying well these days," Tony murmured to himself as he got out and stretched his legs.

The doors to the screen house stood open, revealing a room with concrete flooring where agricultural vehicles were garaged. A Model A Ford, converted by the addition of a plank bed into a jalopy for hauling small loads; a red farm tractor with a badly bent cutting blade; and a front-end loader took up much of the space.

Tony examined the bent blade with the critical eye of one who'd spent his youth working on cranberry bogs. Someone had been careless. Operating a tractor along the steep banks of a cranberry bog was not for the faint of heart. One false move and you might end up in an irrigation ditch, with your neck snapped or your chest caved in. Maybe this guy got lucky; maybe the blade had acted like a kick-stand, preventing the tractor from completely toppling over.

He took a brief tour inside. Other than a half dozen starlings roosting near a broken window pane nobody was home.

Returning to his car he headed for the far side of the bog, steering carefully along a cross dike, navigating between ruts, dodging boulders, always mindful of the vehicle's underbelly. Ten yards shy of his destination he stopped the car and proceeded the rest of the way on foot, to where two men were off-loading empty bushel boxes from a truck and stacking them, upside-down, in a tight pyramid.

The younger of the men wore a baseball cap and spoke with a Portuguese accent. Despite a brisk autumn breeze sweeping across the vines he was shirtless. The second man, somewhere in his forties, wore a wide-brimmed cloth hat and had on a long-sleeved shirt. Even so the sun had bronzed his face and neck a deep red, like the dying leaves on the maples bordering the bog. The shirtless man stood on the ground to receive the boxes as his companion on the truck tossed them one by one.

"Mr. Johnson?"

The man on the truck nodded. "What can I do for you, bud?" He spoke without breaking his rhythm as he deftly tossed boxes to the man on the ground.

"If I could have a minute of your time…"

"As you can see I'm busy. We start picking day after next."

"It's about James Saybrook."

"That son of a bitch," Johnson said flatly, without breaking his stride. Distracted by the interruption, the man on the ground failed to catch a box as it whirled past him. The box bounced off the turf at his feet, its thin wooden slats splintering on impact.

"Careful, Manny," Johnson snapped. To Tony: "Like I told his brother, the bastard left me in the lurch. Harvest a week away and he takes off without a word. How'm I supposed to find a replacement at this late date? Son of a bitch," he reiterated.

"No idea where he might be?"

"If I did I'd kick his scrawny ass," Johnson said.

Tony nodded. "Well, thank you, Mr. Johnson. I wish you a bountiful harvest." He trudged back to his car and with a skill honed by years of practice turned the vehicle around on the narrow track and drove away. There were questions he could ask but hadn't. Like: whose brand-new Chevy was it that was parked outside the screenhouse?

He retraced his route through the copse onto the paved road. He drove a hundred yards before pulling onto a clearing behind a stand of pitch pines. The clearing made a perfect hidey-hole where, judging by the evidence on the ground, lovers trysted and people dumped their trash. If Tony ever needed a sofa for his office this was the second place he'd look, after the salt marsh outside his office window.

He glanced at his wrist. Three-thirty-five. Bog workers started their day at seven a.m. They knocked off at four, except during harvest, when they labored till dusk.

At precisely two minutes past four the Chevrolet emerged from the thicket onto the asphalt and swung right. From his vantage point behind the pine grove Tony could easily make out the driver as the car sped by: Manny, the man with the Portuguese accent. Seconds later Johnson's pickup appeared from the woods and turned in the opposite direction. Tony waited until it had sped off, and the Chevrolet had rounded a curve, before emerging out of his hidey-hole.

Few vehicles were on the road; Tony easily caught up with the Chevy. Windows down and radio blasting, Manny churned along oblivious to his tail. After a few miles of forest interspersed with cranberry bogs and an occasional house they neared the outskirts of Plymouth. Cranberry bogs gave way to gas stations, pizza parlors, real estate offices, a restaurant or two.

Slowing, Manny entered the parking lot of a joint with a sign that read The Tidewater Tavern. Tony pulled in next to the Chevy but waited five minutes before following Manny inside.

The dimly lit interior reeked of tobacco smoke, stale booze, and unwashed bodies. An ancient juke box with a cracked dome stood silent against a wall. As he crossed the floor through a litter of cigarette butts he half expected to be set upon by drunks wielding broken beer bottles. It was that kind of dive.

He slid onto a stool at the bar and ordered a Narragansett. Manny was seated at the far end. If he recognized Tony he gave no indication. Tony reached into his pocket and took out a snapshot of James Saybrook he'd obtained from his brother. Tall and thin like Edward, James was less of a galoot, though that wasn't saying much. Neither was likely to win a Mr. America contest. Nor for that matter was Tony.

He nursed his Narry as patrons trickled in: bog workers and construction crews weary at day's end, hookers beginning their shift. He finished his Narry and ordered a second, then beer in hand left the stool and approached his neighbors. "This guy's missing." He flashed James's photo. "Seen him?" Some of the drinkers waved him off, or told him in graphic terms what he could do with himself. Others merely shook their head. To Tony it made no difference. He had an inkling as to where he might find Edward's prodigal brother.

After he'd questioned those seated at the bar—all except Manny—he went around to the booths where he made a general nuisance of himself, again with no success. If anyone in this bucket of blood knew the whereabouts of James Saybrook they kept the knowledge to themselves.

He moseyed over to where Manny sat staring into an empty whiskey glass.

"Manny! Long time no see!" He thumped the bog worker on the back. "How's tricks?"

Manny swiveled around on his stool and stared at the interloper with bloodshot eyes. "Who you?"

"Manny, it's me, Tony. Say, your glass is empty." Judging by the slur in Manny's speech it had been emptied and refilled several times. "We'll soon take care of that." Catching the bartender's attention he pointed at the glass.

"I no know you," Manny mumbled. "Go 'way."

The bartender, busy with boozers clamoring for drinks, eventually came over and poured. Tony placed some coins on the bar, then said to Manny: "Drink up. Then we'll go outside and talk."

"I no go nowhere," Manny said, eyeing the amber liquid. "But I drink your whiskey."

"That'a boy, Manny." Standing behind the bog worker, he lifted him from the stool.

"Hey, hey, leave go!"

Tony leaned over and whispered in his ear. "That's a nice new Chevy you got, Manny. I mean, a greenhorn like you, fresh off the boat—doing okay for yourself. It'd be a shame if the car got dented, or the paint scratched, or the windows smashed. Not to mention the tires being slashed. Or somebody pouring sugar in the tank. Let's say we take a walk outside, just to make sure everything's all right."

"Okay, okay. We go." With a firm grip on his elbow, Tony guided Manny through the brume of tobacco smoke to the fresh air outside. Nobody paid heed: just another drunk being helped along by his buddy.

"Don't you just love this time of year, Manny? No longer humid, not too cold, just the slightest hint that winter is on its way. Harvest about to begin." He took a deep breath as if to emphasize the sentiment. "Life is good." He had positioned the two of them so that they stood midway between his car and the Chevrolet. "So, tell me, where's the body?"

"Body? What you talkin' 'bout?"

"You know damn well what I'm talking about."

"I tie my shoe." Manny reached down to his boot but instead of tightening the leather thong drew forth a concealed knife. As he straightened he made a clumsy thrust with the blade. His intended target easily side-stepped the blow. Thrown off balance Manny stumbled against Tony's car.

"Don't scratch the paint," Tony said as his assailant struggled to regain his balance. "I've only had the car ten years."

As he spoke he seized the wrist holding the knife and twisted until the weapon dropped to the ground, then slammed the bog worker's head against the side of the Chevy. "Ah, gee, Manny, you got a hard head; I hope it didn't put a dent into your nice new car. Feeling a little green around the gills? If you're gonna be sick, do it on your car, not mine."

"You pickin' on me 'cause I'm immigrant," Manny complained as he regained his senses.

"Whoa now, Manny. Let's get something straight." Tony brought his face up close to the bog worker's. The man's breath reeked of garlic and cheap whiskey. "I'm not prejudiced against immigrants. My grandparents were immigrants. From Italy." He brought his face even closer. "I respected them. They worked hard. They were good, honest people."

He placed his hand on Manny's shoulder and pressed him against the Chevy. "But you know something, Manny? I don't respect you. True, you work hard. But you're not honest. Now, let's start over. Where's the body?"

*****

A week later Tony stood in the shade of a tall oak in a far corner of a rural cemetery, smoking a ten-cent cigar. Although the leaves on the oak had taken on their autumn hues, they still clung fast, and would do so well into December. If the dead who were buried here had messages to send, secrets to share, it was only among themselves.

It had been a nice funeral. One of the blue-blood Saybrooks, a state senator, gave the eulogy, a moving tribute to the deceased that left hardly a dry eye among the mourners. James Saybrook, it seems, had been a brilliant scion of the family. Had his life not been cut so tragically short he would have gone on to achieve great things (in what field, exactly, the senator didn't specify). At that point Tony had nodded off, but woke in time to exit the church with the others and join the procession to the cemetery.

During the graveside ceremony he'd kept a discreet distance; he was after all neither friend nor family. Besides, hypocrisy had an adverse effect on him; it would not be seemly to puke on the coffin. Was anyone truly grieved by James's untimely demise? Certainly not Edward. If anything, the Saybrook family galoot seemed relieved to be rid of his ne'er-do-well brother.

Tony was not surprised when, the majority of the mourners having left, Edward approached him. "It was good of you to attend," he said, though he glanced at the cigar with disapproval.

Tony shrugged. "I witnessed your brother's exhumation. The least I could do was see him decently buried again."

"I never asked exactly how it was you came to discover James's body. What with the shock, and journalists flocking about…"

"Yeah, it's time I gave you a full report." He flicked the ash from his cigar. "I'll keep it short so you can get back to the others. When I paid a call on your brother's employer I immediately smelled a rat. A brand new car next to a battered pickup. Odd, but nothing to arouse suspicion. But then I see a tractor with its mowing blade bent out of shape. Oops. Someone's had an accident. I remember you saying Johnson was paying James under the table. Suppose it was James who'd been operating the tractor when it tipped. Suppose the accident proved fatal.

"If that was the case Johnson would find himself in hot water: the government takes a dim view of employers who don't report their employees' wages, and who don't pay Social Security and Workman's Compensation taxes. Then there's the deceased's family. Saybrooks, with high-powered attorneys, their tongues hanging out eager to initiate juicy lawsuits."

Edward frowned, presumably at the image of Saybrooks and their drooling attorneys, but refrained from comment. "The clincher," Tony went on, "was Manny Sousa, Johnson's bog worker. When I mentioned your brother's name he turned pale; he was so flustered he missed a wooden box he was supposed to catch and let it smash against the ground.

"Manny's an immigrant, hasn't been long in this country. You yourself pointed out that bog workers earn piddly. Johnson, a known skinflint, is probably paying him less than the going rate. So how's Manny afford a new car?

"Answer: hush money. He witnessed the accident and helped his boss bury the body in an abandoned sand pit. His reward for silence: the down payment on a new Chevy."

"But how'd you get him to confess and show where they'd buried James?"

Tony flashed a sheepish grim. "Shucks, it was easy. I bought him a few drinks, made him my pal, and after his tongue was loosened he confided in me."

"I hear from the Plymouth police that he's in the hospital," Edward said.

"Yeah, my fault," Tony confessed. "I let him get a little too drunk. He stumbled in the parking lot and fell." He dropped the cigar stub onto the grass and extinguished it with the heel of his shoe. "Time I got going. Sorry for your loss, Mr. Saybrook."

When Tony returned to his office the first thing he did was look out the window at the salt marsh below. A new pile of trash had recently been dumped. Maybe if he sifted through it he'd find something of value before winter set in.

A Jeweled Anniversary

Cate Moyle

It is generally assumed that a single woman over the age of thirty must be in want of a wedding, Ashley thought agreeably. Assumed, that is, by parents, grandparents, married siblings, and all this familial pressure begins to count increasingly more important each year over a dwindling list of groom qualifications. This kind of free promotion is what she counted on—all the way to the First Centennial Bank and Heritage Trust of Tennessee, to be precise.

Ashley added her company's glossy brochures to the Welcome Wagon table while she waited in the bank lobby, then read the tickertape on a TV overhead. The flat-screen hung below a giant mural of dueling cannons—heavy in a *North and South* aesthetic—an interior, like most buildings in the colonial town of Williamson, boasting the old and conceding the new. She smiled in appreciation of a traditional wood fire crackling within the marble fireplace next to a brand new laser-beam security gate.

"How are you, Miss Austen-Holmes?" said the silver-haired man in line behind her, his breath brushing her neck intimately.

"Fine, Mr. Nolan." She scooted forward. "And it's Miz, or simply Ashley." Her smile softened.

His tremoring hand removed a handkerchief from his pocket. "No, I don't use the term *Miz*. Or call young ladies by given names, either." He mopped his forehead. "Business good? You jumped out of any airplanes lately?" He chuckled at the question.

She knew he referred to the recent magazine article in *Nashville Style*, where her company *eXceptional Events* had been featured in a story about music executives who tied the knot while skydiving. "No, I usually stay groundside and let the celebrants do the jumping. And there aren't many requests for outdoor events in late winter. But with the wedding season approaching, I'll become very busy. Meanwhile, I'm looking forward to planning your anniversary party with Molly."

Nolan grunted and avoided eye contact.

"And yourself?" Ashley prompted.

"Me? Not a care in the world. Just got rid of the wife and I'm scot-free!" He added a devil of a smile.

"Um, excuse me?"

A log in the fireplace burst and flared.

"Next." A teller's voice called out.

Ashley left Nolan's grimace behind, stepping to the teller counter. Despite the second millennial date on the calendar, the teller had a beehive hairdo reminiscent of the 1960s. "Hey, Laura Jean, that's some do."

"It's called the bunker. Do you like it?"

"Very…retro." Ashley passed her deposit under the cashier's window. In a hushed voice, she asked, "Tell me, what's going on with the Nolans?"

"What do you mean?" Laura Jean flipped through the stack of checks.

"I've never seen one without the other. And he's acting strange—like gleeful."

Laura Jean looked to the far teller station where Nolan laughed. "Yes, now that I think on it, this is the third time this week he's been in here without her. And that *is* odd." Her eyes on Ashley, she asked, "Do you think Molly is all right?"

"I don't know. Probably. Perhaps she's just under the weather. Let me know if you hear otherwise?"

Laura Jean nodded her assent as she finished the transaction, handing Ashley a receipt.

"By the way, where did you get that hair done?"

"Sadie at Ellery's Everything Hair. Why?"

"I like to keep track of where to send clients." She pocketed the bank slip in her Gucci clutch and teased her old friend. "Everything Hair has a moneyback guarantee, right?"

Laura Jean frowned and waved another customer forward instead of answering.

*****

When Ashley arrived at *eXceptional Events*, her assistant, Joan, had already unlocked the front door, and she noticed a Sound City Coffee paper cup on her desk.

"Oh!" she cried with joy. "Did you get me The Hermitage?"

"Yeah, happy Tuesday to you." A voice answered from inside a dressing room.

"Thank you! What are you doing there?"

"I picked up Skylar's wedding gown from Nash Couture, which is the reason I was anywhere close to your favorite coffee addiction." Joan appeared from behind the heavy blue velvet drapery. "How you can drink that stuff is beyond me."

"Who wouldn't love a coffee bean roasted with old hickory wood, slow-brewed, then splashed with a shot of Tabasco?"

"Anybody who loves their taste buds and doesn't want to deaden their mouth for the rest of the day. Next, they'll offer a Cajun Caramel-latte with a shot of jerk syrup." Joan made a disgusted face.

"Um, that actually sounds good, minus the jerk." Ashley lifted the lid on her brew, careful of the rising steam. "I don't understand why Gunny's Bridal won't create the gowns we want right here in Williamson."

"Rainbow-colored taffeta dresses? C'mon, that's so not Gunny approved."

"Small town thinking leads to small town income." Hearing her sharp tone, she softened her voice. "Still, my point is—you went above and beyond. Thank you."

"You're welcome. And I don't mind the bustle of the city, sometimes."

Ashley sipped and watched as Joan filed away product flyers left out yesterday and checked the trash bins, moving from one undirected task to another. She knew Joan's high energy well, but this sort of discipline was likely honed during her time in the military. As was her sharp memory. "What time is Skylar's appointment, again?"

"Ten o'clock."

"Good, then I have time to run another errand." Ashley tapped a pencil on her desk—a sure sign she was working through a problem or craving a cigarette.

"You okay?" Joan asked.

"Yes." Ashley gave a rueful smile. "Thinking how to learn more about Molly Nolan. I may know who fits that bill." Ashley picked up her purse. "I'll be back before ten."

"And if you're not?" Joan, the Plan B advocate, asked.

"All the details are in her wedding folder. This is simply a hand-holding meeting. If Skylar's stressed out, then our job is to steady her nerves, and if she's too quiet, be a cheerleader."

"Cheerleader? I'm not exactly dressed for that." Joan pulled on the lapels of her solid gray blazer.

"Ready as always. Just remember—pom-poms." She gestured, then picked up her coffee.

"Yeah, I'm so the pom-pom type." Joan rolled her eyes.

✴✴✴✴✴

Ashley loved the heady scent inside Elinor's Floral. While the store bore Mrs. McDonagh's name, nowadays it was her son Edson who did most of the work. She spied him, neck crooked to clamp an iPhone to his shoulder, repositioning blooms in a vase as he spoke. He looked dapper, as always, wearing an apron atop his pin-tailored clothes.

"Good." He nodded. "It will work beautifully, trust me." He hung up.

"Speaking of trust, Ed," she leaned on the counter, placing her drink down. "Have you heard any news on the Nolans?"

"The retired professor and his wife?" he asked.

Ashley nodded.

"No, not sure I've heard from them since he ordered an anniversary arrangement for her last year. Is there trouble?"

"That's what I wonder. No one has seen her for a week, and when I saw him alone this morning, Mr. Nolan behaved like a kid in a candy store." She picked up a pair of shears and spun them on a finger.

"Okay, that is weird, he's usually a saltine cracker." He took the scissors away. "Come to think of it, I haven't received his annual order of flowers, either."

"For their upcoming anniversary?"

Ed nodded. "Each year, he sends the order through snail mail since he can't drop by the shop alone. He won't even telephone for fear of being overheard. And when he pays his bill in cash, it's sometimes by way of a friend. Feels sweetly sketchy." He winked. "Like a liaison."

"How many of those do you handle, Ed?" she teased.

He blushed.

"Well, last month Molly hired me to coordinate a big 40th wedding anniversary party for them, and now, she's ghosting me. Her generation doesn't usually do that."

He snipped a dead bloom off the bouquet. "You asked Nolan about his wife?"

"There wasn't time, and he was being cryptic. How did he put it? He 'got rid of the wife' and something about being scot-free."

"Eh, not a good response."

"Exactly!" Ashley finished her coffee and tossed the empty cup. "This could be worse than I thought."

"Or it could be better than you're thinking. Maybe Molly Nolan is visiting someone, and he's looking forward to some fishing, or days of no nagging…" Ed's response was met with her doubtful frown. "The phrase scot-free does sound concerning, though," he amended.

"Would your mother know about Molly's whereabouts?" Ashley asked.

"I'll ask. It's likely, since she participates in every church circle she can," Ed said, making a final bow adjustment, "To catch wind of weddings and funerals. My mother has built this business being non-discriminatory about people's denominations and money."

The bell over the door rang as Elinor entered her shop. She smiled and greeted Ashley with the warmth one bestows on a daughter.

"Elinor, how well do you know Molly Nolan?" she asked.

"Molly?" Elinor removed her headscarf. "Why, she's a dear friend of mine."

"How is she doing these days?"

"Fine. Like the rest of us, juggling ailing relatives while trying to keep our own not-so-young bodies together." Elinor handed her pocketbook to Ed, who placed it under the checkout counter.

"Really? Who's ill? I hope not Mr. Nolan," Ashley said.

"No, that old dog will outlive us all. Molly's widowed sister had a hip replacement, so I think she's been caring for her. Or I presume. Is there a reason you ask?"

"Mr. Nolan was acting strangely this morning, so I just wondered if there was trouble…"

"That husband of hers throws a fit when she's gone." Elinor whispered, "I think Molly could use some prayers in that regard."

"Is he—?" Ashley's question was cut short by the entrance of a customer.

*****

Having finished her cup of The Hermitage, Ashley crossed the street to the Route 1 Diner to continue her daily caffeine ritual. As expected, Detective Barnes of the Williamson police sat at the counter finishing his breakfast.

She placed her usual to-go order, then greeted him. "Good morning, Mr. Barnes."

"Well, if it isn't my favorite event planner. How do?"

"Fabulous. Yourself?"

"Can't complain—how's your daddy?"

Ashley's father and Fred Barnes were grade school pals, and she could never talk to him without providing updates. "Big Daddy is staying out of trouble lately—what more could a daughter want?" Ashley smiled, then lowered her voice. "Could I bother you for a moment?"

After his nod, Ashley quietly shared her encounter with Mr. Nolan and her concerns, careful to pause every time someone passed by or stopped to greet them, which meant the telling took a solid fifteen minutes. By that time, the story lost its tension and sounded more anecdotal, even to her own ears.

"Naw." The detective shook his head. "Spencer Nolan and me go way back. He's gruff, but a good guy."

"I know it sounds crazy, Mr—, Detective Barnes, but I have a bad feeling. Could you do a welfare check or something?"

He studied her worried expression and patted her hand. "Sugar, you bet. As soon as I get caught up on paperwork."

Stifling her disappointment in his typical non-committal and condescending tone, she left with a sweet and professional expression plastered to her face.

*****

Ashley should have returned to work instead of slipping into her Nissan and weaving through town to drive past the Nolans' house. She could have turned back before idling in traffic on the Little Harper River bridge—a piece of nostalgia with a 1930s sensibility of form and function. Instead, she found herself parked in front of a simple brick ranch-style house.

The front door opened with the sound of a hockey game blaring on the TV set and a visage of the occupant's startled, angry face. "What are you doing here?"

Ashley had her best smile ready. "Hello again, Mr. Nolan. Sorry to disturb you, but I'm looking for Molly, regarding the anniversary party plans. I've called several times without answer and so when I found myself in the neighborhood…"

"She ain't here. At her sister's place yonder." He flicked his wrist. "In Hoppers Vale. They got poor reception out there."

"Is it possible I could have her sister's name and address?"

"Maggie? A filthy woman: smoking, drinking…"

Ashley remembered that the Nolans were teetotalers.

He reached for a notepad on the hall table and scribbled the house number. "Seeing as you're dropping by." He also handed her a library book. "Wish I hadn't ordered groceries for them either. Damn delivery charges. On top of all *her* sin taxes. Damn government." That said, he shut the door.

*****

Hoppers Vale was a lovely ride into the lush, forested hills surrounding Williamson. Driving past the antique stores that dotted the route, Ashley stifled the urge to stop. Distracted, she lost count of the difficult-to-read rural address numbers. Spotting a mailbox decorated with a plastic crashed witch on a broom, she felt sure this was the house.

A grocery delivery box rested on the stoop and helped confirm the location. Ashley couldn't help a quick snoop: pineapple, mangos, cinnamon sticks, a box of Luzianne tea, a large bottle of bourbon, and cartons that looked suspiciously like cigarettes. 'Sin tax' indeed.

In response to Ashley's knock, Molly called out a welcome and a 'come on in.' Hearing the woman's voice, Ashley felt relief. She tossed in the library book and picked up the box.

"Ah," Molly stood in the kitchen. "Bring that here. I didn't know you were the delivery carrier."

"It was at the front door. I just happened by to talk to you about the party plan."

Through the opened back door, a woman who looked like Molly—more salt-n-pepper than silver-haired—entered using a walker. Outside of the apparatus, her lithe form moved like a younger woman. A veil of fumes fluttered in behind her, giving an ethereal quality.

"Maggie, this is that extraordinary party planner, Ashley. This is my sister."

Her sister harrumphed. "Events are planned…"

"…Parties happen," Molly finished with a giggle.

Ashley set the groceries down on a table crowded with trays of appetizers and cookies. "Well, it looks like you have the makings for one."

"We're hosting the church circle's monthly birthday party this evening," Maggie said, pointing. "Help yourself to whatever."

"And it's also my 40th year in the St. Barnabas ladies' circle," Molly grinned. "I joined as a newlywed." She jingled her empty glass. "We were going to refresh—would you like some fruit tea? Remember, I told you Maggie makes the best."

"Yes, I remember. But no thank you, I'm really a coffee kind of girl and I've had too much caffeine already today." Ashley picked up a coconut cookie and nibbled. *Delicious.* She grazed through the other offerings.

After stirring the iced tea, Maggie raised the clear pitcher into the light streaming through the kitchen window. She whispered her appreciation. "Like a ruby."

Molly accepted an offered glass, garnished with mango. "Thanks, Mags. I just can't stop drinking the stuff."

From prior menu planning, Ashley knew Molly preferred mocktails over cocktails, but she asked anyway. "So, are we drinking spiked ones?"

"Oh, heavens no." Molly chortled.

Maggie picked up her re-filled glass. "I'm not much of a drinker, especially during the daytime." She absentmindedly brushed a mint sprig up and down against the ice cubes. "Of course, that could be construed as unsocial, so I sometimes imbibe." She toasted her sister's glass and said, "Maybe later, huh Molls?"

Molly rolled her eyes and turned away. "Ashley, dear, what was it you needed to talk about?"

Ashley plunged into describing the project she'd fabricated on the drive, asking for photos and mementos to create a timeline of the Nolans' engagement and wedding.

"It was a rushed affair," Maggie blurted.

"True." Molly blushed. "And an elopement, so it's really a story best left untold." She gave her sister a sideways glance. "Not that I regret anything."

"Qué será será." Maggie waved off the point. "I've always maintained, it's better to know as little as possible about the person you marry."

Nonplussed, Ashley wondered if their tea did contain bourbon and the sisters were joshing her. "Well, no problem. I'll find another special way for the anniversary party to reflect the happiness you've built with Spencer."

"Happiness?" Maggie scoffed.

Molly laughed. "In marriage that's entirely a matter of chance."

"Life itself is a game of chance," Maggie added.

The sisters clinked glasses again. Ashley smiled, thinking what a duo they must have been in younger years. When it came time to leave, she breathed easier. Molly was safely ensconced at her sister's house.

*****

Before Ashley opened for business the next morning, Ed hurried out of the back storage room shared by both stores. "Molly Nolan is dead!"

"What?" Ashley practically shrieked.

"Last night—she dropped dead at a party."

"Heart attack?"

"Who knows? Mother said it was some kind of seizure. Maybe related to her diabetes."

Joan, who had walked in, paused, listening.

"But I just saw Molly… Could it be…" Ashley left the question unsaid.

"Could it be skinflint Nolan didn't order an anniversary bouquet," Ed paused, "because he knew Molly's death was imminent?"

Ashley broke the silence. "I thought you said he sweetly ordered furtive flowers."

"True, though he never seemed affectionate. An expected act, perhaps. And there's a fine line between clandestine and covert."

"He *always* seemed like a curmudgeon to me."

Joan cleared her throat. "But isn't everyday incivility the very essence of love?"

Ashley frowned. "What else did your mother tell you, Ed?"

"Very little. She was crying, Ashley, and this morning she was still in bed. I'll learn more *if* she comes to the shop." Ed glanced at his wristwatch. "Then I'll call you."

Joan pulled a project folder from the file cabinet and leafed through it. "Diabetic friendly dinner offerings, all the way down to the low-sugar Red Velvet cake."

"Red Velvet, so overdone," Ashley complained.

"Yeah, but it's their 40th anniversary. A *ruby* anniversary. Hence, the cake color."

There were a lot of treats laid out for that party yesterday. Cakes. Cookies. Breaded things. Ashley wondered if a diabetic seizure could be induced and shared her thought out loud.

"What an inefficient way of doing it—seems easier to poison someone." On hearing Ashley's gasp, Joan added, "In theory. Remember, Nolan wasn't at that party last night."

"Hmm." Ashley looked across the street. "I need coffee."

*****

Not finding Detective Barnes in the diner, Ashley hovered under her storefront awning, out of Joan's earshot, and phoned him.

"I agree. Given our conversation yesterday, it is odd, Ashe, but there is no police investigation. It's been ruled diabetic seizure and that falls under natural causes."

"Seizure is rather generic word, isn't it? And the doctor didn't see her die."

"But plenty of witnesses did and their descriptions were taken into account. Look, Molly was older and her health none too good."

"That doesn't satisfy me."

"Ashe, the more I see and hear, the more I'm dissatisfied with it, too. We just have to live with it."

"And Molly? Does she get to live with it, too?"

Barnes sighed. "Sadly, it's how she lived and died. Her husband confirmed her health had been giving her trouble lately."

"Yes," her voice drifted off, "Of course he did."

"Look, I've seen it before—a sudden death and then the rumors. I hear you, that Nolan was acting strange, but let this be. Rumors never do good."

*****

Later that afternoon, after receiving a text message from Ed announcing his mother's arrival at the florist shop, Ashley dropped in to offer condolences and get more details on Molly's last moments.

"It was dreadful," Elinor said.

Ashley embraced the older woman. "I'm sure."

"We were just talking. Like normal. Then she suddenly had a seizure and died before the ambulance could arrive. So… swift."

Ashley nodded and waited for an appropriate pause. "Were you near Molly when this happened?"

"Yes, on the next seat over, but I was talking with LuAnn and heard someone say, 'Look, Molly's ill.' Then I turned to see Molly struggling to her feet, swaying, before she fell. At first, I tried to support her, as did Maggie, but Molly was shaking, so we pulled furniture out of the way. Then she went still."

"Elinor, how awful." Ashley lowered her gaze like a silent prayer. "What did everyone do?"

"Maggie shouted for us to dial 9-1-1. And LuAnn is a nurse, so she knelt alongside Molly's sister, but when she checked Molly's pulse, there was none. I guess she started CPR, but I remember her saying to Maggie, 'I'm sorry, she's gone.'"

Ed rubbed his mother's back in a reassuring gesture.

Ashley began pacing. "Did you notice what Molly had been eating? Drinking?"

Elinor shrugged. "She ate exactly what everyone else ate—well, a lesser amount. Molly was always careful with portions and avoiding the desserts."

"I'm just wondering if the last thing she put in her mouth is important."

"I really think that concern is up to the professionals, Ashley. Besides, I wasn't watching her." Elinor's gaze drifted. "I heard crunching sounds. Then a gag."

Ashley and Ed exchanged glances.

"But, oh, her face convulsed. Awful." Elinor started to cry.

*****

"Ashley Francis Austen-Holmes, where are you going with this," she scolded herself on the drive home. She shook with a sense of boding, not unlike when her wayward brother had done something very wrong. Still, this wasn't family and likely she was interfering.

But didn't Molly deserve a few moments of questioning? Such as, why would Nolan say 'rid of the wife' instead of 'the wife's away?' Why hadn't he ordered anniversary flowers? Was there any meaning behind the library book he'd sent to her, *Probate for Dummies*?

A knot of doubt fluttered in Ashley's stomach. Maybe she placed too much faith in her intuition. Maybe she'd forgotten to eat lunch again today.

*****

A chardonnay and a shower had taken the whirl out of Ashley's thoughts when Laura Jean called with a bombshell.

"Spencer Nolan came into the bank and wanted to close their account."

"No." Ashley placed her hairbrush down. "Can he do that?"

"Well, not without her death certificate. Then he met with the bank manager, in private, so I officially don't know what happened. But…"

"Gotcha. Mums the word."

"But I looked through the end of day reports and under the list of new account creations was Nolan's name and the beneficiary was Maggie Hudkins."

"Opened an account with his sister-in-law as beneficiary? What's he up to?"

"Is this scandalous or what?" Laura Jean squealed. "His wife's corpse is barely cold."

After hanging up, Ashley immediately dialed Detective Barnes' number, relieved that she knew someone on the force.

He listened without interruption and made a promise that sounded like he'd keep. "Thanks. We've already made some discreet inquiries, so this will be followed up. But, Ashe, please don't share what you know with anyone."

"Rumors, I know." She toweled her hair.

"That, and a detective's best weapon is surprise."

*****

Assured by Detective Barnes that the Medical Examiner would now investigate further, Ashley spent the next few days catching up on work. Once she made it through her messages, Joan placed a stack of project folders on her desk.

63

"Sorry, I've been wrapped up in the Nolans. Was there any more on Skylar's wedding that I need to know?"

"Yeah, she wants some unusual favors for the guest reception."

"You know I *love* unusual."

The front door flew open and Elinor McDonagh walked in with Ed on her heels. Ashley was surprised to see both away from their floral shop during business hours. Must be big, she thought excitedly.

"Ashe, I've been thinking about how often your instinct is right," Ed said. "So, Mother and I have been talking through the evening Molly passed, and she's remembered something that may be important."

Elinor wrung her hands. "It maybe nothing. Just something that struck me as different, but in hurried moments, I set it aside in my mind."

"Go on. Everything is something," Ashley encouraged.

Ed nodded.

Joan looked to be taking notes.

"When we first sat down to eat, Molly ended up with a spiked fruit tea. At least, I assumed so, as she made wry faces after sipping. She accused Maggie of slipping bourbon into her drink."

"Wow, had she?"

"No, maybe Molly picked it up from the wrong side of the table. Anyways, they jested and we all had a good laugh."

"Then?" Ed prompted.

"Then she washed out the glass and got Molly a fresh tea."

Ed began pointing as if the words hung in the air.

"Maggie washed the glass?" Ashley asked.

"Naturally. Listen. Even if the drink was spiked, it was later, when we were nearly finished, that Molly fell ill. And I didn't think Molly would have a reaction to a sip of alcohol."

"Maybe, it was *more* than alcohol," Ed said.

Elinor shook her head. "Edson, please, this was girls-night-out fun."

"Mother, this is the kind of detail that the police need to know. Don't you agree, Ashe?"

Ashley took Elinor's hand and gave it a squeeze. "I think since we don't know details about Molly's health conditions, it wouldn't be right to assume. I'd let the police decide what could, or could not, be harmful."

The older woman shrugged, but nodded her assent.

On another score, Ashley wanted to ask about Mr. Nolan's relationship with his sister-in-law, but she resisted. It was obvious the idea of murder did not resonate with Elinor's understanding of the couple.

Before the McDonaghs closed the door behind themselves, Ashley threw out one last question. "Elinor, do you think the Nolans had a happy marriage?"

"Ashley, there's as many happinesses as there are moments in time," she replied.

*****

Although she rarely visited Gunny's Bridal, the seamstress was a valuable gossip and Ashley wanted details on the Nolans' marriage.

Gunny stood at a dressmaker's dummy, busy working with white satin. Her eyes lit when Ashley asked and she removed pins from her mouth. "Ah, Spencer Nolan. Tall and handsome, once. Served in the army and disappeared in Korea—never thought we'd see him again."

"So, it's a bittersweet love story?"

"Yessiree. She was smitten. As was he." She adjusted a seam pinning. "They had that molten kind of love."

"Molly and Spencer?"

"Molly? No Maggie. His first love. Unfortunately, while he was held prisoner, Maggie came into the family way and married someone else. Spencer wed the younger sister when he returned."

*****

Ashley returned to *eXceptional Events* and shared the newfound secret with Joan. "So, he killed her to return to his recently widowed first love."

Joan pursed her lips. "Or *she*. Poison is as much a woman's weapon as a man's."

Having seen the sisters together, Ashley's response was a cool, hmm. She tapped her pen on her desk. "Okay, back to those reception favors for Skyler's wedding. What's the unusual favor?"

"A variety of Juuls."

"Jewels? Did she increase her budget? Substantially?"

Joan flashed a magazine advertisement. "Electronic cigarettes in a rainbow of flavors: sour apple, bubblegum, and the like." She passed the page to Ashley. "But who are they trying to fool about not marketing to kids, right?"

"Or 'kids-getting-married'." Ashley sighed, taking the ad. "Well, if it's not illegal, we'll do it."

Joan nodded and quipped, "eXceptional Events where off-beat meets main street."

The phone rang and Joan repeated the slogan into the receiver.

Ashley studied the magazine page, whispering, "Mango."

"Detective Barnes." Joan handed her the phone and interrupted her thoughts.

Without saying hello, Ashley and Barnes blurted together, "Poison."

Then also in unison: "How?—"

Barnes began. "You were right, Ashe."

"Autopsy is in?"

"No signs of diabetic-induced seizure, but the medical examiner noted perimortem signs of liver failure, consistent with poisoning. It will take time for the pathology report."

"I bet they'll find a lethal dose of nicotine."

"Nicotine overdose? Naw, that's somewhat rare, unless one's a heavy smoker, or has an accident with a nicotine patch," said the detective.

"Molly never put it in her system. She was poisoned."

"Still, there's no evidence to show how or who administered the dosage."

Ashley relayed the incident that Elinor had shared. "Seems the stuff was in her spiked fruit tea, only the tea wasn't spiked, it was laced. Laced with fruited nicotine."

"Hmm. In all my experience, I've never come across a case of nicotine poisoning. Let's see…" Ashley could hear the detective typing on his computer.

She beat him to it. "WebMD says this alkaloid is an odorless liquid and a few drops of it are enough to kill someone."

Detective Barnes whistled. "Potent stuff. It's a good theory, Ashe. Too bad there's no longer glassware to analyze."

Ashley dropped the pen she'd been tapping. "Yes, but somewhere there are receipts for the groceries that Nolan had delivered to Maggie's place with a carton of Juuls. I didn't think much of it at the time, but I remember he specifically complained to me about the cost. He bought it and she administered."

*****

Under questioning, Spencer Nolan and Maggie Hudkins admitted to their re-kindled relationship and that they'd been poisoning Molly for weeks, hiding the nicotine flavors in a variety of food and drink.

The extent of their perfidy came out at trial, where both were given life sentences. Maggie Hudkins' jail time lasted only one day due to a fatal heart attack. Spencer Nolan lasted another week when he was found hanging in his cell from his belt.

On a local Williamson *Psst Crime Insider* blog, a marketing gem appeared when an anonymous detective acknowledged the force's gratitude for Ashley Austen-Holmes who, by the *eXceptional Event* of her persistence, had been the means of uncovering Molly's murder.

Memindip Solves a Problem
Jay Andrew Connor

1

As my on-again off-again friend, Adagouti, will readily tell you, it is not easy being dead. Especially when your birth tribe didn't follow the correct rituals for your burial before moving on to fresh grazing land. Or that construction workers return after a long while, dig you up, then plant you elsewhere because you are an inconvenience to a fresh water pipe being laid to the Governor's new house.

Adagouti, he says:

– You know, you don't have to be too wise to spot a shifty wraith. And I say this with all the kindness I can muster, you are one really shifty wraith, Memindip.

I look Adagouti as best I can in the eye, given that his tortoise-like face is forever slowly bobbing up and down, making it hard not to focus on the bundles of stringy sinews visible under the sagging skin of his neck.

– My friend – who is likely to slip from that most exalted of positions if he is not careful – were it not for the lack of respect my people showed me after my demise, then both you and I know we would not be having this conversation in the first place.

Adagouti may well be the self-proclaimed foot messenger for the ancient African Animist tribal Gods and Guiding Spirits, but there are times when he needs to be reminded of our positions.

– Be that as it may, I have been told to tell you that you will soon die.

– Again?

– Of course again. You cannot live again indefinitely, can you. All Life has an associated Death invisibly attached to it at birth. It has to be invisible, because if you could see it, you would ask it silly questions such as 'When am I going to die?' or 'How am I going to die?' And anyway, Death can never be trusted. She lies like a hyena giving directions to an abandoned lion kill. As you know, I have wandered and walked the Shashaska for more time that you have existed in one form or another. So respect your elders when they tell you things,

lest the fleas of a thousand camels infest your crotch and you scratch your withered balls off.

I shake what I believe would once have been my head.

– Adagouti, according to those who came long after, you are but a distracting figment of an ancient generation's imagination, and not a very appealing one, at that. My children's children were told of a God who promised them the reward of an afterlife that was a joyful paradise. A land of perpetual milk and honey and sunshine and happiness. Imagine that if you will. All they had to do was turn their backs on you and your kind.

– *But how would you ever survive in such a place when you cannot even swim? And how can you believe in rivers of milk and shores of honey when you know that the rivers are but the fingers of Opoula, the water goddess, who lives in the sea, forever salted by the tears of those she has taken to live with her. What does she care about some childish upstart beliefs? She is forever at war with her brothers and sisters, and to her that is all that matters.*

– At war?

– *Why yes. Have you not seen the violent crashing of the waves upon the rocky shores? Have you not seen the ancient falls, dryer than a desert one day, then overflowing with newly spilled rainwater the next?*

– That I have, it's true. And somewhere in my distant memories lives a boy child who ran around and through those falls, bringing fresh water to his family, the cattle and the goats. And as a man, that Memindip brought a young woman to see the beauty of it all.

– *And now is never the time to hurt yourself with painful shards of the past, my friend. It cannot be changed or altered. If we could do that, then we would be greater than the Gods themselves, and they would become our playthings.*

His image shimmers and wavers as if in the desert heat.

– *It is the time for you to prepare yourself for the transition.*

– But what do I have to do once I have been reborn? Like a porcupine, I suspect such a gift would come with hooks and barbs, of that I'm sure.

– *There has been a wrongful, premature death that has gone unavenged, and you have been destined to be its avenger.*

– But did you not just say that each life has an associated death? So why not ask of her as to who did what and why?

– *And did I not just tell you that Death lies compulsively? She gains as much pleasure from her misdirections as does a warthog wallowing in a pool of mud slop.*

– So why am I being sent to avenge that which I have not seen or understand?

– *Ah, Memindip, were that it were that easy. You will be reborn at a point in time before the accursed thief steals the life from its holder. You will observe, you will deduce and you will conclude as to who the culprit is.*

– Yes, but who is–

Adagouti cuts my anxious question short.

– *Enough of this ineffectual monkey-like chit-chat! Prepare yourself to be reanimated.*

– When?

– *Now, of course.*

And so it was that I was reborn.

Yet being reborn is not like the first time. No wailing aunts, no curious visiting relatives whom you never see from one fruitful season to the next, no shamen waving charms and talismen in the air while drinking something they have brewed up in the back of their summer manzil.

No, one instance my bones and I are trying to get eternally comfortable in the very substandard burlap sack we were dumped into, and the next we are reassembled, re-fleshed, and relocated, spitting out a mouthful of dry soil and dust. As if from the back of a cave, I hear Adagouti's distant voice say:

– *Why is everything so complicated with this one?! Memindip! Stop fidgeting and be still while I try to fix that which has become broken.*

Then everything is black and silent, until:

2

"Mr. Memindip?"

Mister? I open one eye, unsure as to where and how I have acquired it. I open the other, and hope they match.

"Mr. Memindip, another mint tea?"

I look down at the now empty glass cup in front of me, the syrup of half dissolved sugar thick at the bottom, and the sweet taste heavy in my mouth. I flex my jaw.

"Perhaps a refill, if you will." My voice is almost as I remember it, only younger than at my demise.

The waiter disappears off behind me and I catch sight of my wide brimmed hat on the chair beside me. I shoot my cuffs, curious as to the contrast between starched white cotton and my own black-brown skin. Then I see myself in a mirror panel on the wall, and I take in my lime green suit and lemon yellow tie, and for a moment I consider how many ways I would enjoy throttling Adagouti for dressing me like some gaudy forest parrot. I look around 30 years old, with hair again, though cut short and close to my skull – no wrinkles around the eyes or scrag around my neck. Perhaps I should forgive Adagouti some things after all. But my face is not entirely that of my own, of that I am sure.

On the tablecloth near my hand is a paper coaster with *La Veilleuse* printed on it, the lettering circling a hand holding a nightlight on a stick.

The waiter returns with a large pewter tea pot. As he pours the aromatic dark liquid into my awaiting cup, he asks:

"Are you here to see Miss Fontaine, and perhaps admire her fine singing voice?"

"Perhaps."

The waiter nods. "Then you will not be disappointed."

I look across the seating area decked out with small tables and clusters of chairs, across the softly lit but unoccupied dance floor, to the front of the low stage – catching a whiff of kif in the air. The musicians assembled off to the left are creating something that is both cacophonous and tribally rhythmical at the same time, and I remain unsure as to whether I like it or not. And like the rest of the assembled audience, I am not disappointed when Miss Fontaine takes to the stage.

Her voice is like the touch of cooling rain at the height of the drought season – something to be enjoyed and revelled in – a moment to be savoured and forever remembered. She performs three – maybe four – songs. A pause, then she is back on stage for another 'set' to complete the evening's entertainment.

Yet, as her performance comes to an end and the house and stage lights rapidly fade to blackness, there is the distinctive click of a flintlock pistol being cocked, followed hard on its heels by the muzzle flash and cordite smell as the gun is discharged.

Almost immediately the lights come on again. On the stage lies Miss Fontaine, a stain of blood spreading from the fresh hole in her chest.

In the uproar and chaos that follows I remain seated, observing, as like a leopard in a tree observes from the branches. The audience remains seated or standing until realisation finally touches them. Some run to the edge of the low stage, some even climb up onto it in their efforts to help. Others slink away from the whole affair, either abandoning their lovers and mistresses, or taking them out of the club and into taxies – not realising just how reliable a taxi drivers' memories can be from time to time.

Before long, Commandant Monnes appears, flanked by several of his gendarmes, all in camel brown uniforms and with revolvers at their sides. Barely raising his voice, Monnes booms, "Everyone go back to your seats. I said, *Everyone!*"

The chaos continues as more people appear from backstage, herded like goats by several gendarmes.

Commandant Monnes looks about him and waits while the remaining clientele have settled down. Then he walks to the edge of the stage and looks at the crime scene, at the corpse of Miss Fontaine, then over to the musicians. He singles out the trumpet player using his official police stare.

"You, music man. Tell me what you saw – and I don't mean the colour of the notes, or the sound of a clear blue sky at midnight. I mean as to how this poor woman came to be parted from her life."

"Whoa now, your honour, none of us saw what happened. We have the lights in our eyes while we're playing. Then *P'toof!* They get turned off at the close of the set, and we're all blinded by the darkness before the lights come back on."

The clarinet player pulls at the trumpet player's jacket sleeve. "Tell him about the flash, Bippin. Tell the man about the flash from the far side of the stage."

"I was just getting to that, Maylon." Bippin the trumpet player looks back towards the Commandant again.

"The end of the second set all the lights go out. By that time the audience are clapping, whistling and calling for more. Which was when we saw the powder flash."

"From the side of the stage?"

"Yes. With all the noise from the audience we only saw the flash, then nothing more until the lights came back on again. And there she was, lying on the stage as you see her now."

Commandant Monnes turns to look back at the body. The edge of the stage comes halfway up his chest, and although her eyes are now closed, her head is turned towards him, with perhaps a wisp of a smile on her lips.

A young gendarme appears from the back of the stage and walks forward.

"Sir, there appears to be no trace of any firearm. But, to make matters worse, there is a door behind me that opens out onto the side street at the back of this nightclub. It would be the simplest of things to have committed the murder, then made good an escape thought the back."

Concise and complete. The young man impresses me with his efficiency.

Monnes sighs, dismayed by the seeming futility and lack of a ready suspect.

"Start taking statements from those who remain. Give me a full briefing in the morning so I can work out the best direction to take in regard to tracking down this poor woman's killer."

He turns to leave, then sees me in all my re-fleshed and dressed finery. For a moment he looks quizzical, then makes his way over to my table.

"Good evening, Commandant," I say. "Would you care to sit?" I point at a chair, which he pointedly refuses.

"Do I know you?"

"Tomaso Memindip, sir." And like a puppet I find my hand going to the top pocket of my jacket, fingers reaching behind the folded handkerchief to pluck out a business card as if it were an embedded Niger bush thorn.

"And what business do you have here, Tomaso Memindip?"

"I am…." I pause, unsure as to how much I should say. "An investigator."

"An investigator?"

"Of sorts. I am here to right wrongs and give the innocent a voice."

Monnes looks at my card, and for the first time I see that the pasteboard is printed with my name and an address in the Furuke district of the city.

"And if you truly are a voice for the innocent, what are you doing here? Did you know that this murder was about to take place?"

"I can honestly say no," *Because if I told you the truth I would be in danger of being locked up.*

"So it is just coincidence that you should travel from the respectability of the Furuke district," He sniffs at the smoke-tainted air, "To this less than respectable venue?"

"A very sad coincidence, it's true." I improvise as best I can with what little I have. "But Miss Fontaine's reputation is spreading fast, and I wanted to see for myself if the claims were true. Alas they were."

Around and about us, with their statements already taken, the room is rapidly becoming deserted. Against the flow, the City Morgue doctor and two assistants with a stretcher arrive, and fight their way upstream to the stage.

Monnes turns back to me. "Regardless of all the cow dung, I advise you to go back to your safe manzil, shut the door, and keep away from my investigations. Unless, of course," He looks me directly in the eye. "You are the murderer, and wish to confess?"

"It would be a brave fool who would think to pit themselves against you, Commandant."

Monnes stands and looks down at me. "I have a feeling our paths will cross again. I only hope we are travelling in the same direction when they do."

With that he departs – leaving in his wake the doctor, now on stage, and his two assistants.

I watch, mildly angered at the way the doctor prods and pokes, touches and gropes the defenceless corpse laid out before him.

At the edge of the stage, elbow supporting as he leans upon it looking out across the now almost deserted nightclub, one of the stretcher bearers watches me intently. Brown eyes and an olive complexion. I would say, if pressed, that he hails from one of the peninsula islands along the northern coastline.

From his shirt pocket he pulls out a half crumpled packet of cigarettes – Mojha, cork tipped – and a brass Zippo lighter.

"Five minute smoke break, dukturah?" He asks, still looking at me.

The doctor doesn't look up, but mumbles:

"Those things will kill you," as he carefully checks through the pockets of the dead woman's blouse, before adding: "Go. But make sure you're only five minutes. I'm nearly done here, and it's a long walk back to the morgue."

Tobacco in hand he mutters something to the other assistant from the corner of his mouth, then walks by me on his way to the street.

Outside, the air is clearing as the streets and the district in general quieten. Shopkeepers long departed, baker's apprentices setting the kindling – ovens to be ready by 4, bread to be ready for sale by 6. Taxi drivers touting for the last of the late night club business.

Around the side of the building is the smoking assistant, cigarette already a quarter sucked to ash. Without looking at me, he says, "You like what you see?"

My confusion is genuine. "What?"

"On stage, the dead woman. You'd like to look at her? In private? Don't worry, I get to talk to a lot of your kind. Those who like to look at the dead."

"I still don't –"

"Twenty dirham, an hour or so after sunrise."

"You have me wrong. I am here to catch the person who shot her."

"You're not one of the Commandant's men are you?"

"Dressed like this?"

He looks at me for a moment. "Perhaps not. So what's your interest in the dead woman?"

"I am on a mission to avenge her death."

"So soon?"

I nod.

"Okay. But it's still twenty dirham a look. My name is Sully. If anyone else answers your knock, then don't ask for me."

He drops the end of his cigarette onto the pavement and rubs it out with his shoe, then heads back into the nightclub.

I start to walk along the main street, heading in no particular direction. In less than fifty paces I'm level with a large black Chevrolet of undetermined age and indiscriminate parentage if the replacement panels are anything to go by – definitely more scratch than paint. In the maroon red leather driver's seat half sleeps the rag-tag driver – the car windows and his once white shirt are partially open to help keep everything cool.

I knock on the roof of the vehicle to see if he is actually asleep, or worse – thankful that he wakes with a start. He glares at me for a split second, then smiles with both his mouth and his eyes – grateful for any business at this time of night.

"Good," He glances quickly at the clock set in the ivory cream and chrome dashboard, "Morning, Sayidi. I am Marzouk, and I take it you need transport to a place of discrete pleasure? Or perhaps you'd care to dine before taking to your bed? Wherever you wish to be, you will find my charges exceedingly acceptable. In fact, were it not for my aged and infirmed mother, my fees would be even cheaper, were such possible.

"I suspect your aged mother disowned you before you had reached manhood. But that is of no concern to me. I am in search of someone who has the means and wherewithal to transport me in and around this city."

"You mean more than one journey?"

"One journey should be enough to judge your skills. But further employment after that is open to negotiation."

"Okay, Sayidi. Please, step into my office and we will negotiate."

I open the back door and carefully slide onto the maroon leather seat, closing the door behind me. My hand goes back up to my breast pocket and another card is handed over as I say:

"Here is an address I wish to go to. It will be a test of your driving skills and honesty."

"Okay, boss!" Ignition ignites, cranks crank, and we're off.

An uneventful 15 minutes of near misses and colourful expletives later, Marzouk parks up in front of a 5 storey apartment block.

"Here you are, Sayidi. The fee is five dirham – a mere trifle to one such as yourself, but it will put food on the table for my wife and three children."

"And what of your aged mother?"

"Ah, and her as well, Sayidi. She lives with us in our small but happy manzil." He looks at me via the rear view mirror. "So, Sayidi, do my driving skills meet with your approval? Am I to be the one chosen to transport you around this wonderful city of ours?"

I don't want to appear too eager – or needy – so I pause in contemplation before saying:

"I am prepared to put you on a retainer of," I reach into my jacket, take out my wallet, and extract a 200 dirham note. "One hundred dirham."

"Ah, Sayidi, alas I do not have the wherewithal to change such a large amount. Perhaps if you would consider the second hundred as an extension of the first contracted amount – for, say, services that are yet to be rendered at a future date?"

"Allow me to offer yet a further alternative." I fold the brightly coloured note in half, run my fingernail along the fold, then quickly tear the note in two. Not totally oblivious to Marzouk's whimperings, I hand him one of the halves.

"Here," I say. "Take this as a deposit in order to open my account." And before he can say anything more, I put the second half into my wallet, and the wallet safely back into my jacket.

Opening the taxi's door, I get out, and to the still confused Marzouk, I say:

"You now have my address. Call for me an hour before sunrise. I need to be at the city morgue at a certain time in order to meet a certain person."

Marzouk nods, still looking at his half of the violated 200 dirham note with, I suspect, a small tear welling at the corner of his eye.

"Yes, Sayidi. I shall call for you then."

I turn, go through the main doors of the apartment block, nod to the night porter at his desk, and take the lift to the 4th floor.

Once behind the safety of its front door, I breathe a long sigh of relief. Adagouti has done a remarkable job in regard to my rebirth.

I have a home. I have money with which to purchase things I need. And I obviously have a status I would never have dreamed possible for a tribesman such as myself to attain when I was first alive.

3

– Memindip! We have matters of some urgency to discuss.

I am lying on top of a large muskaba, in one of the three sleeping rooms this manzil possesses. Windows open to catch the midnight breeze, I have just slipped into my dream land when I see the spirit form of Adagouti. It is clear he is not in good humour.

– We need to talk about your rebirth and about your host body. There are… Let us say conflicts.

– But surely when I was reborn I was placed in my own body.

– And how is that body supposed to have survived? Answer me that! You died at the hands – and dagger – of a Portuguese trader you had sold quartz to instead of diamonds, in the year 1701. The present year is 1969.

Adagouti has a long, and oft times accurate, memory. I change the subject.

– So whose body am I inhabiting?

– You are living like a hermit crab, in the shell of Tomaso Akriki, from down in the southern lands. This was his hide-away manzil, and it is his ill-gotten money you are spending. He died of a broken neck due to a car accident. He was the last of his line, and this manzil was 'lost' in the accounting.

– And the money?

– You have all that is in your wallet. It will replace only that which you spend from it in one transaction. It will continue to do that until you have solved this crime.

– So Death has already come and gone to both myself and this Akriki? Is there a chance that she will want to reclaim what she already has possession of, without warning?

– For now Death has no direct claim over you or Tomaso. She haggled like a fishwife with the last of the morning's catch, but she finally agreed with the Gods that there were circumstances which made this situation unique.

– But what is so important about this? Why am I here at all?

– Are you questioning the motives of the Gods?

I feel I am about to step into a pit of snakes, whose floor is also made of quicksand. But still I carry on.

– Of course not. But some idea would at least help me to understand.

– Okay. There was a time when Be'kal decided he would once again walk the earth as a Tribesman – a novel experience. During that time, he fell in love with a woman, and as is natural, there came about the birth of two almost perfect children. Twins though one was a boy and the other a girl. The boy was

handsome and fearless, and the girl was beautiful and wise. Although they were half God, they were also half mortal. It is said that it was the mortal half of the boy that lusted after his father's power and greatness – to the point where Be'kal killed him, as a lesson to all men that Gods are still mighty and all powerful.

The daughter, however, grew into a fine young woman. But after she heard of the fate of her brother she feared for her life also. So she hid herself amongst the Tribes. Eventually she married well, and was blessed with children of her own. Time and circumstances pass, until we come to Aziza Fontaine. She was the last of the last, and her murder has ended the line forever.

– So why doesn't Be'kal come back to this plane and avenge her death?

– *Because in this day and age there are very few such as yourself who still believe in the old Gods and spirits anymore. Without belief their powers weaken, hence your re-existence. You were a devout believer, Memindip, despite your underhand ways – some of which would shame vultures were they to hear of them. And for your belief, you are rewarded by helping the Gods themselves.*

In the distance I can now hear a tap-tap-tapping, insistent, like a beetle in a fallen tree trunk.

– So what happens after I find the culprit? Or, more importantly, what happens to me?

The tapping gets louder and becomes a distraction, and I cannot hear Adagouti clearly when he finally replies:

– *This is a valley we will need to cross when we come to it.*

– Adagouti! You cannot –

But the sound of knocking is now so intrusive that I am forced to wake up and realise that someone is at the manzil's front door.

4

I cover myself with a dressing gown and pad to the spy hole set in the painted wood. On the other side is Marzouk. I open the door and he greets me with:

"You said you needed to be at the morgue just after sunrise, Sayidi. So I am here to rouse you from your slumbers."

He is smartly turned out – pressed white shirt, cream cotton suit, brown shoes and tie – and with no sleep grit in the corners of his eyes, unlike myself.

Unsure as to whether his beliefs allow it, I ask, "Have you eaten yet?" And on shaking his head, I tell him, "Over there in the kitchen area you'll find khlea, eggs, bread and good olive oil. While you prepare us breakfast, I will wash and dress for the day."

By the time I have completed my toilet – choosing this time a more subdued

2 piece grey suit and tie – Marzouk has completed the preparations. The strips of meat are beneath the soft fried eggs, the bread cut into wedges, and a thin layer of oil sits in the dish of the plate.

I offer up a silent acknowledgement to Bulhakish and her unending strength in pushing the darkness back from whence it came, even though the hour is early and she has still to bring the morning with her. Then I take up a piece of bread, coat the end in egg yolk, and commence to break my morning fast.

Meanwhile Marzouk chews contemplatively, looking around at the apartment. Swallowing to empty his mouth, he asks:

"Forgive me, Sayidi, but what is it that you do that gives you such things as money in your pocket and an incredible roof over your head?"

I try to remember all that Adagouti told me at the start of this adventure.

"I am a righter of wrongs – a voice for the innocent, and an avenger in search of the truth."

"You are a detective?"

A what? The expression is not unknown to me, but I say:

"Yes, you could say that. I am a diviner of the truth, which makes me a detective of sorts."

"You are a private detective? As in those books the American tourists often leave behind?" Marzouk's eyes are wide as he chomps through some meat and bread. Still having no comprehension as to what he is babbling on about, I just nod and continue to eat in silence, until –

"Sayidi? Are you on a case right now?" Again with the wide eyes and chomping jaw. "Are *we* on a case right now?"

"Alsinujab alsaghir, at the moment there is no 'we' – only I."

"But I am your chosen driver, no?"

"Be that as it may," I wipe up the remains of the egg and olive oil with a fresh wedge of bread. "I think it is time we were travelling to the city's morgue."

Down in the lift – still a novel experience – and as we cross the foyer – myself leading and Marzouk bringing up the rear, as befits our new employer employee relationship – the night porter opens the street door for us. Outside in the cool air, I pause to look up and down the Furuke district. Tidy, well kept, white walls now tingled grapefruit pink from the rising sun. Some traffic already. A large cart selling warm bread and sweet milk to waking households. People moving – those who need to, off to morning prayers, while those of older beliefs have already added a drop of blood to the fresh water as it disappeared from the wash bowl. Both give life. One to the tribesman, the other to the land that feeds him.

Marzouk stands with the taxi door open. "Are you ready, Sayidi? You look distant, in contemplation."

"I am wondering if by nightfall, we shall have discovered who the murderer is, and in doing so, discover why."

The journey is via a winding collection of backstreets. Some are dark and dank, others lead into and out of small areas of peace and tranquillity – the sound of running water underscores the birdsong, valiantly audible over the Chevrolet's engine.

Parking up, I tell Marzouk to wait for me – knowing full well that the other half of the 200 dirham note keeps us tied together like Siamese twins.

The City Morgue is imposing. An old stone structure with a heavy weathered door and slightly tarnished brass address plaque.

I pick out a 20 dirham note from my wallet, fold it three times, then trap it between two fingers of my right hand.

Satisfied, I knock several times and Sully the assistant lets me in, the 20 dirham note changing hands as we shake our greeting. With the note in the pocket of his lab coat, he guides me through to the Autopsy Room at the back. Cold and clinical electric light shines off equally cold and clinical stainless steel.

"She is over here."

I follow him to the gurney where her body rests, a white sheet giving her some well-deserved modesty.

Sully gently rolls down the sheet until the bullet wound is visible. His mouth turns upwards in a sad smile.

"She is still so beautiful, don't you think?"

I look down at her, and wish that I'd had the chance to run my fingers through her long black hair, or gently brush her lips with mine, if only in a final parting kiss.

I look up. "I understand the bullet was fired by an ancient pistol."

Sully shakes his head. "Pistol, true. But it was no bullet or ball shot that killed her." He goes over to the evidence locker and picks out a brown manila envelope. He shakes the contents onto his palm, then picks up the object between thumb and forefinger. "It was this pearl. As smooth and as round as any lead musket ball."

Sully comes over and places it in my upturned hand and we both look down at it in silence for a moment.

Then Sully softly says, "It has age. See how some of the layers have been worn away with time, creating small imperfections. It also has the slight greenish opal tinge to it. This never came from the Eastern Coast – the water is too cold. Or from the Northern Coast, because those thieving Spaniards would have taken it for themselves. No, this is a glorious thing from the Western Coast."

I hold it up to the fluorescent light, and see the tiny indentations of its original claw setting. "Yet here it is, unaccompanied by its rightful or wrongful owner."

With the pearl back in the evidence locker, I leave Sully to his cold world, and go back to the waiting Marzouk.

"Did you have any success, Sayidi?"

"In some respects yes. I discovered Miss Fontaine was killed by a pearl of extraordinary beauty."

"And this pearl belongs to?"

"That, alsinujab alsaghir, is our next task. Without the pearl it would be futile to try and find the jeweller who sold it – though I suspect were I to describe it then it would be easily recognised. No, I need to talk to the musicians, and the owner of *La Veilleuse*, to find out more about Miss Fontaine."

5

In daylight the street on which the nightclub exists is quiet. Neon signs are turned off, doors with posters pinned to them are closed, no hustle, no bustle. At 9 o'clock in the morning, Marzouk is the only taxi not passing through on its way to some other destination.

I step out onto the curb as Marzouk says:

"It looks like it's all locked up for the day."

I nod, then head to the side street, down and around to the back of the club. The back door is cracked open, and around it are four men – plaid work shirts and labourers' blue denim – smoking. One, pinched face, chin pointed and dimpled, takes nips from a flat metal flask. All four eye me warily.

"Gentlemen," I say, offering them one of my business cards. "I believe you are the musicians who played here last night?"

No one commits to a reply. Then Pinch Face says:

"I remember you. Green suit, wide brim hat. Are you one of Monnes' men?"

"No."

Mylon, the clarinet player, takes my card then joins the conversation.

"You look too straight and officious to be hipster. What do you want anyway? We already told the gendarmes all we know."

"Yeah," adds the trumpeter, Bippin. "All we saw was a flash from the wings, then the lights come back up and Aziza is lying in her own blood."

Pinch Face half smiles. "As dead as our careers are now." He takes another nip, swallows, but adds nothing more.

The long thin gentleman with skin as white as the inside of a turnip, lights a cheroot. "Mister Dreckler is correct in what he says. Without the vocal skills of Miss Fontaine, we're just another quartet with leanings towards modern jazz – which barely pays the bills. Though at weekends we sometimes whore our talents out to social events."

Bippin smiles. "Eloquently put as always, Professor."

I cannot help myself. "Professor?"

"I originally studied at the Musique et Musicologie at the Sorbonne."

It is a loaded comment and I refuse to show my ignorance by asking where that is. Mylon fills in the hole in my knowledge, saying:

"That's in Paris, France. And Joachim," he indicates Pinch Face, "Is a real German. But he was born in 1940, so he never got to be a proper Nazi."

Jochim glares at Mylon – his anger hot and obvious – then he spits onto the pavement at Mylon's feet.

Bippin quickly pushes himself away from the wall. "Gentlemen, please, we have a guest. Let's leave all the scratching and clawing until we have some privacy." He turns to me. "So, what can we four humble musicians help you with?"

"Tell me about Miss Fontaine. How did you meet her? Did she have any boyfriends? Lovers? I need to know more before I can begin to understand this whole affair."

Bippin settles into the subject.

"She came to us four years ago now. We were the house band at the Marquis Hotel. We'd just started in on a version of Lovin' You Blues, when she comes from the back of the room, tight red satin and hair up high, singing as she walked through the audience to the front of house."

The Professor gets lyrical:

"You're making me crazy,

You're driving me mad.
The only way of loving you,
Is with a good love gone bad."

Back to Bippin. "By the time she finished she owned the room body and soul. While the applause continued, she made her way on stage, winked at us, then called the next tune. And the next. All the way to the end of our regular set. She'd done her homework and knew our pieces – even calling us out for solos. After that, we sat around the bar, and by the end of the night she'd become our new singer."

I nod and point to the building. "And here?"

"Yeah, well, the Marquis wasn't into good music."

Jochim snorts. "They just wanted pap for the masses, while we wanted to go in another direction. Three weeks later we broke our non-existent contract, changed our name, and went to the first venue that would hire us."

Mylon looks down at his hands. "And now we're back to being a four piece no hope."

Bippin shakes his head. "At least we still have the recordings." He turns to me. "We made a recording of our set. Rented a tape recorder, bought two spools of magnetic tape. The Professor set it all up – three microphones – and we went through our show from beginning to end. Twelve songs in all. Enough for a full sized album."

The Professor adds, "I took the tapes to Northstreet Studios and had an acetate cut. A demo disk. We're still waiting for Obelisk Records to complete the contract."

"Still waiting?"

"They want exclusive rights, content control, not forgetting a promotional tour. Whether they'll want us now is more the question."

"And did Aziza have admirers?"

With a quick glance at Bippin, Mylon says:

"She had lots of admirers – stage door callers, letters, and presents nearly every night."

The Professor joins in. "She was a singer with beauty in her voice as well as herself. She had an attraction that many could not resist."

"And was one of those gifts something set with pearls?"

Carefully Bippin asks, "Why are you interested in such?"

"I have my reasons." *And it will be common knowledge once the newspaper jackals get their teeth into her.*

"She got jewellery – gold, silver – some with stones. Most of it was nothing special, and I suspect that all of it has been removed as evidence. You'll have to ask the gendarmes, provided you have the baksheesh for them to reply."

The four drop into a morose silence, so I ask:

"Is Miss Fontaine's dressing room through there?" I point at the half open back door.

Bippin says, "Help yourself. You can't miss it – it's the one with the star on it."

I move passed them, closing the door behind me, and wander down a narrow passageway. There are two doors set into the wall – the farthest ochre painted with the word *Management* in black lettering – the closer has a faded gold star on dusky pink paint. I open it and walk into the small dressing room, turning on the overhead light as I enter.

No windows, a closet to one side and a dressing table with a large mirror on the other. Across the table top are jars of make-up, several lipsticks, paper tissues – no doubt all disturbed by searching gendarmes. I sit on the wooden chair and look at my reflection, then focus on several photographs taped to the frame. Black and white, a family gathering – two daughters, now reduced to one. Is part of my re-existence to be the messenger who passes on grief and sadness to those still living? Is that what this avengeful role entails? A voice for the innocent – and a purveyor of tears for those left behind.

A search of the room produces nothing except stage clothes, a clarinet, trumpet and double bass in their respective cases. Scattered around in small piles are various pieces of sheet music, some with *The Marquis Hotel* stamped on them in indigo ink. One catches my eye. Across the top in a confident hand is *Sing this only for me – with love – Bippin*.

6

Back in the morning sunlight the four musicians have disappeared – maybe to sleep until the evening's performance – maybe just to sleep and hope that tomorrow night will not be cancelled as well.

As I turn to close the street door I see someone in the shadows, watching as I leave. Our eyes meet, and he steps forwards.

"Can I help you? I am Nabil Harrak, the manager. What are you doing backstage? Are you one of those ghouls who flock to see places where violent death has occurred?"

He's clearly angry and upset, so I forgive his unfounded accusation. In reply I take something which Marzouk had said earlier, and use it to my advantage.

"I am a detective."

"I've said all I' going to say to Commandant Monnes. Has he sent you to spy on me?"

"No, nothing like that." I step out of the sunlight and back into the passageway. "Forgive me, but is there somewhere more appealing where we can talk?"

"There is the Café Lubar, three doors down from here. Go there and I will meet you after I have sorted something in regard to this evening's closure."

I nod, and leave the way I came.

Turning onto the main street again, I pass by Marzouk – appearing to be asleep far too convincingly for my liking – and carry on until I get to a small row of tables set out on the pavement. As I pull out a chair a waiter appears from the relative cool of the building, bringing a tray of glasses, a bowl of sugar cubes, and a large teapot of mint tea. The pot and bowl are placed on the table, and I hold up three fingers.

"One for my guest, one for myself, and one for the driver." I point to Marzouk's taxi.

"Very good." He moves off with the third cup now full of tea and six sugars as Nabil sits down on the chair across from me.

In the mid-morning sunlight he seems listless, eyes slightly bloodshot and possibly red rimmed. He puts four cubes into his glass as he says:

"I don't have much time and there is so much to do. She has no family here to bury her in the proper Muslim way, so it is left to me to do the best I can in the circumstances. It seems only right."

"She was a Muslim?"

"She never told me so directly, but in this city it stands to reason."

"She has family. I've seen the photographs in her dressing room."

"That is true, there are old photographs. But Bippin has their last address, somewhere in Mombasa."

"Did you know her before you employed her?"

He takes a gulp of his tea. "No, she was part of the band. They auditioned, and when I heard her sing I knew she was something special. More than special…"

His voice trails off and I let the silence take hold while I drink some of my tea – which is a mistake as Nabil stands.

"I have to go. If you want to talk more then I suggest you make an appointment first."

As he walks off I see Marzouk's taxi also heading down the street, and a handsome young gendarme coming towards me. He's almost at the table when I ask:

"Tea?"

Torn between etiquette and business, etiquette quite rightly wins out. He sits in Nabil's vacated chair and waves the waiter forward with a gesture of his hand.

Tea poured, sugared, tasted and approved of, I pre-empt him by asking, "What can I do for you?"

The Commandant wants to speak with you."

"But I spoke with him last night"

"He says the two of you spoke, but you told him nothing. He's not amused."

"And he sent you to find me?"

"No. Apparently you are less than important, merely an insignificance to him. But, should we find you during our daily travels, we are to, and I quote, 'haul your ass in for questioning.' It's just my good fortune to have found you." He drinks more tea. "However, although it is a shame to waste such a quality beverage as this, I suggest it is time I started hauling."

I pin a five dirham note under the teapot, and follow the gendarme up the street, his head shaking in dismay.

"Why is there never a taxi when you want one?"

7

It is a fifteen minute walk to the police station, and at the end of it I am grateful for the coolness provided by the desk and ceiling fans. Eventually I am deposited in a chair in front of the Commandant's desk, but he deliberately ignores me for five or six minutes. He does nothing constructive in that time – merely pretending to read papers that he has no doubt read previously. It is just a show of power, such as is played out at any tribal meeting.

Finally he puts the document down and says:

"What is your purpose here? And don't give me any more of that voice for the innocent, because I'm sure that dung beetles follow you waiting for you to come out with that again."

"I have been tasked to find out who killed Miss Fontaine."

"Tasked by whom?"

"I'm not at liberty to say."

"What?" He leans forward in his chair. "If you tell me, then you don't get paid, is that it?"

"No, it's just that I don't really know myself."

"You see? Right there," He points to a corner by the window. "The beetles are gathering already." He sighs and leans back. "Look, I don't have any time for all of this. If you find out anything then you let me know, otherwise stay out from under my feet."

I look at him and smile my most welcoming smile. "And is this sharing of information mutual?"

"And have me do your work for you? Get out of here! Mutual exchange of information indeed! You are the offspring of a fox in all but colour and fur!"

Outside the police headquarters it is getting too close to midday for it to be anything other than very uncomfortable.

Before I can step off the curb, Marzouk arrives behind the wheel of his taxi.

"Get in Sayidi, before the tyres stick to the tarmac."

I get in the back, and the heat is almost as stifling. The taxi jerks, and we are headed out of the district and back to the apartment block.

8

"So tell me, Sayidi," Marzouk asks when we are settled at the table in the kitchen area, taking food. "Is detective work always this strenuous?"

It has been less than 24 hours since I found myself in *La Veilleuse* drinking coffee.

"No, alsinujab alsaghir, most days it is worse."

Marzouk smiles. "That is good to hear, otherwise I was afraid I would become bored." He takes another bite of cheese, following it with some bread and a mouthful of mint tea. Then:

"Who do you think murdered the singer?"

I'm about to speak when there is a knock on the front door, and almost immediately Marzouk is at the spy hole, his right hand in his jacket pocket. He swallows to empty his mouth, then says loudly:

"Who are you, and what do you want? State your business, or go away."

From the other side comes the muffled voice of the clarinet player, Mylon.

"I'm here to see Tomaso Memindip. I have business to discuss with him, not his dog."

Marzouk looks at me and I nod to let the musician in. As Mylon enters, I point to the third chair around the table as Marzouk bring a fresh glass and the pot of tea from off the stove.

I wait for him to add sugar and sip, all the while noting the tension in his face and hands.

"This is a most excellent tea." He nods his appreciation to both Marzouk and then to me. Another sip is followed by a heavy sigh.

"Ah. This is not going to be a pleasant social call. I am here to tell you that the band has broken up. The record label has sent a messenger to tell us that they have retracted their offer and cancelled our contract. It's all down to the fact that Aziza is no longer with us. With her death there can be no promotional tour. Radio stations are not the marketplace for modern jazz, and we cannot afford the finance to have it produced ourselves." He drinks more tea and the frustration starts to leave him as he talks his anger out.

"If we had found somewhere that paid better, then maybe we could've pressed up a short run. Maybe sold it at the club. But I doubt much would sell beyond that, even to the most devoted of fans. That was why we left before you'd finished talking to that old lecher, Nabil. There is no reason for us to stay. As it is, the Professor is already heading to India. He says if it is good enough for the Beatles, then it should be just fine for him. Jochim is packing up and moving back to Germany, with his travelling companion, Rolf. Apparently it is a European thing." He takes a long breath, the sadness of their parting heavy in him. "Bippin and me? We've been together since the orphanage. We've always looked after each other. We'll probably head south – maybe form up another band – play Jo'berg perhaps. If they let us."

I backtrack, and ask, "You say Nabil is not all he seems to be?"

"He's a lecher. Even had a spy hole from his office into the dressing room. The Professor spotted it after we'd come back stage from our second or third night. It had been a twinkle of light that'd given it away. Rather than cause grief over it, Aziza hung a picture to cover it. He could complain and expose his fetish, or stop looking at Aziza as she changed into and out of her stage clothes. As far as we know he didn't have another one drilled."

I remember the sheet music with the inscription, *Love, Bippin*, and see if Mylon can supply any further information. But he is surprised.

"Bippin and Aziza were together for a while, but it just didn't work for them. She wasn't prepared to settle down and have his children. She wanted the big career, like the American singers. Quite quickly they decided to stop seeing each other, just after the recording was made." He pauses, then, "Hey! You didn't think Bippin had anything to do with this, did you? We were on stage all the time, so you know he couldn't have done it,"

Marzouk pipes up. "What about an accomplice?"

"No, not a chance. Anyway, we all needed Aziza and her singing. Why would any of us do something like that?"

I change direction. "Where is Bippin now?"

"He's back at *La Veilleuse.* He said he was going to pack up her things and send them back to her family."

Mylon takes a long sip of his tea then stands. "I need to be away. I have a sack truck to pick up so we can take the boxes to the National Parcel offices."

As he leaves, Marzouk starts to tidy away the drinking glasses. When he finishes curiosity gets the better of me.

"What is it in your pocket?"

"Ah, Sayidi, it is nothing."

"Show me."

Slowly he withdraws a 6 inch mahogany and tarnished steel hilt. He moves his thumb across the handle and a thin double-edged 5 inch blade snaps into view.

"It is my protection against thieves and bandits who might try and rob me of my taxi money."

"And would you use it?"

"I have done so in the past Sayidi."

I nod. "It looks like I might have misjudged you alsinijab alsaghir. Not a little squirrel, you are more a little scorpion."

9

With the sun now resting on the horizon, the heat is coming out of the air, the journey to the nightclub isn't as eventful as previously experienced.

I find Bippin in the dressing room, gathering up sheet music and packing them in a box of Aziza's clothing and possessions. He looks up at me as I enter.

"Mylon visited me earlier. I'm sorry to hear about the recording contract being rejected."

"Well, if it was going to be then it would still be. Anyway, we're going our own separate ways for a while. Easier to travel when there's only one, or two of you."

"I understand you'll be heading south? Taking Mylon with you." Band leader, tribe leader, they both deserve respect.

Bippin smiles. "If I don't look after him who knows what trouble he'll get himself into."

The bond of brotherhood, regardless of parentage, forged through shared experience. I look around at the wall with the dressing table against it, and above the mirror is a framed postcard – a ballet dancer, leg up on a box as she adjusts her shoe.

"Is that where the spy hole is?"

Bippin nods. "Nabil is sick. He gets pleasure from secret voyeurism. At least that's what the Professor says. Even after that, he had the audacity to propose to her. Aziza said she'd thrown the ring back in his face, then walked out of his office. He stopped following her, or pestering her after that."

"How long ago did this happen?"

"About six, maybe eight weeks ago? Something like that. I wasn't sure when you asked about jewellery and pearls. The ring was antique silver, with a large pearl in the centre, surrounded by a circle of peridotite."

"And what happened to it?"

"I'm not sure. I suspect Nabil may well have taken it back to the jeweller and asked for some kind of refund. But that's just my supposition rather than fact."

"Nabil? Is he here?"

"Last I saw he was at the bar, sorting deliveries and doing his stock audit. Before that he was out, making arrangements for Aziza's burial."

"So the police have released her body already?"

"I doubt it, but he's adamant she should be buried as quickly as possible, even though she wasn't of the faith." He looks at the box of clothes – Aziza Fontaine's last possessions. "If you'll excuse me, I need to get her belongings packed up and despatched via the overland post by this evening."

I nod and walk out, leaving him to tape up and address the cardboard boxes. Instead of making my way back to Marzouk, I check on Nabil. He is still at the bar area, invoices and paperwork in several piles around him. While he is preoccupied, I feel now would be a good time to look around his office.

The door isn't locked, but one of the old pine desk drawers is. All it takes is a little leverage with the ornate paperknife, to flex the frame, and the drawer is eased open.

Inside, under handwritten letters and the remains of a small posy of wilderness flowers, is the ring case, next to a small five chamber revolver.

I take up the case and push the lid open. Inside is the silver band, slightly tarnished as befits its obvious age, the peridotite translucent green, but the claw mount is missing its pearl. The receipt of purchase is carefully folded into the domed lid.

The door opens, and Nabil stands in the doorway, a look of anger underscored by regret. As he steps into the room, I close the ring case and slip it in my jacket pocket. It is, after all, evidence in a heinous crime.

As he moves into the room I move away from the side of the desk, unsure as to what he'll do next.

"So you found it?" There is both sadness and relief in his tone. He sits down behind his desk and I move towards the doorway – a memory of the small revolver still sharp in my head. I try for a distraction:

"You must have loved Aziza deeply to have purchased the ring before proposing."

"When I heard her sing at the audition, I fell in love with her then. Her poise, her grace, and when she smiled it seemed she was smiling just for me."

I remember her final performance from the night before. Her smile had tried to capture my newly beating heart, but I knew the futility of it all. Love is a barb that works its way under your skin, and is unbearable when it inevitably gets ripped out of your flesh.

With his hands in front of him, Nabil starts to softly cry at his loss and the realisation of what he has done. "She led me on, her eyes, her lips, all promising so much. Or so I believed."

"But she turned down all your gifts?" With my back to the door I slowly reach behind and feel for the doorknob with my fingers.

"All but the very last. I wanted her to accept that beautiful pearl. A gift of true love. in the only way left to me."

"So where did you get the flintlock pistol?"

"How did you know I'd used a flintlock?"

I want to tell him they were in common use in my day, but I don't. "I heard the click of the hammer as you cocked it. I've also seen the pearl. As round and as smooth as a musket ball. Where did you get the pistol?"

"It was in an old props box. I found it while spring cleaning and it was in the bottom of an old wooden tea chest. A day or so later and I found the two barmen out the back, loading it with flash powder and shooting dried peas at discarded tin cans. That's when I had the idea to use the pearl." His chest heaves as he carries on. "But something went wrong. I must have put too much powder in, or tamped the cotton wool down too much. It was only meant to surprise her. From my heart to hers. Only it killed her instead. Why are we so stupid in love, and always regretful in death?"

I leave the question unanswered, and ask one of my own. "Where is the pistol now?"

"After I fired it I tossed it up into the gantries. No one looks up there, and there's no requirement to use them when all I put on are live bands and singers. You say you've seen the pearl? Where?"

"A morgue attendant showed it to me just after sunrise. It would have made a beautiful wedding ring."

Nabil takes a long breath, and releases it slowly. "Now, as all the arrangements have been made for her once the police release the body, I have one last thing I need to do." He reaches into the open drawer, takes out the small revolver and lays it flat on his desktop blotter. "If you would please leave."

I close the door behind me on my way out, and looking down the corridor I glimpse Bippin as he stacks the second of two cardboard boxes onto the two-wheeled sack truck steadied by Mylon. They vanish around the corner of the building as I step out into the fading sunlight. Moments later, behind me, I hear a single gunshot. I shut the back door, walk calmly around to Marzouk, and say:

"We need to go to the police station. I need to talk to Commandant Monnes about a murder."

10

I am back sitting in front of the Commandant's imposing desk. In the centre of it, between the green shaded swan neck lamp and his 'In' tray, sits the ring box, with the unfolded receipt beside it.

"And you say he shot himself?"

"I didn't go and check, but it's a pretty good assumption."

Monnes leans back in his chair. "I have gendarmes on their way to the nightclub as we speak. They'll know if your story is genuine or not."

"It's genuine." *The Gods have seen to that.*

"So," he picks up a paperclip and turns it around and around between the tips of his thumb and forefinger. "Is this the end of your interfering?"

"I'm not sure. It all depends."

"Ah, yes, your mysterious, anonymous benefactor."

If only you knew, Commandant. But I say:

"That, and whether or not I decide to stay in this city for a while." I cough slightly, then add, "I can appreciate that someone such as yourself – overworked and so woefully underpaid – may value an independent investigator for those times when your caseload become overwhelming."

Monnes looks sharply at me. "I'm not paying you any money, if that's what you're hunting for."

So much for the rewards of information mutually exchanged.

"The money would mean nothing. My satisfaction would lie in the knowledge that I have righted a wrong, or brought someone to justice."

"I'm still not paying you."

"Perhaps the next time?"

11

After the two gendarmes have deposited me back on the street, the young gendarme from the cafe passes me on his way to see the Commandant.

"You were right, he committed suicide. He left a short note before he shot himself."

"Difficult to write it afterwards," I say with a smile.

He turns, about to reply, then carries on into the headquarters building, shaking his head and smiling.

I push myself into the chaos and mayhem of early evening, and approaching Marzouk I see he has company in the form of an irate businessman, judging by his stance and angry hand gestures. Talking to him in a firm voice, Marzouk says:

"And I tell you again, I am not for hire. I am waiting for my passenger to return."

In his surviving wing mirror he sees me approaching. "And here he is now."

I get in the back, and Marzouk drives away, leaving behind a very confused man.

"Where to now, Sayidi?" he asks as he bullies and barges his way into the traffic, all the while attempting to push the horn button through the steering column and into the engine compartment.

12

The apartment is thankfully cool by the time we arrive, and despite his disapproving expression, the doorman lets Marzouk in without question.

Over freshly boiled tea, I ask:

"Do your wife and children not object to your long absences?" I watch as he graces me with a slight blush of embarrassment.

"Sadly, Sayidi, they do not exist. Hopefully one day. But for now…."

Marzouk offers no more information, so I say:

"And what of your mother?"

"She is real, and old, and is the incarnation of a honey badger when slighted. My brother, Kalim and I live with her, but we are out of room, which is why I took up the taxi work. I work – they sleep. I sleep – and my brother looks for work."

"And this arrangement is not likely to improve?"

Marzouk looks at me, his mouth still half full of bread and black olives. "What do you think?"

"Here," I reach into my wallet and take out the other half of the 200 dirham note and push it across to him. "If you take this to the Main Street National Bank, they will exchange it for a whole one."

"No, Sayidi. Consider it as your copy of our contract."

"So the 200 dirham?"

"Is a lot of money to us. But I have my pride. A contract is a commitment to be honoured."

"And if I were to employ you full time?"

"Me? A private detective?"

"A private detective's assistant."

"It's a demotion, but I'm prepared to accept it."

I look at him. He is all mouth and ragged-arsed trousers, yet he has been honest and optimistic, with no knowledge of what he was getting involved in.

"If it's a demotion then you will not be needing the use of the spare rooms and facilities I have here."

His humour fades. "Is that a truth, Sayidi?"

"You'll be on call, night and day. You know this city, whereas I do not. Therefore I need you as my assistant."

The sparkle is back in his face. "For 100 dirham a month, Sayidi, I will consider your offer. Maybe we should think of it as a business merger."

"Be careful, alsinujab alsaghir, you're not the only potential assistant in this city."

13

With Marzouk off to tell his mother and brother about their good fortune, I settle myself down in my chosen sleeping room, lay on the bed and eventually reach my dream land.

I am at the point of wondering how I will ever eat the whole bowl of dates being proffered to me by an interesting young woman, when I hear the voice of Adagouti as he approaches. Even at the distance I can see he is less than best pleased with something.

- Adagouti, I have found the culprit. Sadly he dispatched himself before he could be called to justice, though I suspect Be'kal has something special planned for him, regardless of when he arrives at his next destination.

– *There has already been much discussion amongst the Higher Powers regarding your success, so consider yourself to be in their good favour for the time being.*

– For one such as myself that is always good to know.

Adagouti glares at me and I realise I have interrupted his speech.

– *However, all is not how it should be. But with you it is never a simple matter, is it? Far from it.*

– But what have I done to incur displeasure? The Gods like me. As a tribesman, what more can I ask of life?

– *And that is the very problem! It's not Life, but Death. Your Life should no longer be! Nor should Tomaso Akriki still exist in this world in any form. The pair of you are supposed to be dead, and yet here you are!*

– So you have come to take me back to my land between worlds?

– *How can I? On one side you are blessed with the benefaction of those far greater than I. Yet you have also managed to become an irksome thorn in Death's side – one that she will see plucked out as soon as possible.*

– I still do not know what I have done, but I am more than willing to do whatever in order to make things right again.

– *Don't you understand? You have lived, died, and lived yet again. That is what you've done. When you died the first time, Death severed her bond to you. Now you are alive again there is nothing to which she can attach herself to. So, until Be'kal makes a decision you will remain deathless.*

– But what if I ceased to believe in you and the Higher Powers that supposedly made myself and the world I used to live in? Have they not already been ousted by the newer beliefs?

– *Then you would also cease to exist in perpetuation. Your tribal line would disappear, as if it had never existed at all. Your name would be forgotten from the racial memories of your tribal tree. Not that the name of Memindip was in their thoughts and on their lips in the first place, but it would be even less so were you to attempt such a denial.*

– So what you are saying is that my beliefs have become my 200 dirham note?

– *Yes, Memindip. You need to keep believing in the old ways and traditions, otherwise you will cease to exist – and that is without Death herself stepping in and taking you yet again.*

– I can see now why Fate is always a dubious ally. Fickle at best.

– *Have you been too long out in the midday sun?*

– No, I am just contemplating my predicament.

– *What?! Are you treading in camel dung? No! Are you tending goats and getting regularly bitten on the ass by flies? No! You have a manzil like no other. You may no longer have an ever refilling wallet now that the murderer has been brought to justice. But there is money enough for you to live on in your new manzil, albeit for a short time. But I'm sure someone as resourceful as yourself will find some kind of employment. And, of course, you now have Marzouk. When did you ever think you would own a slave?*

– Marzouk is not my slave!

– *Then why trap him with his own greed?*

I remain silent, unwilling to answer in the knowledge that it would show me a part of my own flawed being that I do not wish to acknowledge as existing.

Adagouti clicks his tongue in admonishment.

– *Whatever, Memindip, it is now out of my jurisdiction. Like the ceremonial male gazelle, I am passing the buck upwards. It is for those above us who will ultimately decide your fate.*

– And when will I know their decision?

– *Who knows? Who can tell what whims and foibles the Gods are prey to? It could be in the next minute – or the next ten years.*

– And until then?

– *You are to continue uncovering the hidden truths, helping others by your detections, and wherever possible righting wrongs. It is something you appear to be good at.*

– So I am still a private detective?

– *No, Memindip. You are still one very shifty wraith, who appears to have gotten away with a successful reanimation. At least for now.*

Learning Vocabulary With the Jence Brothers

Bob Ritchie

One day in the spring of 2016, I introduced ten new vocabulary words to my ESL students. Their first assignment of the day was to write a sentence with each word, and to connect those sentences to form a kind of short story. Using a classroom computer, I took part in the exercise, and tapped out my ten loosely connected sentences (which disappeared the moment I turned off the machine). I so enjoyed the exercise that I decided to do it again, this time in a longer form. The true challenge would have been to maintain the words in alphabetical order, but I'm not that obsessive. Quite.

Atheist   n.   person who does not believe in god

Darrell became an atheist when he was barely nine years old. It happened one day, a Sunday, in fact, when he had been forced, again, by his parents to go to the old Baptist church down in Redlands. He was probably disposed to not like church because of his parent's insistence that he attend, and maybe because of the long trip: There were churches over in Big Bear. Lots closer than the one in Redlands, and not requiring a rollercoaster drive down the mountain. Except, truth, the drive was fun. All that aside, Darrell understood that his parents could not be credited with his newfound awareness.

His best friend, Dennis, asked how it had happened. And in the asking, showed his disapproval: "Don't be a dork. How can you say there is no God?" Dennis bounced the basketball he held hard against the asphalt court to punctuate the question.

Darrell could hear the capital G when Dennis said the word, "god." The regular "thwap" of the bouncing ball echoed in the cleared land that surrounded Dennis's house.

"I was listening to the people pray," explained Darrell, "you know, during the church service?"

Dennis paused to swivel and shoot. The ball swished through the net, not touching the rim at all. "And people praying made you an idiot?"

Darrell laughed because he knew that he was supposed to, but then he answered, all serious, "No, it's that, well, like they were just saying, 'We know we're dirty sinners, but since we're admitting it here, in front of you, god, well, everything's okay.'"

Dennis opened his mouth to reply, maybe to jeer at his friend; then he ran over and retrieved the ball, panting from his efforts, but otherwise silent. "What are you talking about?" he asked.

Darrell took a string of red licorice from his pocket and chewed. "What kind of god would let people get away with doing all kinds of bad stuff and then let 'em forgive themselves? Let 'em do the whole thing again the next week?"

Quaff   *v.*   drink heartily

Old Tom stood on the balcony, quietly surveying the tree-filled valley before him. A faint glow lit the sky, a good six miles away: Big Bear. "And too big for my tastes," he said. He sipped hot coffee from the heavy ceramic mug. "Ahhh!" Thunderous footsteps erupted behind him. Without turning, he shouted over his shoulder, "Darrell, you and your friend need to slow down. You're in the house, now. And you know that your mother isn't feeling well."

The elephant crashes became quiet cat feet. He heard the refrigerator open and knew that Darrell would be removing the jug of orange juice. Tom smiled and shook his head; the boy could quaff an entire jug of juice without breathing. "Just like me, when I was his age," he said to himself.

On the other side of the valley, a twist of smoke rose above the small stand of trees that marked the edge of his property. Always aware of what went on around him, Tom knew that the Jence brothers were camped out there. He didn't think they were bad men—had no reason to believe otherwise. Glen, the older one, was too smart to stay a 7-Eleven clerk, though. A fly lit on Tom's neck. He slapped at it, missed, and cursed when his own action resulted in a sharp sting. The stream of sweat there transferred to his palm, and he wiped the moisture on the front panel of his jeans. Ellie would have trouble getting the sweat stains out, but what was a man to do? It gets hot, you sweat.

Darrell and his friend stampeded through the living room and raced outside, ready to live the day, once again. Darrell had invited the other boy—Dennis—for a sleepover. Ellie had not been pleased but had acquiesced so she wouldn't have to endure her son's pleas.

"Be dark in an hour," the man called after his racing son, "you and Dennis be back for supper or there'll be some sad boys tonight."

Percipient   adj.   perceptive; insightful

Glen Jence stared across the small clearing at his brother, Steve. He grimaced when Steve, trying to get his battered Yamaha to remain erect, slammed his ankle against the bike's kickstand and yowled, seeming unaware that metal stands up pretty well to mere flesh and bone. Not the most percipient of men, his brother, but Glen loved him and had thrashed more than one person who had insulted the Jence name by calling Steve "dim." Glen threw some sticks down into a pit where he had laid a fire. It would be dark, soon, and though it never got too cold in the elevated valley at this time of year, the morning rain had come in on a chill and left enough water to enforce it. Plus, it would be better to have some illumination during the black night to come. Steve didn't do well in the dark, and Glen couldn't spend another night comforting his little brother.

The sharp sound of a bouncing basketball reached from Old Tom's place all the way into the stand of trees that Glen and his brother were occupying.

Glen flicked the flint wheel of his disposable lighter, got the kindling going. The webbed tinder was damp, as were the sticks and branches that he had laid neatly on top. But the blackened walls of the ancient pit provided protection from the gentle breeze making the trees titter, and soon, the wood burned, the flames leaping, seemingly bent on escape.

When it got dark enough, Old Tom, and Old Tom's son, and Old Tom's pretty, young wife would all retire into the huge house that marked the far northern edge of Old Tom's land.

When the dark had come, and a little more, Glen and Steve would creep in, quiet as they could be, and liberate Old Tom of his son, Darrell. The boy would bring a mighty large ransom. Old Tom doted on him, wouldn't see any harm come to him.

Steve's bike crashed to the dirt, and he scrabbled to get it back up.

"Steve!" Glen hissed. "Just leave it be. We have to cross the valley on foot, anyway."

Whining, Steve said, "It's getting all scratched up!"

Glen suppressed an exasperated snort, "Scratched up! That thing has more nicks, dents, and scrapes than a bumper car at the fair. Anyway, it's mud you need to watch for, now. The ground is still wet."

Steve sat back on his heels, face screwed up as if he were about to cry. "Jeezly!"

Glen threw some more wood on the fire and ignored his brother. *I went to college for this.* The last edge of the sun sank behind Butler's Peak. Steve whimpered. Glen dusted bits of bark from his palms, ignoring his brother's distress. Time to get moving.

Staunch   *adj.*   loyal; faithful; dependable

Darrell heard something thrashing about in the brush.

"Dennis," he shouted, not afraid, but remembering his mother's warning about coyotes and bobcats and such. *Wouldn't come here, out in the open,* he thought.

The basketball caught him full in the chest, knocking him to the ground.

At the same time, the thrashing became pounding footsteps. Hard hands and arms wrapped around his upper arm and knee, hoisting him in the air as if he were nothing.

"Dennis!" Fear. A staunch friend, Darrell nevertheless realized that he would desert Dennis in a second if only his mother's gentle, encompassing arms could replace the hard ones.

A voice on the other side of the court half-shouted. "Glen, I got 'im!"

"No, I do. You got a friend, I guess. But that's perfect: Two for one." A shout, next to Darrell's ear.

Darrell struggled, but the man holding him tightened his grip, arms like padded steel bars, and turned, hustling into the forest.

Furrow   *n.*   groove

What Steve didn't know about children would fill a library. Even the one down in Redlands, which was big and old. Like Old Tom. Well, he was big, anyway, *And older-n me,* Steve thought, *so, old.*

"Glen," he whispered, mindful of waking the two boys. Or consciousizing them; he didn't guess that you woke up from getting knocked out. Did you?

Glen didn't answer, so Steve tried again, putting some force into his voice this time: "Glen!"

"Shh!" Glen's admonition slapped out of the darkness and scared the bejeebers out of Steve, who jumped forward in startlement.

A scratch sounded and an inch of flame erupted. Glen was leaning over one of the boys. He extended his hand to the boy's still form.

Steve opened his mouth to apologize for making noise. *Stupid, stupid.* But Glen said, "Never mind! Look at this!" Glen ran his finger along a deep, bloody furrow in the boy's forehead.

Instigator   *n.*   troublemaker; person who entices others to do something, usually not acceptable or good.

He liked his father but had never liked listening to his father. Well, *get'cher fishing clothes on* and *come in for supper* were fine. It was the *clean your room* and the *dry the dishes* Darrell objected to.

What he wouldn't give.

He huddled against the cold tree trunk that the smaller of the two men (smaller like Sugarloaf Mountain is smaller than Mount San

Gorgonio—not-as-big smaller, but not actually small) had set him against. Heat radiated from the fire that crackled in the pit only a foot away, but Darrell wasn't warm. Fear had taken his spirit in its large cold hands and squeezed. His eyes slitted so that the men would think he was asleep, Darrell contemplated the still form next to him. Something had happened to Dennis. Darrell sent his hand across the dirt, slowly enough that the two men wouldn't notice it.

Dennis was breathing. So, not dead. Darrell pushed down on the sigh of relief that whooshed up his throat. Without turning his head, he sent all his eye-tention to the right corners, trying to get a glimpse of his friend.

"Wha'd I do, Glen" said the bigger one.

The not-Glen bigger one stood with his arms and hands hanging loose. He looked confused, Darrell thought. Like he wasn't much used to thinking.

The other one, Glen, was at the edge of the clearing, in shadow. Darrell, with his eyes slitted and the small, below-ground-level fire providing little light, couldn't make out the man's face. He could see the man rubbing his shin bone. He groaned, turning it into a growl. "Jesus H, Steve. You haven't a clue, do you?"

"Mamma says don't take the name of God in your veins." Steve, San Gorgonio; Glen, Sugarloaf. Darrell reeled his hand back in, as careful in the pull as the push.

Colloquial   adj.   local and informal (often used to describe language)

Eleanor said, "Thomas, did you remember to ask Darrell to set the table? Him and his friend?" She plucked a tissue from the box on her lap, blew. Darn cold.

"Sorry, Ellie, I forgot. They're outside. I'll reel 'em in," Thomas answered. He strode to the door and then stopped, his fingers already gripping the knob. She saw his eye go to the shotgun that he kept in the umbrella holder that her grandfather had carved by hand out of a felled bough of black oak. Grandfather had called it a spear holder, but Ellie had never owned a spear. That Grandfather belonged to the Serrano people made Ellie a Serrano person; she had always felt that she was just a person. What did she need a spear for? Thomas leaned over and grabbed up the shotgun. She nodded. Night was coming on, and she had heard the screech of a mountain lion last night, never mind the wolves that roamed the area. How had Thomas let Darrell stay out so long?

One of the door's hinges screeched when Thomas pushed open the door; Eleanor started, though it happened every time. Thomas stomped through the opening, swinging up the shotgun as he went. "Wait here." His voice had lost its colloquial equanimity, becoming edged. Of course she ignored him and followed him out to the long driveway.

"What is it, Thomas?"

He remained focused on something a few yards from the basketball hoop he had set up for Darrell. "Get back inside." He gestured backwards with the stock of the shotgun. Though aimed forwards, the newly acquired sharpness of his voice reached her, and she inhaled with a suddenness that made her dizzy.

Dotard   *n.*   foolish old man

Tom saw blood. Oh, he wanted to see oil, shining in the oblique rays of the setting sun. Or a puddle of water left by this morning's shower.

Blood.

"Ellie, I mean it. Get back in the house." He stepped forward, beyond the cement of the driveway/basketball court and into a clearing that separated the property from the forest. Close enough to see the fresh scrape mark on a breaching, ancient root. The edges of the small pool were sharp black in the moonlight.

"They must think I'm some kind of tired, used-up dotard." Thomas had easily tracked the men—two of them, with a motorcycle that leaked oil—to the clearing where he had met and wooed Ellie. According to her grandfather, Ellie's family had occupied the area for well over a millennium. That first encounter, Tom exploring, getting a feel for the land he had just bought, Ellie had been uncovering a fire pit that might have been originally excavated as many as 20 centuries before. By one of her far-distant ancestors.

Tom leaned against the same tree that he had leaned against when he had met his wife. He bent, hovering over the very fire pit Ellie had found, and sniffed, inhaling the scent of burnt wood. He straightened and sent the dancing beam of his flashlight around the small open area, swiveling until a disturbance in the ground cover caught his attention. There. The beam showed the deep imprint of motorcycle tires accompanied by a hash of footprints; all led to the southeastern border of the clearing. He dropped to his knees and studied the mess. Only one kid-sized set. *Dear God....*

Misnomer   n.   misapplied or inappropriate name or designation

Though Glen had hiked these hills, valleys, forests every summer from the time he could walk, he had gotten lost. The one boy, Darrell, was on foot, stumbling and slow, but self-locomoting. The other—"Dennis," the conscious boy had called him—flopped loosely against Steve's shoulder.

Glen decided to try again. "Steve," he said, speaking over his shoulder.

His brother grunted. He caught one foot on a sky-reaching root and stumbled. The bike fell and the boy nearly did. Steve's shoulder thudded against a tree trunk, preventing him from joining the motorcycle on the wet, pine-needle covered ground. He dropped his flashlight.

"Steve, the roots. You already put a gash in that kid, the last time. Leave the bike. We'll come back for it."

The walking kid, voice tremulous: "Is he okay? He's a great basketball player."

Apropos of nothing, thought Glen, who had graduated from Cal State San Berdoo with a degree in communication strategies for the 21st century, but who hadn't had a steady, non-blue-collar job since... ever.

Ahead, Steve retrieved his flashlight, straightened, and trudged on, leaving his motorcycle. The moving circle of light from the electric lantern that Glen carried kept Steve and the kid—and Glen—in a pool of clarity, safe. As if light were a defense against all strange and bad things. Glen's ears picked up a faint rustle close behind. *If that isn't a deer, we're screwed.* He picked up his pace.

The rustle became a crackle, and the old man, Tom, came plain into the light. He held a shotgun at waist level, angled up enough to blow the head off anything about six-feet tall. The mouth of the barrel seemed to leer at Glen. *Safe?* it chuckled, *something of a misnomer, yeah?*

*Vilification   n.   * blackening   someone's   (or   something's) reputation

The tableau. Frozen in the light that seconds before felt impregnable, the Jence brothers and Darrell looked like statues to Phobos, god of fear.

Darrell broke through the marble of terror and ran to his father, throwing himself at legs and waist. Tom reacted by swinging the shotgun to the side but also tightening the finger that hovered over the trigger. The roar of the weapon filled the valley, assaulted the trees that surrounded the men and boys, pounded a ringing silence into the ears of all living creatures within the gun's jurisdiction.

Steve burst into tears, swinging the unresponsive Dennis off his shoulder and into a cradling embrace. He buried his face in the boy's shoulder. "I don't want this!" He cried, his voice muffled by meat and bone. He crumpled, like a blow-up lawn Santa bleeding air.

At the limits of the blast radius, Glen collapsed, a dozen pellets buried in his right arm and side. Though the lead shot didn't pose any significant danger, Glen would bear the scars of his injury throughout his life—the least woeful outcome of the incident, as it would turn out. While imprisoned, he would suffer the naïve vilification of his brother, who would tell all in hearing distance of his and Glen's despicable deed, about what terrible men they both were. And Steve avoided Glen—both in prison and after their release—couldn't look him in the eye. Decades later, as a bedridden senior, Steve would have to move into Glen's tiny apartment in Yucaipa—the illegally converted garage of the judge who had sentenced them both. The silence would be deafening. Anyway, Glen was deaf, so, perhaps, not a big deal.

Dropping his gun, Tom rushed to the sprawled form of the larger man. Darrell dashed after. The head and torso of the boy, Dennis, were free and clear, but the light from Tom's lantern highlighted an evil-looking injury that appeared to start at the boy's hairline, meandered down his cheek, and came to a stop at the corner of his mouth.

"Dennis!" Darrell, first to reach his friend, fell to his knees and began tugging at the one free arm.

Tom knelt, one knee coming down on a mound of pine needles, the other digging in the wet dirt, the bare forest floor. He laid a palm on the boy's untouched cheek. Warm. But warm and cooling or warm just warm?

Children grow. Dennis and Darrell would remain friends for a few months after Dennis's release from the hospital. That their paths would diverge was not the fault of the Jence brothers and their flawed plan. Dennis would become obsessed with chess, eventually joining the All-America Chess Team. Darrell would lose himself in the youth circus down in Redlands, becoming skilled at the teeterboard, unicycle, flying trapeze. Children change.

Leaning away from Tom to twist the dimmer switch on her bedside lamp, Ellie asked, "You locked both locks?"

Tom touched his fingers to her shoulder. Warm skin and tenderness. He nodded, though Ellie couldn't see it. "And set the alarm."

Several times during the long night, Ellie and Tom tiptoed down the short hall to Darrell's room. To verify that he was present. That he was sleeping. That he was safe.

Darrell stopped being an atheist when he was barely nine years old.

The Devil's Accountant

Michele Bazan Reed

If the devil dwells in fire, can you find traces of him in the ashes?

I did, one July afternoon in 1924.

The heat that summer was unrelenting. It frayed nerves and ordinary people did desperate things, whether maddened by the rising mercury or hoping the general lethargy would help them get away with it.

There'd been a spate of violence, mostly petty stuff, tempers fraying on hot nights. But the big news in our city was a ring of burglars and second-story men, breaking into houses and businesses. Homeowners with windows left open to let in a night breeze found they let in more than they bargained for.

As the heat intensified, the heists became even bolder. Just that Sunday, daring yeggmen pulled off the biggest theft in Syracuse history, cracking the safe at E. W. Ellis department store and making off with 20 thousand dollars.

The oppressive heat also meant that people were reluctant to drag themselves up the four flights to the sweltering offices of Harry Jerome, PI. Business had picked up a bit after the case of 'The Lady in Black,' but most of it was people asking me to find their missing relatives. Not exactly big money cases, hence my less than posh digs.

I decided to take advantage of my sparse agenda that Wednesday to knock off early.

I slapped on my boater and headed out, looking for a cool alternative to the heat. Three short blocks away, I rapped three times—two long, one short—on the door of a large brick mansion. 'Nellie sent me,' I said with a nod to the gent who opened it.

'Sorry, only members allowed,' he said, deadpan, as I slid a foot over the threshold.

'Knock it off, Charlie. You know I'm Art's best customer.'

He grinned, gave me a slap on the shoulder and muttered, 'Yeah, and we both know why.' He let me into the marble foyer anyway.

Three flights of oak staircase later, I was admitted to the speakeasy Arthur ran out of a parlor with Oriental carpets, furniture from Gus Stickley's factory down the road, and oil paintings on flocked walls. A mahogany bar ran the length of the room, serving cocktails like the Mary Pickford and the Sidecar.

I slid into a leather Morris chair with a view overlooking Jefferson Street, and ordered a whiskey, neat.

A stranger sat opposite me, nursing a gin rickey. He looked to be about 50, with a pomaded head of brown hair and a trim mustache to match. His linen suit fit him well, and he managed not to look rumpled, quite a feat considering the scorching temperatures outside.

Ruthie handed me a whiskey from her tray.

'Put it on my tab, toots,' said the swell in the chair across the marble-topped table.

Ruthie raised her eyebrows at me, and I nodded. Art had been giving me drinks for free, ever since that day in '21, when I tipped him off to the approach of Federal agents. Arthur spilled his wares out the window into the snow, while Prohibition Enforcement Agency cops were climbing over the transom. All they found inside the elegant rooms were a group of 'businessmen,' smoking fat cigars as they discussed the day's stock market prices. Art rewarded me with the promise of free drinks for life. And the look on the G-men's faces when they came up empty-handed? That was just a sweet bonus.

But if the man in the linen suit wanted to pay, who was I to deny Arthur a bit of profit? 'Much obliged, fella,' I said in his direction. 'And to whom do I owe the honor of this libation?'

'Phillips. Edmund Phillips.' He tapped the ash from his cigar into a brass floor ashtray. 'And you're Harry Jerome.' He said it, not asked.

'Didn't realize I was so famous.'

'"The Hound," best finder in three states?' That could have been a smile or a sneer that curled the edges of his mouth as he sipped the gin.

'Four, but who's counting? So, what do you do, Mr. Phillips?' Just being polite. The guy bought me a drink, after all.

'I'm an accountant. Freelance, I guess you'd say.'

My ears perked up at the odd turn of phrase. 'You don't say. Lotta work here in Syracuse for … freelance accountants?'

'Lately, yes.' He studied his drink, swirling it around and watching the condensation form rivulets down the side of the tumbler in the humid air.

If he was going to elaborate on the subject, I never got a chance to find out. Just then, Art came over and gestured toward a private room off the bar. With a wave of apology to Phillips, I followed.

Art made the introductions. 'Harry, Mr. Lloyd Watkins of the Statewide Insurance Agency here has a problem. I told him you could probably help.'

I nodded, non-committal.

'There's been a terrible fire, Mr. Jerome. A small newsstand and office building on Water Street burned two nights ago. The entire building was gutted, and the four office tenants lost all their possessions.' Watkins was short and rather stout, dressed in a simple blue suit. His hair was plastered to his face with sweat and his eye twitched in a nervous tic.

'That's a shame. But what's it to do with me?'

'Mr. Watkins was underwriting the policy, and his company stands to lose a big payout. He thinks the fire seems suspicious,' Art said.

'All right, Mr. Watkins, you have three minutes to present your evidence. Why are you so suspicious of this particular fire?'

'The landlord swears it was the ring of burglars, dressed all in black with masks on their faces. He was at the store late, cleaning up and stocking the shelves for the next day. The thieves were surprised to find anyone there, so they panicked, he says. They knocked him over the head and set fire to the building in an attempt to destroy the evidence— and the only witness. But it just smells fishy. For one thing, this burglary ring hits big-money targets. With 20 grand from Sunday's job, why would they break into a downtown newsstand the very next day?'

He leaned forward, ticking off his points on the fingers of one hand. 'I can understand they clouted the guy, but why set a fire, rather than escape through the window? Most of the thefts this month have been pretty slick jobs, no violence and little damage. And anyway, he wouldn't have been able to identify them with disguises on.'

Now that Watkins was talking, he loosened up a bit, even took a swig of a needle beer he'd been nursing before I came in. Must be the insurance company didn't give him much of an expense account. That near-beer injected with a jolt of hooch was worse than no booze at all, if you ask me. The cheap drink didn't bode well for a hefty fee for me, either.

'You've got a point there,' I said in agreement. '*The Herald* said the earlier break-ins were pretty methodical. In and out. No muss, no fuss.'

Watkins looked down at a small leather notebook with the company's logo. 'The owner said he came to when the smoke set him to coughing and gagging. He escaped into the street and set up a hue and cry. A passing policeman called the fire squad, but it was too late to save the building.'

It seemed to me a good thing, tragedy averted. Watkins confirmed that.

'You can imagine how relieved we were to not have to pay the death benefit in a case like that. You see, we hadn't done much of an inspection when the policy was written back in '17, short-staffed during the war, you know.'

'Well, that's all good news. What do you need me for?' I eyed him over the rim of my glass.

'It's just suspicious, like I said. If we can prove that the fire was set on purpose by the building's owner to collect insurance money, the company wouldn't have to pay. The policy was worth $1,500, so if you prove it's fraud, that would be a cool $150 for you.'

If the job was as straightforward as he promised, it shouldn't take me long. And it's not like I had a line of clients beating a path to my door. We shook on the deal, and I said I'd get right on the case.

*****

The fire was on Monday and the city was moving slowly on demolition of the ruin, but it was scheduled to come down within days. I figured I'd better get over and sift through the ashes, see what turned up.

Later that afternoon, I showed up at the building on Water Street. I'd taken the time to ditch the boater and linen pants, donning instead a workman's cap and dungarees, and grabbing a pair of gloves for the rough work.

According to the information Watkins had given me, it had been a two-story wooden structure: newsstand on the first floor, four small offices above.

I'd asked him for the names of the tenants, and their current whereabouts, so I could interview them about anything they'd seen or heard.

Watkins promised to meet me at the site at 5, but until then I had the place to myself. The police had cordoned off the area for safety and posted it for no trespassing, but they hadn't bothered to set a guard. For now, the place looked deserted.

When the building came down, the remnants of the landlord's and tenants' belongings ended up in the basement, covered by beams and parts of wall. I pushed around a few of the smaller pieces of debris, but was careful not to dislodge anything that looked like it might be load-bearing.

Digging through the ashes, I found a small metal box from Hydrox Cookies. The paint on the outside was charred in places, but I recognized the blue and gold pattern. This was the owner's cash box. When I pried it open, I found some coins, receipts, and the insurance policy. Mr. Roberts, the owner of this establishment, had indeed insured his building for $1,500. Under the policy, I found several pink pieces of paper, dunning notices. This shopkeeper had bills, and they were seriously overdue. I ran a quick tally in my mind. Roughly $1,300. A handy fire would take care of that.

I sat back on my heels, a low whistle escaping my lips. I'd seen too much of that recently. People caught between bills and the threat of jail, desperate for relief. While the stock market was booming for some, and flappers and swells were putting on the Ritz, the majority of people were just scraping by. Something The Hound knew well.

I pulled the papers out and stuck them under my hat. Watkins was due any minute now. I wanted to buy some time for Roberts, and myself.

Searching through the ashes, I found some objects belonging to the tenants. Apparently, one was an architect. A T-square and compass were among the rubble, unhurt. I put them aside.

Nearby, protected from the fire by a plate of steel from the woodstove on the floor above, was a green cloth-bound ledger. I pulled it out and flipped through the pages. The first ledger page listed dates and initials along the left-hand column, with amounts varying from a few hundred dollars to several thousand, along the right.

On another page were more initials, and these had smaller amounts next to them. They repeated, some the same from one entry to the next, and the dates aligned roughly with those on the other page, usually a day or two following the first-page entries.

Incoming and outgoing columns. Perfectly balanced, everything accounted for. Like a certain profession? My mind started swirling this around, like the slick at Art's was swirling his gin rickey, a thought niggling at the back of my mind.

I turned to the front of the ledger to see if it was inscribed with the owner's name. But the endpapers, of heavier marbleized paper, had stuck to the glue of the linen cover from the heat. I pulled out my penknife, jimmied it under the corner of the paper and carefully slid it along the periphery. When the paper came loose, I sucked in my breath. Two initials, inscribed neatly in fountain pen, according to the Palmer Method. EP – Edmund Phillips, the freelance accountant. I should have known.

Just then the insurance man showed up, looking the opposite of the figure that occupied my thoughts, flustered and sweating in the 80-degree heat.

Watkins waved a sheaf of papers at me while he caught his breath. 'I have the names of the tenants right here, Mr. Jerome. Most have residences in the city, but one I couldn't find any reference for. A Mr.

Phillips is apparently a new tenant to this building, and he left no forwarding address.'

'Lemme guess, he showed up, oh, about 3 three weeks ago, took a short-term lease on the office, paying top dollar. Cash in advance?'

He nodded.

'If you do a little more digging, you'll find any references he gave his good landlord here were faked.' I fanned myself with the smoky ledger. 'Oh yeah, and he listed his occupation as … accountant?'

The shorty, sweaty man in front of me let his mouth drop open, but whether it was in awe of my deductive skills or just the heat, I wasn't sure. 'Well, yes, but the landlord swears he never saw any clients go in or out of that office. Guy was a night owl, too—staying well past the time the landlord closed up shop downstairs. He thought it was pretty suspicious, but a paid-up tenant, who didn't cause trouble? Why rock the boat? How did you know all that about him?'

'You forget I'm The Hound and I know how to sniff things out. Speaking of which, if you'll excuse me, I think I know the most recent whereabouts of our mysterious accountant as well. I'll return his ledger to him while I'm at it.'

I headed back to my office to change into more presentable clothing and study the account book more closely.

On the way, I stopped off at the shopkeeper's home. When I told him I was investigating the fire for the insurance company, he protested his innocence. 'Mr. Jerome, I told the police the honest truth. I was set upon by the thieves from that burglary ring. They had to be. Coshed me over the head and left me for dead, they did. And then set fire to my store.'

I pulled the papers out from under my hat. 'Mr. Roberts, I found these in a box under the rubble of the fire. You have a lot of bills and that insurance money could save your hide.'

'I know it looks damning,' he said. 'And to tell the truth, I was secretly glad the place burned. If I can get out from under these bills, I can start again, no problem. But if I go to jail for debt, it's all over. I didn't torch the place, but I'm damn glad those thugs did.'

I wanted to believe him, and I told him so. 'But for now, you're under suspicion, unless I turn up some evidence to prove your side of the story.'

I asked him about The Accountant, as I had come to think of Phillips, and he described a mysterious tenant, who came in late and stayed later. 'I tried to spy on him, but I couldn't prove a thing. He noticed my snooping and confronted me with it one night, and I can tell you, the look in his eye was frightening. After that, I steered clear of that one.'

*****

Back in my office, I went carefully through the ledger, trying to figure out what it might mean. One thing was certain: I agreed with the landlord. This accountant was a suspicious character. I was convinced he was up to no good – but what, I didn't have a clue. Yet.

I studied the lists of incoming and outgoing sums. The initials meant nothing to me. They didn't correspond to any known businesses or wealthy Syracusans, who would be an accountant's clients. It must be a cipher, but how to break the code?

When I was with the agency, I had some experience with codes. The Caesar Cipher was the oldest known to man, and was the simple way Julius Caesar kept his troop movements secret. He would shift the letters of the alphabet by a number picked at random – 4, 7, 9. To crack the code, all you need is that number. But how to find it?

I decided to focus on the dates instead. Grabbing the pile of *Heralds* that I'd saved in the corner, for insulation in the upcoming winter, I started to crosscheck the dates in the ledger against events in the newspapers.

At first, no real pattern emerged. Some dates had no corresponding news. But as I checked more dates, it became obvious they coincided with the recent robberies.

Sunday's entry—$20,000—was designated with the initials, MEM. That would have to be the robbery at E. W. Ellis Department Store. Making a chart of the alphabet, I lined up the E with the M. A shift of 8.

I decoded the other initials, using the chart I made shifting, 8 letters. They still made no sense. Think, Harry. What would an accountant do? I started playing with different combinations of the entry dates and amounts. Then I noticed it. Each line of the ledger had been printed with an identical number on both the right and left edges of the sheet, so the accountant could fill in other columns without getting off track. The 20,000-dollar entry was line 8.

Assigning each entry a shift corresponding to its line number revealed the other victims of the robbery ring. The third robbery, EF, would be BC – Baker and Charles Store; the fifth, PM, would become KH – King and Harris tools. DAN was WTG – Walker Taylor Garrity department store, the seventh victim. They matched the newspaper accounts of the burglars' heists.

In the distributions list, The Accountant had disbursed about an eighth of what he took in, divided among a crew also identified only by initials. I decoded them as well, using the same system, and one caught my eye. MW from the Garrity's theft became FP, which had to be Frank Patrick, a thorn in the police chief's side ever since he was caught at the age of 13 robbing a Salvation Army kettle. The other initials were probably known to the police, too. It looked like our friend The Accountant ran a ring of more than 20 petty thieves, no doubt youths he recruited right on Syracuse's streets. In any factory town like ours, there were plenty of kids bored, out of work, and ready for a little adventure – and a quick buck.

It really got my hackles up to see kids set on a life of crime, risking their freedom for a pittance, while a criminal like The Accountant raked in the fruits of their labor and then left town.

After the vicious attack on the shopkeeper and the fire they set, these kids could be up for attempted murder, guaranteeing they'd spend most of their lives in prison if convicted.

I shook my head. Freelance accountant? More like the devil's accountant, if you asked me.

Eight heists were accounted for. At the bottom of the first page was one more, with initials alongside. The date was Friday, just two days away, and the initials read BBK. Shift 9 and that made it SSB. Salina Savings Bank. Friday was payday at a lot of big industries in town. The bank would have a ready supply of cash for workers' pay envelopes.

That would also explain The Accountant's choice of office space. The newsstand was directly across the street from the bank, perfect for keeping an eye on the place and planning this, the biggest job of his Syracuse foray. When this job was done, Phillips would likely take off for the next town, leaving his young lackeys to face the music on their own.

Who knew how many cities he'd hit, how many kids he'd made thieves of? Well, that was going to stop here in the Salt City, if Harry Jerome had anything to say about it.

With no forwarding address for The Accountant, I headed back down to Art's to see if I could track my quarry.

I ordered a whiskey and headed to my favorite spot. As luck would have it, The Accountant was back in his easy chair, too.

'Sniff out anything interesting this afternoon, Hound?' Phillips drew the last word out in a lazy drawl, and, making a show of lighting up a new cigar, blew smoke in my face.

'As a matter fact, yes.' I accepted a glass from Ruthie's tray and savored a swig. 'Investigating that fire on Water Street. Found a ledger belonging to a certain E.P. in the ashes. Police might find it interesting, especially entry number 9, set to be filled in on Friday.'

He scoffed. 'I'm an accountant, like I said. That ledger proves nothing other than that I was doing my job.'

'Then why do the dates and amounts correspond to the recent robberies? And number 9 on Friday? The biggest job of your 'freelance' assignment here? But the worst of it is those kids you employ. Sure, they're all petty thieves, but you've transformed them into criminals facing a life in prison.'

I fixed him with a steely stare. 'Why don't you come along quietly now, and we don't have to disrupt Arthur's business?'

His eyes flashed, and I caught the look that so terrified the landlord. But it didn't scare me. I started to rise and reach for him, but Phillips was quicker. He jumped up, shoving me back into my seat, and headed for the door.

Scrambling up from my chair, I followed, now three steps behind. He rushed down the oak stairs.

I could see him just ahead of me on the second-floor landing, then disappearing as he headed down the lower staircase. I heard an 'Oof!' from Charlie at the entrance as The Accountant shoved him aside. The heavy oak door hit the marble wall with a thud.

I reached the bottom steps in time to see The Accountant, looking over his shoulder at my pursuit, run into Jefferson Street. Straight into the path of the No. 9 trolley. The impact flung his lifeless body into the roadway.

'Electric trolleys,' I said, shaking my head as I helped Charlie pick himself up off the foyer floor. 'You never hear 'em coming.'

*****

The next day, I headed for Salina Savings Bank to cash a check. A key found in Phillips's waistcoat led police to a locker at the train station, where the 20 grand was stashed, ready for The Accountant's getaway, earning me a $200 reward from the department store.

On the way, I stopped to survey the smoldering ruins of the newsstand. The bitter scent of ash stung my nose, but I smiled. The devil's accountant would be freelance no more. Yesterday, he met his employer in person.

Cruel as the Grave

Eve Fisher

Laskin, South Dakota, is in the middle of nowhere and Jackie's house lies ten miles beyond that. From her living room windows you look out on mile after mile of prairie and sky. Jackie says it's the same as having a house on the ocean, only without the tourist problem. The wind blows across the sloughs and lakes, giving a bayside tang to the air. In summer, seagulls and pelicans gyre in the sky. Now it was winter, and all I saw was snow. Jackie loves the view no matter what the season. She says it's restful. I say it's the abomination of desolation. I don't visit her much in winter.

But there's always an exception, and this was it. Jackie needed me as a friend but even more as a lawyer. She'd already been questioned by the police about Clare Harrison, one of those acquaintances we'd made twenty years ago and haven't been able to shed since. Clare's lover, Lewis Ford, had been murdered last week in Minneapolis and Clare was the chief suspect. Fine. The trouble was that Clare had gone to Jackie's the day after the murder and, after keeping her a day or two, Jackie had put her on a bus out of town.

The first thing I asked was, "You don't have her hidden up in the attic or something, do you?"

"Nice to see you, too, Karen," Jackie said, leaning on her cane. "No, I don't."

"Thank God for small favors."

"Mmm. Give me your coat and I'll give you some coffee."

I threw myself down on the couch. "Oh, no more driving. How wonderful. So where is the little bitch?"

"I love it when you cut straight to business. No, how are you doing, how —"

I cut that off. "Considering the police may be back out here any minute, I'd better be."

"Don't worry, it'll just be Sheriff Hanson. He and I are pals."

"Don't count on it. Just tell me the story."

"Edited or from the beginning?" Jackie asked, handing me coffee.

"Define 'edited.'"

"What I told Hanson, what else?"

I sighed. "All right, start from there."

Jackie perched herself on the arm of an armchair and began, "Well, about two weeks ago Clare called me up —"

"Two weeks ago? Lewis was shot last week."

"Yes, but Clare had made arrangements to come up here for a visit the week before. She said she was fed up with Lewis and getting out of town was the only way to get rid of him. Now that did sound strange to me. You know Clare. She's always just moved out and on –"

"And in with another," I interrupted.

"Yeah. Well, she asked if she could visit, I said sure, especially since Steve was heading out for a long haul."

"I wondered where he was," I said, trying to sound like I'd thought about Jackie's husband before now.

"Yeah. Anyway, we all agreed it would be fine, and Clare came on up a week ago. We had a great time, she reiterated that she was done with Lewis and had left town to prove it, and then I took her down to Sioux Falls and put her on a bus out of town to start life anew in, say, Arizona or Saskatchewan, I'm really not sure and neither was she." Jackie smiled brightly and set down her mug.

I nodded. "So, how much of that did the sheriff believe?"

"Well," Jackie said, lighting a cigarette, "he pretended to believe all of it."

"He was probably just being polite."

"I was afraid of that."

"So what's the true story?" I asked.

"Well – she did call me two weeks ago, we did make plans, and she did come up the day she said she was coming, but when she got here she was a wreck.”

“She shot him.” I made it a statement of fact.

“No, Karen, she didn’t,” Jackie said sternly. “And the dead man isn’t Lewis Ford.”

I took a couple of deep cleansing breaths. “All right,” I said. “Let’s hear it.”

“Clare was fed up with Lewis –”

“Just out of curiosity, why?” I asked. “He was a weird son of a bitch, but he had plenty of money and he didn’t seem to mind spending it on her.”

“Well, I gather the biggest problem was they hadn’t had sex in almost a year, God knows why –” Jackie sighed.

“Oh, my. How was she surviving?”

“Picking up strange, what else? She figured since they weren’t doing it, she was back on the market. He was probably screwing around, too. Who knows. Anyway, he didn’t take too well to that… real dog in the manger, and Claire’s never put up with that. So she figured that the only way to get rid of him was to get out of town.”

“I always think the words ‘get rid of’ have a sinister ring, don’t you?” I smiled; Jackie just shook her head.

“Look, the night before she came up here, they had a party at their place –”

“Clare and Lewis.”

“Yes. A farewell party of sorts, though I’m not sure anybody knew that except Clare. Anyway, there was this cute guy there and she snuck off with him in mid-party – you know how Clare is – and they had a party of their own.”

“They go to his place?”

“No, they just went in the closet.”

“Oh, God.”

“It’s a large closet.”

“How do you know?”

“Well, I haven’t been in it, but that’s what she told me.” Jackie stubbed out her cigarette and continued, “And then he went back to the regular party. She was going to do the same, but she passed out."

"In the closet?" I asked politely.

"No, in her bed. She said alone. The party was still going on, she could hear the noise from the living room. She assumed Lewis was still around, too, although she admitted she didn't see him. She passed out and didn't know anything until she got woken up about four in the morning by an extremely loud noise."

"The gunshot."

Jackie nodded. "She got up to go see what it was and just about fell over the body in the living room. No one else was around and there was this body lying there with its head blown off. She panicked, grabbed some clothes and left. Drove like a bat out of hell till her car broke down in Sleepy Eye. She hitched a ride with some guy there and got here as quick as she could."

I got up and walked over to the windows and looked out. Driving out, the clouds had been darker than the snow, creating a distant dark gray horizon, something to focus on over the miles of emptiness. Now it was twilight, and the snow and the sky were the same eerie blue. The horizon and all reference points were gone. "It's a dicey story," I finally said, "but it fits Clare to a tee."

"I knew you'd understand."

"And she says it isn't Lewis' body?"

"That's right."

"Why?"

"There were certain anatomical differences."

I turned around and asked, "What, he had two of them?"

"Don't be silly. The corpse had a large mole on his dick. Lewis didn't."

"His head's blown off and she was looking at his privates?"

"Well, it beat looking at where his head had been," Jackie said.

"And she saw the mole. What did she do, get on top of him?"

"It was a large mole."

"Must have been a natural French tickler. No wonder she had so much fun in the closet."

Jackie was tracing out the carpet pattern with her cane and ignoring me. "I keep wondering how the police identified the body. Why they say it's Lewis Ford's when Clare swears it isn't."

"Well," I said, "it might be that they found something, like his wallet. Or they checked his fingerprints. Or his distinguishing characteristic was already known to them for some reason." Jackie giggled at this point. "Basically, what I'm saying is there's a good chance that Clare lied to you. That it is Lewis' body and for some reason, like because she did it or because some guy she knows did it, she's covering. Stupidly, but she's covering."

"I thought of that," Jackie agreed, which surprised me. Jackie's always been pretty gullible where Clare's concerned. "But I can't see Clare covering for any man. Now if I killed someone, she'd lie till she was blue in the face. She might even do it for you." I choked on my coffee. "She really might," Jackie said, smiling. "But for a man? Never."

"No loyalties possible."

"None whatsoever. To Clare, men are for sex and money, and that's it." Jackie looked off into space, an analytical look in her eye. "Actually, if your definition of orientation is based on emotions rather than sex, she makes you look just a tad heterosexual."

"Don't compare me to Clare. Don't you *dare* do that!"

"I didn't mean it that way –" Jackie protested.

"Just —" I got my temper back under control. "Let's move on to the next topic. Why did you get her out of town?" Jackie shrugged and looked away. "Look, putting her on the bus is fine and dandy as long as you didn't know about what had happened back at her place. But you did. Or at least, you'd heard Clare's story. Now I understand perfectly well why Clare ran like a bat out of hell. That's the kind of person she is. She runs. She bolts. She gets the fuck out of Dodge every goddam time. But you... Clare trusts you. If you told her to jump off a building she just might do it. You are the one person who could have talked her into staying, into going to the police with this whole tale of parties and closets and moles. Why didn't you? Why did you put her on that damned bus?"

Jackie continued staring at her hands. Finally, she looked up at me and said, "Clare's not the most believable person in the world." I nodded. "She's got a long rap sheet."

"I'm well aware of that," I stated. "You made me represent her in that last DUI."

Jackie winced slightly. "Yeah. Well, how would you, as an attorney, interpret her criminal record?"

"Alcoholic, rowdy, part-time hooker and full-time party girl." Jackie looked away and I hastily added, "In the eyes of the law enforcement officials of our fair land."

"Exactly. Who's going to believe her? She was terrified of being arrested, of being railroaded. She begged me to help her get away… And I know Clare, I know she'd never do anything like that. I mean, really, Clare picking up a *shotgun* of all things and blowing somebody's head off? Never. So I figured okay, get her out of the loop for a while, give the investigation time to get cracking. I mean, surely they'd find the killer without Clare having to be…" She grimaced, and then burst out: "It never occurred to me that it would take them so long to find the body! That they'd identify it as Lewis. That Clare would be their one and only suspect. Karen, they're not even *looking* anywhere else."

"You don't know that," I said. Then the devil made me say, "Though, if they're not, there might be a damn good reason why."

"I know. But I don't believe it. Okay?"

"Okay. Meanwhile, though, you're an accessory."

"To what?"

"What do you mean, to what? You put a murder suspect on a bus out of town. Helped her get away. Aided and abetted a fugitive from justice. That's what."

"They're going to have to prove it."

"It's what you did," I said wearily.

"No," Jackie said earnestly. "That's what they're going to have to prove. That I knew all about it. And they can't do that. If they ever do find Clare, she'll swear I didn't know anything about it. So will I. That leaves you. How much of a retainer will it take to make this whole conversation privileged information?"

I glared at her. It didn't take much to figure this one out. Jackie was going to protect Clare with her last breath. God knows why. Clare's always been a worthless tramp, but Jackie's always been crazy about her, so that was that. On the other hand, I was going to protect Jackie with my last breath, so that was *that*. Jackie was worth it, even if I had to (and, possibly, to be honest, if I could) throw Clare to the wolves to do it.

"Okay," I said, sighing. "I guess we'd better make it official. Give me a buck." Jackie dug down into her pocket and handed over a dollar. I tucked it away and said, "Now I'll give you my first piece of professional advice. Stick with the story you gave the police."

"I was planning to."

"Good."

"What's your second piece of advice?"

"Get Clare back here." Jackie raised her eyebrows. "And don't even try to tell me that you can't, because I know you know where she is, or if you don't, you know how to get in touch with her. You get her back here ASAP. This farce has gone on long enough."

"Okay. Anything else?"

"Yes. Feed your attorney before she passes out."

"Good God!" Jackie cried, scrambling to her feet. "Why didn't you say something earlier?" She headed to the kitchen, then turned around and hugged me hard. "Oh, God, Karen, I'm so glad you're here. I've really needed someone to talk to about this whole mess. I've needed *you*. Thank you so much for coming up."

"Any time," I said, my arms wrapped around her. "I just wish you'd called me sooner."

"I was hoping to keep you out of it." Jackie broke away and headed towards the kitchen again. "But, now that you're here…"

"Yes?"

"I need you to do me a favor."

"Depends on the favor," I said.

"I want you to get a look at the autopsy report or the police report, whichever." I must have looked surprised, because she added, "Well, don't you want to know if that dead guy really does have that mole on his dick?"

Well, it made sense, although I wouldn't have bet on whether sense or prurience was Jackie's primary motivation. I went off and called a friend of mine in records while Jackie started cooking.

"I now owe Officer Wickham one beer," I told Jackie as she was working in the kitchen.

"Speaking of beer, there's some in the fridge." I raised my eyebrows. "Don't give me that look. Clare bought it, along with a few others. And drank them all. Well, almost all. The one in there is the one that got away."

"Figures," I said. Clare knows Jackie's a recovering alcoholic, but does she care? No, she just does what she wants. She probably waved it under Jackie's nose the whole time. "I don't need any," I said.

"Go ahead," she said. "It doesn't bother me." So I dug it out. "Sit down. Dinner's ready." She pulled out a chair at the kitchen table and waved me to it.

After we'd started eating, Jackie asked, "What about the mole?"

"Not sure about that. They called it a blemish. And he seemed to have them all over."

"But was one on his penis?"

"Yes." Jackie punched the air. "Approximately the size of a quarter."

"In a flaccid or erect state?"

"He didn't die with a hard-on, Jackie."

"Boy that was some kind of a mole."

"The victim was nude except for a t-shirt. Lewis Ford's wallet and keys were found on the dresser in Lewis' bedroom. He and Clare appear to have had separate rooms."

"She said they weren't screwing anymore," Jackie said.

"No signs of robbery, nor any signs that, say, Lewis had taken off."

"What about fingerprints?"

"The trouble with fingerprints," I pointed out, "is that in order to use them, the person you're trying to identify has to have been fingerprinted at some point in his or her life. Lewis Ford appears to have been an upright, sober citizen who was never fingerprinted in his entire life."

"Upright, sober my ass," Jackie said. "He just never got caught."

"That's what one of the guys at the station said. You do know he was a drug-dealer, or rather, suspected of it, don't you?"

"I'm not an idiot," Jackie said. "Lewis had a high-octane lifestyle, and as far as I could tell he didn't do anything in the nine to five range."

I nodded. "The cops in Minneapolis have been trying to nail him for a while. No luck. Anyway, back to the corpse, who had never been fingerprinted, either." I laid my notes down and leaned back. "Which may not mean anything, except that there hasn't been a single appearance of Lewis anywhere in town or out of it since the murder. No money taken out of his bank, no charges on any of his credit cards. Face it, Jackie, the options are, one, the man is dead. Two, the man has vanished and is living on air. There isn't a third one."

From the look in Jackie's eye, it was just as well the doorbell rang right then. There was a third option: Lewis had been a drug dealer, so, if he was still alive, he wasn't living on air, he was living on stash. But where, why —

"Tom! What brings you out here? Has something happened with Clare?"

I made it to the kitchen door before Jackie finished closing the door behind a uniformed officer.

"Not as far as I know," he said, taking his hat off. "They've traced her to Fargo, but they lost her there. Bob'll be out to see you in the morning, you betcha."

"Great." Jackie saw me and waved me to them. "Karen, this is Deputy Tom Jensen. Tom, this is Karen Sloan, my personal attorney."

I put out my hand for a handshake, but he couldn't seem to figure out what to do with his hat. "You don't shake hands on duty?" I asked.

He dropped the hat and shook my hand. "I was j-j-just… I-I-I'm…" he managed to stammer out.

"Oh, give me that hat and sit down, have a cup of coffee," Jackie said. She turned to me and said, "I wish you could have seen Tom here last week, tearing up the dance floor with Clare at the VFW Ball. They were playing red hot rock and roll oldies." The deputy's face was so red I thought it would explode. I'd never seen anyone blush like that in my life.

"Jackie," he pleaded.

"Sorry," Jackie said tenderly. "Come on, have some coffee."

"I can't," he said. "I've got to get home. I just wanted to let you know." He put his hat back on. He looked very young. And very big. "If you hear anything from her…"

"I'll tell her you're still in the fan club," Jackie assured him. "Though, of course, you might hear from her first."

Suddenly his face, so soft and little-boyish when it blushed, changed, hardened, aged about ten years. "I doubt it. Like I said, just let her know."

"Okay, Tom. Thanks for coming by." Jackie shut the door behind him.

"My, my, my. What would his sheriff say?" I asked.

"About what? Oh, you mean him coming out here to tell me about Fargo?"

I nodded. "It's not standard procedure, honey. He could get fired."

"Well…" Jackie shrugged and limped back into the kitchen. "I can always claim I heard it from Vi down at the Norseman's Bar. She hears everything in town and spreads it just as quick as it comes in. Besides, he's got his reasons."

"Another of Clare's devotees."

"Those VFW gigs have a lot to answer for. Mingling the outlaws with the law, all to hot music and a lot of booze." Jackie laughed. "Though how far it's gone hasn't been proven. Yet."

"I can guess," I said sourly. "It's pretty far gone when a law enforcement official goes out of his way to collude with an accessory –"

"Oh, quit being such a fuddy-duddy."

"All right."

"You know," Jackie mused, "I wonder who the hell he was."

"Who?"

"The dead guy. The one with the mole. The one Clare had carnal knowledge of in the closet."

"Clare didn't tell you his name?"

"No. But then, I'm not sure she knew. Clare doesn't always ask, you know." I kept my mouth shut. "I wonder – you think missing persons might have something?"

"On what?" I asked. "A guy with a mole on his dick?"

Jackie and I looked at each other for a moment and then we both started laughing. We laughed until we hurt, or at least until Jackie straightened up and said, "You know, it's not that damn funny. The man's dead."

*****

When I woke up the next morning everything was just a little too bright. It was all that damned snow. When Jackie first moved to Laskin, she told me that the light was more intense there than anywhere she'd ever been. Now I could see what she meant. I could also see Jackie, wrapped from head to toe, leaning on a great wooden staff, limping through the snow from the windbreak, her breath coming out from her muffler in great white puffs. I watched her until she got to the house. Then I turned away from the window and the room seemed dark as night. Downstairs I heard the back door close with a bang and I could smell coffee. I got dressed as quickly as I could and went downstairs.

"Good morning," Jackie said cheerfully. She was standing by the stove, and had exchanged the staff for her cane. She looked wide-awake and disgustingly hearty.

"Morning. So. I'll bet you've been up for hours. I saw you outside, walking."

"It's beautiful out." She poured me a cup of coffee and put it down in front of me at the kitchen table. "Fifteen degrees."

"You're nuts."

"Yes, but it was nice. I saw two deer and a rabbit."

"Bambi lives, Black Elk speaks." I clicked mugs with her.

"Breakfast?"

"Sounds good to me."

Jackie made muffins and scrambled eggs. As I ate the day seemed to get warmer, even though the weather forecast was grim: cold and snow and everything I hate. The only reason I stay this far north is because of my friends, my community, my job, but every winter I reconsider the whole deal. Florida…

The doorbell rang before we'd finished breakfast. We both groaned, and Jackie went out, and returned with a cold draft of air and the sheriff.

"Karen, this is Bob Hanson. Bob, Karen Sloan. A very good friend of mine. And my attorney."

"An attorney?" he said. "Well, that's certainly your right."

"I know," Jackie replied.

"Although this is all –"

"Unofficial?" Jackie asked.

"Oh, Jackie. Let's call it official but friendly."

"Exactly. Would you like some coffee?"

"Thanks," he said. "It's mighty cold out there."

"You know, you really should wear earmuffs in this kind of weather," Jackie commented. "Most of your major heat loss is through your ears, and you need to cover them up or you'll catch pneumonia."

"I've heard that," Hanson replied.

"Well, it's true. Here, have a muffin while you're at it."

"Thank you." He helped himself to muffins and we sat there, watching him eat. So friendly. So familial. So Mayberry. "These are good. Home baked?"

"Yes, thank you," Jackie said. "Now, what can we do for you today, Bob?"

"Well, I suppose first off, you should know that we managed to trace your friend up as far as Fargo."

"Fargo?" Jackie seemed surprised.

"You said she was going to San Antonio," Hanson commented.

"Well, she'd mentioned it. I can't believe she'd head north in this kind of weather. She's never been big on winter." Jackie reached for her cigarettes. "Do you mind?"

"It's your house," Hanson reminded her. Then he fished out a pack himself and asked, "Do you mind?"

"Not at all." Jackie turned to me and grinned. "We're going to smoke you out, Karen." I shrugged. "Karen quit smoking ten years ago and has been telling me how awful my lungs look ever since."

"What are friends for?" I murmured.

"Speaking of friends," Hanson said, "If you don't mind my asking, Jackie, how did you meet Miss Harrison?"

"We met at a party and hit it off," Jackie said.

What she didn't say was that it was a party at our place, and that Jackie had spent most of the evening in the kitchen, drinking heavily. That night had been frightening. It was shortly after the accident that crippled her, and she was in a world of her own with no intention of coming out. And then Clare came bouncing in. I don't know what happened – I was in another room, I'd had it – and by the time I came back into the kitchen to get some more ice, the two of them were old pals. Jackie was even drinking coffee.

They stayed up talking most of the night. Discussing, if I remember correctly, some new-age mish-mosh of astrology, free-will, immortality, and colors, along with their favorite albums, hottest ranking rock stars, and God only knows what else. I don't know. I do know it seriously disrupted the plans of the young stud who'd brought Clare to the party in the first place.

"I see," Hanson said. He sounded dissatisfied.

"Something puzzling you?" Jackie asked.

The young stud finally did manage to drag Clare off for a brief fling, or rather, Clare had taken him off to give him some to shut him up – and right then I remembered that the fling took place in one of our closets. Clare's story might have some truth to it after all. Anyway, when they emerged, Clare shooed him off like a pesky fly and went back to Jackie.

"It's just that you don't seem like the type of friend she'd have. Or her you."

"Well, you never know," Jackie said.

The stud finally got Clare to leave with him, but thirty-six hours later she came back, looking for Jackie. We've never been rid of her since.

"Friendship's a lot like love," Jackie said. "You don't choose it, it chooses you, and afterwards everyone wonders what on earth they see in each other."

"Do you know Miss Harrison, too?" Hanson asked, turning to me.

I cleared my thoughts as quickly as I could. "Yes," I said. "I met her the same time Jackie did."

"Are you good friends with her as well?"

"No."

"You see, Karen and I were roommates when Clare and I became friends," Jackie explained, and I wanted to shut her up more than just about anything I'd ever wanted in my life, "but Clare and Karen never hit it off. I've never been exactly sure why." She looked at me and added, "Maybe I just haven't asked the right question to find out."

Hanson asked, "Have either of you ever met or heard of a man named Gerald Lee?"

"No," Jackie and I said together.

"Who is he?" Jackie asked. "Is he connected with Clare?"

"In a way," Hanson said. "He's the corpse."

"What?" Jackie erupted. "And you let us all believe that it was Lewis Ford's body? How long have you known?"

"Found out last night," Hanson said, watching her.

"Meanwhile, Clare's been under suspicion for murdering her lover –
"

"Now, Jackie –" I tried to smooth her, but it didn't work.

"Last night? Why didn't you call me? I've been worried half to death about this mess!" Jackie cried.

"Let me explain how this all happened," he said.

"Please do."

"They haven't been sure whose body it was from the beginning," the Sheriff said. "After all, his face, well… it wasn't there." Jackie shuddered. "And remember, they're out-of-state cops. They're not going to tell me everything. I wouldn't necessarily tell them everything, either, you betcha."

Jackie nodded. "I understand. It would make a perfect sense, him being Ford. After all, late at night, half naked…" Hanson's eyebrows went up. "Karen checked the police report."

"Did you get the coroner's report, too?" Hanson asked, amused.

"No," I said.

"Well, that's what cracked it. Once the coroner found out he'd had AIDS, they started hunting doctors –"

"What did you say?" I asked.

"The guy had AIDS," Hanson said. "Full-blown. He had those lesions all over him, uh, Karposi's sarcoma?"

"Kaposi's sarcoma," I corrected automatically. Jackie had turned into white stone.

"Yeah, whatever. Anyway, when they found that out, they started checking with hospitals, doctors, etc. They needed a firm ID of the victim, and truth is, they didn't have fingerprints or a face to go by. They finally found the right guy, a Doctor Williams, who identified the body. The lab work confirmed it. The man who died is Gerald Lee. Whoever he is. You don't know, either of you?" We both shook our heads. "Well, I hadn't gotten my hopes up too far. Nobody seems to know who he is."

"Not even his doctor?" I asked.

"No. Turns out Mr. Lee used a post office box for an address and didn't have a land line, just a cell phone. The doctor says he's seen that before. There's still a stigma to having it, especially in some circles."

"What about Lewis?" I asked. "Are they trying to track him down now?"

"Miss Sloan, they've been trying to track Mr. Ford down ever since they found this out. Nothing. I'll tell you what, if you could find Miss Harrison, that would really help. She might have some idea where he went."

"I can imagine," I said. "But would she be interrogated as a witness or a prime suspect?"

"I think they'd just like to talk to her," Hanson replied blandly. "I'd like to talk to her first, if possible."

"Talk to her or book her?" Jackie asked.

"Talk to her. Just talk to her. Please, if you hear from her, ask her to call me, okay? You know me, Jackie. I'll play straight with her. I won't pull any fast ones..." He got up and we rose like courtiers. "Well, I'll leave you two now. Thanks for the coffee.”

“Any time,” Jackie managed to say. We all walked him to the front door, where we stood in silence while Hanson gathered his coat and muffler and hat and started bundling himself up.

“How long do you plan to be in town?” Hanson asked me.

“I don’t know,” I said. “Depends on how long Jackie needs me. Or wants me.”

Hanson nodded and left.

Jackie closed the door after him, looked over at me and simply said, “AIDS.” Then she turned on her heel and thumped her way into the kitchen, where she sat down in her chair and brooded over her coffee cup. I leaned against the counter. I didn’t know what to say, and even if I did, I wasn’t sure I should say it. Everything was dead quiet, except for the ticking of the kitchen clock. Jackie looked like she’d died with her eyes open, which was unnerving because I wasn’t sure why. It had just been proved that Clare had not killed Lewis, so that problem was solved.

“Oh, the hell with it,” she said. “Let’s take a drive, go out to Pipestone. The falls are all frozen over, it’ll be beautiful.”

“And cold,” I couldn’t help saying.

“Wuss. We’ll take a thermos. I’ve got plenty of blankets, in case we want to camp out.” She was silent a moment, then she said, “I need to get out, get away for a little bit.”

“All right.”

We were all bundled up and ready to go when Deputy Tom drove up. Jackie saw him and she called out, “Tom! Why didn’t you tell me?”

“Tell you what?” Tom asked, getting out of his car.

“That they found out whose body it was!”

“What?” Tom sounded absolutely stunned. I rolled my window down, a triumph of curiosity over warmth.

“That’s right – it’s not Lewis at all. It’s a man named Gerald Lee. Didn’t you know that?”

“If I had, I’d have told you. They must be keeping me out of the loop. Oh, God, Jackie –” He and Jackie walked towards each other and they met half-way between the two cars. “Did Bob – did the sheriff say anything about me?"

"No. Why?"

"You know," Tom said, and I had to strain to hear him as his voice sunk. "About me and Clare."

"Oh, come on, Tom," Jackie's voice sailed out. "One night after the VFW does not make you an automatic suspect."

Tom was blushing again. Against the snow and the blue-gray sky, he looked like a large Nordic beet. "It's not just that," he managed to say. "Your friend – I met her before."

"So?" Jackie asked.

I got out of the car. "Look, I'm freezing out here," I called. "Why don't we go back inside if you're going to talk all day?"

Tom started to say something, maybe hello, maybe not, but the radio in the squad car let out a loud squawk. He almost dove for it. When he emerged a minute later, he said, "I got a call out at Harv Ullman's farm. I gotta go."

"Okay," Jackie said.

"Can I talk to you later?" he asked urgently. "Like maybe tonight?"

Jackie shrugged. "Sure. We're going out to Pipestone but we should be back before dinner."

Tom nodded and got into his car. "Watch out for the weather," he advised. "Blizzard's coming." He waved goodbye as he peeled out of the driveway and onto the main road. Jackie shook her head and came over to me.

"Now what do you think that was all about?"

"Sounds like he met Clare before," I said. "And was worried about his boss finding out about it."

Jackie nodded. An old grey pick-up slowed down as it came to Jackie's drive. "Oh, great! Who the hell is *this*?" she snapped as it stopped. We stared at the truck and, presumably, the driver stared at us. Then the pick-up started again and went on down the road.

"Lookie Lous," Jackie said, getting back in the car.

"You know," I said, fastening my seatbelt, "I just can't see Clare with an officer of the law."

"Why not?" Jackie asked. "He's young, he's single, he's a good-looking cuss if you're into the Viking type."

"He'll be overweight in five years," I said. "His stomach's already rolling over his belt."

"Well, he's not my type, that's for sure," Jackie said, pulling out into the road. "God, I wish Steve were back." She put a tape in and Vivaldi came flowing out of the speakers. Ten miles down the road she let out a deep sigh. "Isn't it beautiful?"

I looked around. There was the snow, the sky, and a few bare cottonwoods etched between them. It was the ultimate embodiment of the word 'wilderness', and she loved it. Something in it set her free. She once told me that flying down a country road was the closest thing she'd come to doing grand jètés across the stage. And we were flying now all right, flying far too fast for my peace of mind. I snuck a glance at the speedometer and saw it hovering around eighty. I snuck a glance at Jackie. She wasn't smiling. She was looking at the road and the landscape with a fixed intensity of will that frightened me more than the landscape.

"Halloween," Jackie suddenly said.

"What about it? It's February," I reminded her.

"No, Halloween is when Tom must have met Clare. She came up for a couple of days and she went to the Halloween dance at the Norseman's Bar. They must have met then."

"Great."

"Yeah." We went on flying. "I wonder... What if Tom's been seeing Clare all along?"

"Tom lives in Laskin," I pointed out.

"Yeah, but he goes to Minneapolis a lot. What if he's been going up to see her? What if he was at that party?"

"Oh, God," I groaned. "You think the whole world was at that party?"

"No, just Tom. And why not? Clare draws 'em in, you know. Like flies on honey."

I didn't say the other thing flies are attracted to. Instead, I pointed out, "Well, if he was, he isn't going to admit it to anyone. Except maybe to Clare."

"I don't know, he sounded like he was pretty close to admitting something this morning. And he's worried sick. Good God, if he was at that party – and he is the jealous type, believe me – what if *he* -" Jackie stopped talking.

"What if he shot this Lee guy?" Jackie nodded. I shook my head. "Come on, Jackie." She gave me a blank look so I said, sternly, "Jackie you are out of your mind. It's pretty obvious now that Lewis shot him."

Jackie nodded. "Yeah, you're right."

She kept on driving, but it was barely a minute before she burst out, "It's not that, Karen. Think about it! AIDS! And she slept with him! What was she thinking?"

Jackie pulled over to the side of the road, stopped the car, and burst into tears.

I pulled her into my arms and held her while she cried. Her hair smelled of shampoo and smoke. I kissed it softly. The slight tremors of her weeping raised up her scent, a scent of mulled honey and cloves and musk. I was drowning in it. I closed my eyes and rested my face in her hair, to breathe her in as long as I could, as long as I could stand it, as long as I dared. Her body, so warm and shaken, so fragile, as I ran my hand down her arm, my arm molding across her back, curved and carved and warm, so warm…

It didn't last long. Only a few moments passed before she had straightened up and out of my arms, wiped her eyes, blown her nose, and was staring out at the road with eyes as bleak as the landscape.

I started to say, "I'm sorry," but I stopped myself. I wasn't sorry, except to see Jackie hurt. I started to say, "Don't worry," but there was plenty to worry about. I started to say, "I'm here," but she knew that, and while she'd be polite, even I knew it wasn't enough.

"Oh, this is ridiculous," she said, and pulled out of my arms. "Let's get some lunch." She started the car, pulled back out on the road, and gave me one of those rare, sweet, genuinely loving smiles that stab you to the heart.

The Norseman's Bar was a typical bar, bad Western art, dark, almost empty at this time of day, but Jackie seemed to find it okay. The waitress, named Vi, came over and took our order, and then asked, "Hey, what's the latest on that friend of yours?"

"Nothing much. Still in trouble," Jackie said.

"Well, that's a damn shame," Vi said. "Some people might've thought she was a little out there, but I liked her." I made a sort of choking sound and Vi looked me over: a quick, judgmental summing up that seemed to go against me. "You hear from her, you tell her I'm sorry to hear she's in trouble."

"I will."

"So," I said, "Clare hit all the hot spots of Laskin while she was here."

"Yep. Just trying to make sure she had a good time." Jackie's fingers did a little tap across the table, and I knew she wanted a beer.

"Great. She's partying hearty while there's a dead man rotting in her living room."

Jackie sighed. "Look, she was damn near hysterical when she got here, and that was enough. I thought a little distraction wouldn't hurt."

"She distracts easy."

"Besides, it would have looked suspicious if she hadn't gone out and about."

"Ah, the perils of maintaining one's reputation."

"Karen. Please."

"Hey, Jackie!" A man called out. "How's Steve?" Jackie excused herself to me and went over to chat with him. She didn't come back until Vi showed up with our lunch. Jackie smiled and said thanks.

"Sure thing. You want anything else, let me know." Vi turned away and then back. "Hey, did you hear that your friend flat cleaned Ronny out? He'd never seen a woman could shoot pool like that in all his life. He was telling some guy all about it last night."

"Ronny was bragging about losing to a woman? To another man?" Jackie shook her head. "The end of the world's coming, Vi."

"I know," she agreed. "But he hasn't changed any. An hour later he was trying to hustle my cousin, Diane, and I had to warn him off. He'll be back in here tonight, doing the same damn thing, too."

"Probably right," Jackie agreed.

"I know I am," Vi said stoutly. A bell rang and she went off to the kitchen.

"She is, too," Jackie said, picking the onions off of her burger. "Ronny's just like a dog in heat. I thought he and Clare might hit it off, but it was way too competitive."

"You were trying to fix her up, too? Was that another distraction?"

"No. Oh, I don't know. Look, these are about the best burgers in Laskin. Let's not ruin them by talking about all this stuff. I'm sick of the whole thing."

We ate silently and steadily, watching other people come and go. When we were done, Jackie made a slight gesture with her hand, and Vi came over with the coffeepot and refilled our cups. Jackie lit a cigarette and leaned back in the booth.

"You're smoking too much," I said.

"Beats drinking," she said. "I'll try to cut down tomorrow. Or the next day. Whenever this mess gets sorted out."

"In other words, in the next decade or so."

"Yep. You know, the more I think about it, the more there's something wrong with the whole story. A dead guy with AIDS. Lewis missing and not a sign of him for all this time. Not even a money trail, and Lewis can't survive without money."

"Neither can Clare," I pointed out.

"And why was he killed?"

"Who? Oh, Lee. Jealousy, I guess. Lewis caught him in Clare's bed –"

"No, that's where it all goes wrong," Jackie interrupted. "First place, Clare has enough sense not to be sleeping with some guy with full-blown AIDS. Not to mention whether said guy could even do it. I would doubt it, myself, but I'm no expert on how long sexual function lasts with HIV. Second place, Clare and Lewis hadn't been sleeping together for a year, and she was screwing around all over the place. And he knew it. Why would he suddenly have a fit of jealousy and blow this guy's head off?"

"Jealousy hits people in strange ways, at strange times."

"Thank you, Ann Landers."

"You asked."

"It's not jealousy," Jackie said. "Remember, Clare didn't sleep with the dead guy."

"How do you know?"

"Because she described a young hard body. Not a man dying of AIDS. So she didn't sleep with him, so there's no fit of jealousy to fuel the murder. So it has to be something else. Lewis must have killed this guy for a reason that had absolutely nothing to do with Clare. I figure it's got to be drug connected, which means that Clare had nothing to do with it."

"It's a thought."

"Yeah." Jackie got up and Vi appeared before us. "You girls want anything else?" she asked.

We both shook our heads. Vi made out our bill and Jackie paid it. Then, out of nowhere, she asked, "Vi, who was it Ronny was talking to about Clare and the pool game?"

"You mean about getting beat?"

"That's right."

"Some stranger," Vi said.

"A stranger? This time of year?"

"Weird, huh? Said he was from Texas, but he sure didn't sound like Texas to me."

"You should know," Jackie said. "What did he look like?"

"Mmmm. Not bad looking, if you like 'em tall and skinny as a rail. Myself, I go more for the mountain man type, same as you." I was startled to hear Steve described as a mountain man, but I suppose he is, in a way.

"Dark hair?" Jackie asked.

"No, blond hair, kind of thin on top. Why?"

I felt a cold shudder run down my spine as Jackie said, thoughtfully, "Well, I was thinking that somebody might be looking for Clare. Besides the police."

"No kidding?" Vi was interested.

"Might be. Listen, Vi, if he comes back here, would you do me a favor and give me a call?"

"I sure will. You think someone's coming after her?"

"Might be," Jackie said.

"Figures. Ronny said she had the kind of eyes a man would kill for. And by God somebody did, didn't he?" She nodded happily as she walked off to deal with another customer.

*****

Outside, the wind hit us like a moving arctic wall. Jackie almost lost her footing despite her cane, and I wasn't much better. We dug in and crunched our way across the new light dusting of snow that shifted and moved and s-curved and double-helixed its way across the icy ground. By the time we got to the car, I was shaking from head to foot.

"My God, it's cold," I gasped inside the car. My nose was running, but I wasn't about to take off my gloves until the heat got cranking. Instead, I wiped my nose on my wrist like a three year old.

"Hot shower when we get home. It'll warm you right up," Jackie said, backing out of the parking lot and moving onto the state road. "My knee says we'd better get home quick as we can."

The roads were crap, the weather was worse, and I was never so happy in my life to see Jackie's driveway. I know Jackie felt the same way because I heard her murmur, "Thank you, Lord." Then she said, "Whose car is that?"

A Chevy Blazer was sitting by the side of the house. "You mean you don't know?" I asked.

"Don't be a smart-ass," Jackie said. "I know people, not cars." We pulled into the garage.

"Maybe it's the jerk who passed us earlier."

Jackie switched off the engine. "God, I hope so. I'll cane him to death."

"Wait a second," I said, as she climbed out of the car.

"What?"

"There's nobody in the truck," I said.

"They're probably inside, getting warm, drinking up all my best booze," Jackie said.

"Well, do you think we should just go barging in?"

"It's my house," she pointed out.

"That wasn't what I meant. I mean, some strange car is sitting out there –"

"Let's just go inside and see who it is," Jackie said in a reasonable tone that was entirely unreasonable.

"If you lived in the city," I muttered, walking behind her. I looked across the snow-swept yard and saw a grey pick-up driving slowly down the road. For a moment, I wondered if it was the same one from before, but decided it was enough to worry about one truck at a time.

Jackie opened the door and went in, beating the snow off of her boots with her cane as she went. I followed slowly, and then I heard an all too familiar laugh. I looked past Jackie's shoulder and saw a woman leaping up off of Jackie's couch and into her arms. A wave of relief swept over me, and then, as always, the urge to kill her.

Clare, of course.

"And there's Karen!" Clare cried gleefully. She leaped forward and hugged me hard. My response was more delicate. "Don't worry, darling," Clare said, smiling. "Everything's going to be fine. Nothing to worry about at all, at all." Yeah, right, I thought, as she stepped away and looked me over from head to toe. "You look great, do you know that? Doesn't she look great, Jackie?"

Jackie was standing with her arms folded, smiling like some rural Mary Poppins watching her charges display proper nursery etiquette. "Karen always looks great," she said. "So do you."

Clare preened and said, "You're just saying that to make me feel good. I know how bad I look. I haven't even freshened up and it was a mighty long trip back here."

"From Fargo?" I asked.

"Kind of. This nice young man, he's a real sweetheart, he drove me down here." She leaned towards Jackie and said, "He's using the bathroom right now and then he'll get right on out of here. I only let him stay to keep me company until you got back home, you know, just in case. But now that you're here, I'll send him on as soon as he gets out."

"That's probably a good idea," Jackie said. At that moment the young man came down the hall. He was young all right, tall, thin, pale, a little unkempt. He stopped when he saw us and looked warily at Clare.

"These your friends?" he asked.

"Yes, sweetie," Clare said. She went over and took his hand and led him down to us. "This is the mistress of the house, Jackie, and this is our very dear friend Karen, and this is Bedford. He lives just outside Fargo, and it was such a lucky thing I ran into him because he's going down to visit his cousin in Sioux Falls, so he could give me a ride. Now wasn't that sweet of him?"

I was beyond speech. Jackie said, "Nice to meet you," and shook his hand.

"Nice to meet you, ma'am," Bedford said. "You've got a real nice place here."

"Thank you. Would you like a cup of coffee?" Jackie asked politely.

"No, thank you, ma'am," he replied. "That's why I had to use the facilities, too much coffee. I'm about wired for sound. Now a beer, maybe…"

"Now, sweetie," Clare interrupted, putting an arm around him, "you know you've got to get on down to Sioux Falls and see your cousin before she goes completely hysterical and calls up the highway patrol and starts a manhunt for you."

"Aw, she wouldn't do that."

"You might think she wouldn't, but I know all about cousins like her. She's worried stiff about you. Can't hardly wait till you get there."

"You think so?" He was blushing. Must be a South Dakota thing, I thought.

"I know so."

"Well, but…" His eyes were yearning, but Clare shook her head firmly. "You've got my number, right?"

"Oh, yes, I do," Clare said, and I knew that was gospel.

"Well, whenever you're up around my way," he said.

"You'll be the first one I call, sweetie," Clare said.

The poor boy twisted around on his heels, but Clare was inexorable. I could see why he didn't want to go: Clare was hot. Her jeans were tight, her shirt was loose, her blonde hair was in a loose knot, with little tendrils falling down in what appeared to be a casual arrangement. As always, she looked fresh-faced and healthy. It took close observation to see how much expert make-up that required. And in the center of it all her eyes, brilliant blue, drowning blue, danced as innocent as a child's reflecting nothing of her true self. Don't ask me how.

The young man finally shuffled out the door and climbed into his Blazer, a last smudge of Clare's lipstick clinging to his lips. Ah, youth. Ah, romance. I watched the truck pull out of the driveway as Clare said, "I am kind of worried about him with this weather and all. I do hope he makes it okay."

"Regrets already?" Jackie asked.

"Too young."

"Since when?" Jackie asked.

"Jackie! No, really. It'd be like robbing the cradle." I wrapped my arms around myself and kept my back to them so that no one would see me roll my eyes or make faces. "You know, Karen, you look like you're freezing to death."

I looked at her over my shoulder. "I've been cold all day. Jackie wanted to take me out to Pipestone."

"On a day like this? Jackie, what were you thinking about, anyway? You know Karen's delicate," Clare scolded. "We've got to look after her. Both of you come right on in the kitchen. I've made some fresh coffee, which is just what you need, Karen. It'll warm you right up, especially if we put a little something in it."

I followed and watched Clare erupt into housekeeping. Pouring two cups of coffee required an immense amount of bustling around on Clare's part. You'd have thought she was serving a twelve-course feast. Finally she sat down and opened a bottle of beer – her fourth, according to the empties lined up on the counter. I looked at the empties and thought that if it hadn't been for that damned murder, Clare might very well have gotten arrested for another DUI or drunk and disorderly after the party. She could have been in jail right now and out of our hair. Yet another reason to deplore the violence of today's society.

"So where have you been staying?" I asked.

"Oh, here, there, everywhere," Clare said.

I looked pointedly at Jackie, who was tuning in the weather channel on the TV. "Don't look at me, Karen," she said, muting it. "I have no idea where she's been. We just had an arrangement that she'd be back within a week, tops."

"You expect me to believe that?"

"It's true."

"Of course it's true," Jackie said in a nice, calm, rational tone. "I always tell the truth. I haven't officially lied to the police once."

"It's just that they've never asked you the right questions." She nodded. "Figures," I began, but Jackie hushed me, pointed to the TV, and cranked the sound up.

I don't know why she did that – it's just music to the local forecast – but we read about the possibility of four to six inches of snow, blowing winds, sub-zero windchills. Well, I could look out the window and see that.

"Not too bad," Jackie said, switching the TV off. "Gives us a damn good reason to stay put."

"How are our supplies for the duration?" I asked.

"For overnight?" Jackie laughed. "Don't worry. We've got plenty of food and we might even have enough to drink, if Clare can ration herself."

Clare reassured her on the last point. "I brought a case of beer. They had a sale at a discount liquor place up the road. And they're all long-necks."

"Great." Jackie got up and got herself some more coffee. "Clare can drink beer, Karen can drink whatever she likes, I can drink coffee, and we can all pop corn and play Monopoly."

"I think we should play Clue," I said. Jackie glared at me, Clare ignored me. "Speaking of clues," I continued, "maybe we should discuss what Sheriff Hanson said this morning."

"What's that?" Clare asked. "Who's he?" Her first mistake, I thought.

"Sheriff Hanson, Clare," Jackie said. "Tom's boss. He came out this morning and told us that it's definitely, positively not Lewis' body in the morgue."

"Told you so," Clare said, taking a hefty swallow of beer.

"It's a man named Gerald Lee. You ever heard of him?"

"Nope. But then, Lewis had a lot of friends I didn't know."

I took a deep breath to start the interrogation when the doorbell rang.

"Shit," Jackie said.

"I'll go," I said.

"No," Jackie said. "I'll go see who it is." She grabbed her cane and went into the living room. "Damn it, Tom, what now?"

And Deputy Tom's voice saying, "Is she here?"

Jackie asked, "Who?"

And Clare leaped to her feet and raced into the living room.

I followed, and almost ran into Clare's back.

She stopped at the doorway and called, "Tom!" He looked across at her, his eyes wide as saucers, and called back, "Clare!" Then they both said, simultaneously, "Where have you been?" or something like that – it was actually pretty incoherent – and hurled themselves into each other's arms.

I looked across at Jackie and said, "Just like in the movies."

"Tom," Clare breathed. "You won't tell on me, will you? You won't tell them that I'm here?" Before he could answer, she hugged herself into him again and said, "God, I've missed you. You don't know how much. I've been so worried and alone and frightened. Hold me. Just hold me. Hold me tight." I glanced at Jackie; her face was a study in sardonic amusement. "It's been terrible," Clare continued, with a perfect little catch in her voice. "You don't know how horrible."

Jackie broke in, saying, "Why don't you take off your jacket, Tom, and have a cup of coffee?" Tom didn't even hear her. His eyes were fixed on Clare's, shifting once in a while, like a tic he couldn't control, to me. "Your jacket, Tom," Jackie repeated.

"Here, I'll take it, darling," Clare breathed. Tom slipped out of his jacket and handed it to her. I figured the pants were next.

"Now," Jackie continued, "how about some coffee?"

"Oh, Jackie," Clare said, hanging the jacket on one of the pegs by the door. "The poor boy deserves a reward after wrestling with that blizzard, don't you think? He needs a beer at the very least." She slipped her hand in between his arm and his body. "Right, darling?" she asked, turning into him. With the coat gone, they could get closer than ever. "You're not on duty, are you? You can have a beer?"

Her eyes were blue flames; his whole body was hard. "You bet," he said.

"Good. Come with me."

They walked arm in arm into the kitchen. Jackie started to follow them, but I stopped her at the door, saying, "Shouldn't we give them a moment?"

"I think we'd better be chaperones."

"Why?" I asked.

"Because."

I put my hand on her arm to stop her. Jackie looked at me, surprised. Thank God the telephone rang. Jackie went to answer it and I wandered over to the bookcase and acted like I was reading the titles. Poor Deputy Tom, wrapped in the coils of Clare. That was his whole story. I stood there and thought about all the young men Clare had had in her life. Or at least the ones I knew about, and I don't claim Jackie's exhaustive knowledge of Clare's lovers. Still, it made a pretty good list, and I tried to organize them in some category other than youth. There didn't seem to be one.

Jackie hung the phone up.

"Steve?" I asked.

"No. Someone from our church, wanting to make sure I was doing okay with Steve out of town."

"That's sweet," I said.

"Yes. They're a good bunch in this town. Found a book yet?"

"Actually, I was just standing here thinking about Clare's taste in men."

"Young," Jackie said.

"Exactly. Young and innocent, like the good deputy. You know,

Laskin's about the only place Tom could be a lawman, outside of Mayberry. He wouldn't last a day in the Cities."

Jackie shook her head. "You're so gullible."

"What, he punches little old ladies on the side?"

"No, but part of the reason Tom's in law enforcement is that he likes to fight and a badge makes it legal. And as far as innocence, well, his pick-up lines are unsophisticated – or so I've heard – but they work. He and Ronny have been vying for the title of town stud for the last six years and it's been a damned close contest the whole time."

"He blushes if you look at him," I protested.

"Yeah. It really turns the women on. Nothing like corrupting a choir-boy for erotic potential. And it's even nicer when it turns out he's already corrupt and knows exactly what he's doing."

"And who's been telling you this? Clare?"

"Of course. But I've also heard it from Vi down at the Norseman's Bar." Jackie smiled at me.

"Okay, fine," I conceded. "I'm naïve about blushing deputies. So now we shall go and talk to the not-so-good Mr. Jensen and find out his story."

"Too late," Jackie said as Tom and Clare came out of the kitchen, hand in hand. Then she smiled at them and asked, "Are you staying for dinner, Tom?"

"He can't," Clare said, pouting prettily.

"I promised my brother I'd stay at his place, nights, until he gets home from Omaha," Tom said. "Sally gets nervous being by herself, and with this storm going on, she'll be having fits."

"That's nice of you," Jackie said.

"Well, somebody's got to do the chores and all," Tom said. "Listen, Vi told me about that stranger down at the bar. The one asking questions about Clare and all? I told Ronny to keep an eye out for him, give me a call. You know Ronny. This guy comes back, he won't be going any place until he's answered some questions."

"Thank you, Tom," Jackie said.

"Yeah, well, this is no time to have strangers hanging around unaccounted for." Tom picked up his hat and coat and put them on. He turned and looked into Clare's eyes. "I wish I could stay here with you, you know that, don't you?" They kissed, and for the second time that day, a young man went out with Clare's lipstick on his face and a glazed look in his eyes.

But Clare's not the sentimental type. She sat down and said, in a disgusted tone of voice, "*God*, men are adhesive."

"Yes, but they are fun," Jackie replied. She was leaning against the counter, holding a cup of coffee, and the steam rose up around her face like a witch's mist.

"I don't know," Clare said, pulling her feet up under her on the kitchen chair. "I'm about ready to give up on them."

"Take her temperature," I said to Jackie.

"No, really," Clare said. "They're always in the way. And you know, it's all a bunch of crap, all that stuff about how all men want is sex. Let me tell you, I've been looking for that guy all my life and I haven't found him yet. I mean, if all they really did want was sex, it'd be great, but they want so much more than that. They want you to love them and they want you to baby them and they want you to be their little kitten." Clare made a nauseated face. "It's disgusting. And you can't trust them at all. I mean, take Tom."

"You take him," Jackie said. "He's not my type."

"Darling, I already have," Clare reminded her, with a wicked grin. Jackie grinned back, and their eye contact stretched just a beat too long.

"What can't you trust about Tom?" I asked, breaking it up.

"Oh," Clare said, "For one thing, I don't know that I really buy that story about his brother wanting him to sleep out at his place. I think his brother's being awful trusting or he doesn't know anything about it. What do you think?"

What I thought was that wasn't what Clare had originally planned on saying.

Jackie answered, "I think Sally's eight months pregnant, and his brother is off getting him a little because Sally hasn't let him near her since she hit six months and one hundred eighty pounds."

"Oh," Clare said.

"Oh," Jackie mimicked.

"I'm more concerned about what Tom might say to Sheriff Hanson," I put in. Clare gave me an oh-please look, and Jackie laughed into her cup. "Sorry," I said. "I wondered if his profession might get the better of his passion, but that was a crazy thought."

"Especially since he'd have to admit he was there the night of the party," Jackie said. Clare, spooked, glanced at me, then back at Jackie. "Wasn't he, Clare?"

"How did you know?"

"I guessed," Jackie said. "He's been running around like a scared rabbit ever since this whole story broke, and the only thing that scares Tom is getting caught. And he wouldn't run the kind of risks he's been running for you unless his ass was on the line, too." Jackie sat down across from Clare and said, companionably, "Tell me about him."

Clare shrugged. "Well, it was after the Halloween dance."

"Told you!" Jackie crowed to me.

"I went over to his place, you know. But I wasn't really sure I was going to do anything. I just wanted to see where he lived. Check out his bathroom and stuff. You know, you can tell an awful lot about a guy from the way he keeps his bathroom."

"I'll keep that in mind," Jackie said.

"You can!" Clare insisted.

"I believe you," Jackie reassured her.

"Well, I went over and the next thing I knew I had this wild man on my hands! I mean, he was all over me. Don't get me wrong, nothing violent, just… determined. And hot. I didn't think they raised them like that out on the farm. He's got this way of rocking his hips…" Clare closed her eyes and seemed to be doing a little rocking herself on her chair. Jackie cleared her throat, and Clare brought herself back to a more decent position. "Anyway, the rest is history."

"It's the history I want to know," Jackie said. "How often has he been coming out to see you?"

"Not a lot," Clare said. "Some. Enough to have some fun."

"Uh-huh. Was he the guy in the closet?" Jackie asked.

Clare looked at both of us, then sighed. "It was the only way to shut him up. He was determined to come to the party, you know? I didn't really think it was that great an idea, if you know what I mean, but he insisted. He was…"

"Keeping an eye on you."

"Exactly. That's what I mean. They're so adhesive. There he was, looming around. Pissed off that I wasn't spending every minute with him. Freaked out by everything, you know. I mean, it was embarrassing. And we had to hide all the dope. I mean, really. So I took him off into the closet, which at least shut him up for a while. And then I sent him home."

"How?" Jackie asked.

"I told him to go," Clare said, as if it was the easiest thing in the world.

"And he just went?"

"Yes." Jackie gave Clare a level stare. Under it, Clare's eyes finally switched away and she said, "All right, I told him I'd meet him later at his motel and spend the night with him."

"But you didn't."

"No. Okay, look, I had no intention of spending the night with him. I mean, he's fun, but… you know. So I just went on about my business at the party, and later I passed out in my bedroom. And then when I woke up — " Clare shuddered. "Tonight's the first time I saw him since the party." Jackie nodded. "Listen," Clare continued, "I'm dog tired, it's been a hell of a day. I know you're going to ask me questions all night long, but for right now, could we just take a break and let me take a nap?"

Jackie looked Clare over carefully. I figured she was calculating her chances of getting another ounce of truth out of Clare if she kept on. She made her decision and said, "Sure. Why not. And you can take that shower, Karen, and finally get warmed up."

Well, when you're sent to the showers, the only polite thing to do is go.

*****

Clean, dry, dressed, and even warm. Between wind howls, I could hear kitchen noises: Jackie was cooking dinner. The only question was what her brain was cooking up.

Downstairs Clare was curled up on the couch, sound asleep, her head pillowed in her hands, her blonde hair sprayed out against the dark fabric of the sofa. Her face was young and soft and happy. She looked like Alice, dreaming of Wonderland. Nothing to worry about… I shook my head and went into the kitchen.

Jackie looked up from stirring a vat of soup. She had a glass of wine in her hand. An ashtray with a lit cigarette in it was on the counter next to her. She smiled at me over her wine glass and asked, All clean?"

"And toasty warm," I said. I wondered if I should say something about the wine, but frankly, I didn't have the heart. Or the guts.

"Good. I knew that would work. You want some wine?"

"Sure," I said, getting a glass down from the cupboard.

"It's in the fridge," she said. "Would you get me some more grape juice while you're at it?"

"Damn you," I said. She laughed, bright and clear.

"Oh, I thought about it, believe me. But I decided that I didn't want to go back to treatment, so I settled for the container, not the contained. Fooled you."

"Fuck you."

She gave me a quick hug. "I'm sorry. It's all right. Don't worry. I've been through rougher shit than this without a drink."

"So far," I said.

"True. Well, we'll deal with it as it comes. Dinner will be ready in about fifteen, twenty minutes."

"Sleeping Beauty's sound asleep on the couch," I said, refilling her glass with white grape juice and pouring myself some as well. "Should I wake her up and make her set the table?"

"We'll make her wash the dishes later," Jackie promised. "Here, have a sip of this and see what you think." She held up a spoonful of soup. My reflection, blonde in white, shimmered across her dark irises. I smiled, blew on the soup, and sipped. Beef with barley. "A little more salt?" she asked.

"No," I said. "It's perfect."

"Good." Jackie put a lid on the vat and leaned back against the counter. She hasn't worn make-up in years, and the lines around her eyes, not to mention the shadows under them, were clearly visible.

"You look tired."

Jackie sighed. "Nothing I can't stand. I don't sleep that well when Steve's out of town."

"God, you and Steve."

"Oh, we're joined at the hip. Go wake up Sleeping Beauty. Dinner's ready."

We had dinner. Clare complimented Jackie over and over again, almost enough to make me lose my appetite. Clare's always been like that around Jackie. She flatters and fawns all over her. I don't know how Jackie stands it. And it's not just words. She hangs all over her. She never misses a chance to put an arm around Jackie, or hug her, or push back a lock of her hair. Basically, any excuse to touch her. Jackie acts like she doesn't notice, but…

Were they ever lovers? I'd give anything to know.

Almost twenty years ago, I came home late one night and found Clare and Jackie in Jackie's bedroom. They weren't in bed. Nothing so obvious. Jackie was sitting in a chair in front of the bureau, her back to the mirror. Clare was standing over her, literally between her legs. They were fully clothed. Dressed up, in satins and silks, ready to go out on the town, which they did. Later. Clare's hair was piled high and golden, Jackie's dark and short and sleek. The whole room smelled of perfume and powder and women. Their faces were inches apart, but they weren't kissing. Not then, at least.

I stood, hidden behind the door, and watched as Clare put make-up on Jackie's face, slowly, carefully, lovingly, lining her eyes with soft strokes of the pencil, putting gentle sweeps of mascara on the lashes. Then she took a lipstick and painted Jackie's mouth as if ripening it into something red and full and luscious. Finally she soaked a cotton ball with perfume and touched it behind Jackie's ears, under her jaw, trailed it down her throat, down the cleavage of her breasts… And their eyes never looked away from each other's.

It was unforgettable. It was sensual. It was the most erotic moment of my life. And I wasn't even a part of it.

*****

After dinner we took our coffee in the living room. Outside the wind was up to a solid roar, but Jackie's house is old and solid as time. There were no drafts. The house was warm, we were comfortable.

"So," Jackie said. "About Tom."

"You got any good stories about him?" Clare asked. "I love hearing stories about my lovers, don't you?"

"Personally," I said, "I like my privacy."

"Of course you do," Clare said soothingly. "And nobody's going to interfere with it."

"Getting back to the party, you said that you and Tom drifted into the closet –"

"There was no other way to make him shut up and behave." Clare stated.

"And then you shooed him off into the night. Are you sure he went?"

"What are you trying to do?" Clare asked indignantly. "Get that poor boy in trouble? Tom can be a pain in the ass, but there's no way he'd take a shotgun and blow someone's head off! *He'd already left.* Long gone. And I am *not* going to have him set up for doing it, do you hear me?"

It was my turn to be soothing. "Nobody's trying to set Tom up, Clare."

"They better not be," Clare said.

"Nobody is," Jackie added. "Nobody's going to set up anybody. What about Lewis' drug connections?" Clare ignored her. "Well?"

Clare started picking at the toe of her socks.

"You keep doing that and they'll unravel," I said.

"I was never involved," Clare said, without looking at either of us.

"I didn't say you were," Jackie said. "But I thought you might know enough to have an idea of where his stash is. And where he is."

Clare shook her head. "Lewis was sweet, but he didn't trust people. I have no idea where he is."

"And it's not like he's going to come forward," I put in.

"True," Jackie said. "Especially if he's dead."

Clare and I both gasped out, "What?"

Jackie sighed and said, "It complicates things, like where's his body, and if he killed Gerald Lee, then who killed him, but it's definitely a possibility. It would explain why there's no hide nor hair of him and hasn't been since the night of the party."

"That's crazy!" Clare said. "You're talking about two murders!"

"Well, it's been known to happen," Jackie said. "He might have killed himself. He might have run after someone else came in, killed Gerald, and then that someone went after him and killed him –"

"You think some stranger would walk in and kill Gerry for no reason?"

"I wasn't really thinking about a complete stranger."

"And if that happened, then why am I still alive? Some kind of homicidal maniac comes in my house! I'd be dead, too."

"Exactly. That's the six million dollar question no matter which way you slice it," Jackie said. "If Lewis killed Gerald because he thought he was your lover and he was jealous, why didn't he kill you, too?" Clare shrugged nervously. "And if he wasn't mad enough to kill you, how could he be mad enough to kill someone over you? And if he did make a mistake and repented of it, why didn't he take you with him?"

"Oh, for crying out loud, Jackie!" Clare almost screeched. "We weren't even sleeping together, I told you that!"

"Then why would he be so jealous that he killed a man over you?"

"Because he's a man!" Clare was screeching. "Men are nuts! Oh, for Christ's sake, Jackie, what are you trying to do? Convict me? I'm innocent, I swear I am. *I didn't do it!*"

"I know that," Jackie said, and at her tone, Clare gulped back anything else, and I wasn't about to jump in.

So we sat, listening to the mantel clock tick.

Finally Clare said, "He must have gotten up to go to the bathroom, and Lewis was maybe having a cigarette or something in the living room and saw him and thought he was the other guy and blew him away. Right?"

"Maybe," Jackie said.

"Maybe!"

Jackie didn't answer.

"What are you thinking?" I finally asked.

"Mostly that it doesn't make any sense. Frankly, I don't buy it." Clare opened her mouth, but Jackie waved her down. "The whole thing is simply that we've got to find Lewis. I suggest you get on it."

"*Me*?" Clare asked.

"Yes, you. You need to figure out where Lewis might be so that somebody can find him. Like the police."

Clare stared at Jackie, glanced at me, then at the wall. She took a deep breath and said, "I can't do that."

"Why not?" Jackie asked.

"Because. How in the hell am I supposed to know where he is?"

"Oh, for crying out loud, Clare!" Jackie snapped. "You've been living with the guy for three years, you should have some idea of who his friends are, where he hangs out, where he might go."

"Well, yes, but –"

"Listen to me," Jackie said urgently, leaning forward. "You need to figure out where he is before he finds you."

"What do you mean?"

"I mean that if Lewis is the killer, and it does look like it, you are the prosecution's chief witness. He might not like that. He might want to prevent it. He might want to take you away with him. Or just take you out."

Clare's eyes were wide. "No, that's not –"

"Isn't it? Listen, murderers do not like getting caught. They usually do what they can to prevent it. They run, they hide, they lie, but they also turn like a snarling cat when they're in danger. And when someone's killed one person, a lot of times they don't mind killing again if it can save their ass. They don't see it as wrong any more. They see it as necessary. Right, Karen?"

I jumped away from the vision Jackie had conjured up of a trapped, desperate murderer. I took a deep breath and said, "It's been known to happen," as the wind slammed into the house and all the lights went out.

*****

The darkness hit so suddenly and completely that Clare jumped – on me. Jackie cursed fluently, and I could see the tip of her cigarette glowing a hot trail as she moved around the room. Clare and I both let out a sigh of relief – and she let go of me – as Jackie lit one candle, then three or four more and placed them around the room. It wasn't nearly enough light (although in other circumstances I suppose it would have been romantic), but it beat the hell out of total darkness.

"Damn blizzard knocked out the power lines," Jackie said.

"What about heat?" Clare asked.

"Oil-burner," Jackie said. "And the stove's gas, so we'll be able to cook. If the power's still out in the morning, we'll put the refrigerated stuff outside. We're fine."

"I wish I'd brought more than a case of beer," Clare said. Then she slapped the arm of the couch and said, "Damn it!"

"What?" Jackie asked.

"I never got a bath," Clare said. "Now what am I going to do?"

"Well," Jackie said comfortingly, "if you hurry up and take one now, there'll still be plenty of hot water. You can bathe by candlelight." She dug out more candles from the cabinet – there must have been dozens in there – and put them in small iron candleholders. "There you go. Go loll. But you know, when you get out, we're going to talk some more about this." Clare didn't say anything. "I mean it, Clare."

"Oh, all right," Clare agreed. "How romantic!" she cried out as she lit one of the candles. The light lit her like an idol. "Now all I need is a bottle of champagne and Javier Bardem."

"I thought you were giving up on men," I couldn't resist saying.

"Movie stars don't count," Clare said firmly, and marched out. We could hear her singing "Sixty Minute Man" as she went down the hallway.

"She's incorrigible," Jackie said.

"That's putting it mildly," I replied. "Do you think Lewis really is dead?"

"It's just a working theory."

"Got any more?"

"Well. Like I said, it keeps worrying me, why Lewis didn't go after Clare, too. It just doesn't make sense."

"Jackie, you're making the mistake of looking for rational behavior out of human beings, and that's nuts. People do the damnedest things for the damnedest reasons, even when they know it's the stupidest thing they can do. And God knows, that's Clare."

"Are you two ever going to get along?"

"In our next life we'll be close personal acquaintances."

"I can hardly wait."

"But to get back to the subject of murder," I continued. "Okay, sometimes murder is a rational act. It can make sense, no matter what anyone tells you. Maybe for money, for freedom, for –"

"Killing the guy who's attacking your kids. Killing the guy who's beating you up. Killing Aunt Linda because she's 95 and you'll inherit a million –"

"Exactly. But what we're talking about here is an unpremeditated murder, and those usually make no sense at all. What's sensible about some guy offing another guy in a barroom brawl? Nothing. Or somebody shooting someone dead over a pair of Nikes? Or walking into a school yard with an Uzi? Murder isn't a game or a logic puzzle, where everything has a reason and one thing has to follow another. An unpremeditated murder usually has a motive. The trouble is, the motive is emotional, not rational, and when it explodes, everything gets messy and unpredictable and totally irrational. And you can't build back logically from the end to the beginning. It just doesn't work that way." I set my coffee cup down with a firm little clunk. "Thus speaketh the attorney for the defense."

"You're probably right," Jackie said. "But still and all –"

"Listen," I interrupted, "here's something that might explain the whole thing. What if Clare was the intended victim?"

"Clare?"

"Think about it. Listen, here's the scene. She says she and Lewis had been having a bad time of it lately. Fine. But, you know, much as I hate to admit it, Vi was right. Most guys don't let loose of Clare easily, God knows why. And I can't believe Lewis was much different. He was probably hoping things would work out, or at the very least he could figure out something that would make her stick around. Meanwhile, there's the party. And he's hoping things will work out. But he sees her and Deputy Tom, and he knows it's hopeless. I mean, he probably knew it before, but, say, when she went in the closet with Tom, that did it. The last straw. And for all we know, there was a showdown, between Clare and Lewis, and she said something unforgivable to him. She's been known to do that. And he loses it. He storms out of the house, trying to think things out, *before* Tom leaves the party. And then he comes back. Everything's quiet. The party's over, everyone's gone. Clare's lying alone in bed, but he doesn't know that. In fact, he's sure – I mean, he knows what Clare's like, so he's sure there's someone with her. He's in the living room, quiet, but crazy, okay? And there's the shotgun right there. He picks it up. Maybe he was going to go into the bedroom and blow her away right there. Maybe he was going to blow his own brains out. Either way, out of the shadows she comes, padding her way to the bathroom. Or so he thinks. He's crazy, remember, absolutely burning with it. And he lifts the shotgun and fires without thinking. Without even looking to see who it really is. He doesn't expect it to be Gerald, you understand? He's been obsessing on Clare so hard, so much, that he *knows* it's Clare. And then, too late, he sees that it's not Clare, maybe even while his finger's squeezing the trigger. But it's too late, and he's killed the wrong person."

"Gerald Lee."

"Exactly." I took a deep breath and went on. "So what does he do? He panics and runs out of the apartment, probably with the shotgun still in his hand. It all happens in a flash. All over in a minute. Clare comes running in, and there's the body, dead on the floor. *She* panics and leaves. Now, I don't know what happened to Lewis afterwards. But that's the way I figure it. What do you think?"

"It's brilliant." Clare's voice made me jump. She was standing in the hallway door, barefoot, wrapped in an old peach satin bathrobe. "That must have been just how it happened," she said, walking past us, and falling into the arm chair.

"Did – did you hear the whole scenario I pitched?" I asked.

"Oh, yes," Clare said, bunching herself up in the arm chair.

"So, what do you think?" Jackie asked.

"I think it sucks to think that someone could be so mad at me they'd want to kill me. But I guess it could happen. It's strange," she mused. "I've never thought of anyone… I mean, I've dumped a lot of people in my life, and a few have dumped me. Don't you dare ever tell anybody that. But I've never taken it seriously. I mean, that whole 'if I can't have you, nobody can'. What a bunch of crap. It doesn't make sense. I mean, there's always somebody else, isn't there?"

"So far," I muttered.

"I mean, you just cut your losses and move on," Clare continued. "That's the way I've always seen it. No lover is worth that kind of craziness. You can always get someone else to sleep with. For God's sake, even Frankenstein got married. But I guess not everyone thinks that way."

"No, they don't," I said.

"No," Clare said wistfully. "And it's a damned shame."

"True," Jackie said. "Back in a minute." And she stumped off to the bathroom.

Clare promptly reached under the couch and pulled out a pint bottle of bourbon. She had the cap off and a healthy dose in her in no time. I'm sure she needed it.

"Want to share?" I asked. Clare nodded and handed me the bottle. I poured some into my cup.

"Got a cigarette?" Clare asked.

"I quit, remember?"

"I know," she said. "I was just joking." She took the bottle back and took another sip. I swallowed a mouth full of bourbon mixed with cold coffee. Not bad. "How are you doing?"

"Oh, great," I replied. "How about you?"

"Tired."

I got up and looked out the window, just as if I wasn't bored to death by the scenery.

Behind me Clare's voice, choking, said, "I wish Jackie knew everything."

"No, you don't." Then I turned around and said, as gently as I could, "And I wouldn't advise telling her. You'd just hurt her. There are some things even Jackie might not be able to handle."

Clare looked at me for a moment, then looked away. "Could be."

Jackie walked back in a couple of minutes later. Clare had put the bottle back under the couch as soon as she'd heard Jackie's cane on the hardwood floor of the hallway. I crossed my fingers and hoped she wouldn't smell the liquor on our breaths.

"Well," she said, sitting down and pulling out a deck of cards. "Who wants to play gin?"

We played until ten-thirty when Jackie, who as I've already said is no night-owl, decided it was bedtime and started wrestling with the problem of who was going to sleep where. Since there was only one guest room, someone would have to sleep on the couch. Surprisingly, Clare volunteered for it. Usually Clare does her best to wheedle her way into the most comfortable of anything available. But ours is not to reason why, so Jackie got out a pile of bedding for her. Then Jackie and I went to our respective rooms.

"Hey, Jackie, tell me something," I said, wandering into Jackie's room. "Would you happen to have a gun of any kind in this place?"

"Why? Who do you want to shoot?" Jackie asked, taking off her outer sweater and throwing it on the bureau.

"No one in particular," I said reassuringly. "I was thinking more in terms of our collective self-protection."

"Like I said, who do you want to shoot?" She yawned and stretched like a cat.

"Well, actually, I was thinking about Lewis." Jackie raised her eyebrows at me. "Like you said, he might show up here looking for Clare."

"Yeah, well, it's a possibility." Jackie sat down on the bed and started stripping off her socks. "Although with the blizzard outside, he'd have a hard time getting to us. We don't even know where he is. He might be under a bar stool in Fargo."

"Yes, but the blizzard's going to end sometime. And when it does, Lewis might be the first person at the door."

"I thought you didn't really take that idea seriously."

"Well, not at the time. But anything's possible." Jackie made a face. "So… we should perhaps have a plan in hand if he were to appear."

"If he does, I'm sure we're not supposed to just shoot him, tempting as it sounds," Jackie said regretfully. "Of course, if he actually broke in, it would be self-defense, wouldn't it?"

"It's always wise to plan your defense strategy ahead of time with your lawyer."

"And if we did happen to shoot him on the front porch," Jackie mused, "we could always drag him into the living room. Or maybe we could arrange for him to fall inside."

"You have such a grasp of the legal technicalities," I congratulated her. "So, do you have a gun?"

"There's a shotgun over there in the corner." She waved towards the window.

I walked over and picked it up. "It'd be a hell of an irony to shoot Lewis with a shotgun, wouldn't it?"

"It would rank," she agreed.

"Can you shoot this thing?" I asked.

"Are you kidding?" Jackie snorted. "That's Steve's. If I tried to use it, I'd end up on the floor with a hole in the ceiling, a broken shoulder, and an enraged homicidal maniac on top of me. You want it, it's yours. But don't shoot every time you hear a weird noise, because it'll probably be me going to the bathroom in the middle of the night, and I'd hate a repeat of mistaken identities."

"Agreed," I said, and picked up the shotgun and left.

*****

In my bedroom I propped the shotgun carefully against the wall by the dresser before getting into bed. I thought I'd lie awake but I must have been exhausted, because a tremendous crash shook me awake. I jumped out of bed and came lurching out of my room at the same time that Jackie came lurching out of hers. We probably looked about the same, disheveled, sleep-drunk, startled, panicked. The only difference was that Jackie had her cane and a flashlight, while I had a shotgun. We looked at each other and then down the hallway. Jackie's mouth tightened, and we went down into the living room.

The flashlight honed in on the source of the crash at once: Clare and Deputy Tom, entangled together on the floor, next to the coffee table they doubtless had overturned when they fell off the couch in their excess of abandon. Or perhaps they'd been on the table. That looked very uncomfortable, but who am I to judge? They also looked panicked. Buck naked, and their eyes were wide open and blinded by the flashlight. It reminded me of when I was a young girl and I'd go with my cousins to shoot rats down at the dump, and I started laughing. I couldn't help it.

Meanwhile, Clare was screaming at the top of her lungs, "No! Please, God, no, don't shoot! Karen, for God's sake, don't shoot!"

Jackie played the flashlight around the room, but there were only the four of us. Clare, still screaming, scuttled away from Tom like a crab. "Calm down, Clare," Jackie ordered. "Karen, put that damn thing down. You're scaring her to death."

I shook my head and set the shotgun against the bookcase. Clare quit screaming and concentrated on breathing. Tom was trying to find his pants without exposing himself, and wasn't doing too badly.

"Would you please light some candles, Karen?" she asked me politely.

"Certainly," I replied in a similar tone.

In the candlelight, everything looked less sordid but more chaotic.

"What a mess," Jackie said in her best Bette Davis voice as she surveyed the battle scene.

Clare had managed to regain her wind enough to gasp, "Jackie, I can explain."

"Yeah. Later. First get some clothes on and get this mess cleaned up." There was a side table still standing, with the pint of bourbon on it. Jackie honed in on it, picked it up, and stumped into the kitchen, thumping her cane down hard for emphasis with every step. I assumed she wasn't talking to me, so I followed her, taking the shotgun with me. She automatically flicked the light switch and the lights came on.

"Alleluia," she said. She set the bottle down on the kitchen table and got a glass out of the cupboard. She reached for the bottle, but then shook herself and filled the glass with water. Clare walked in, a Fellini-esque image of sex. Her robe was barely on, her hair was a wild tangle, and her mouth was swollen with use.

"Jackie," she said, "it's not what you think."

"Really?" Jackie sighed and dug a pack of cigarettes out from a drawer. "What the hell am I thinking?"

"I don't know," Clare said. My ears pricked up at the thin line of desperation that was crackling through her voice. "I don't know, but it's wrong."

"Then what's right?" Jackie was trying to light a cigarette, but the matches weren't cooperating. Some of it was that her hands were trembling. Finally she got the cigarette lit. "Look, just quit playing games and spit it out, okay?"

"I'm not playing games, Jackie. I swear it."

"Cut the crap!" Jackie slammed her hand down on the kitchen table. "You have been bullshitting me from the beginning, and I've had enough of it! I think I've finally figured out what's going on –"

"No!" Clare protested. From the nest of her tangled hair, her face and voice were like that of a wounded bird. "It's not like that at all. Tom was just worried about us, worried about me –"

"The whole world's worried about you, aren't they?" Jackie leaned back and closed her eyes. "You set this up before he left earlier."

"No, he came over all on his own." Clare's voice was shaking. "He wanted to see me."

"Yeah. Because he can't live without you, even for a night. Or is it because you're buying him off so we won't know about –"

Clare turned and fled from the room. "I think she was crying," I said in a neutral voice.

"See if I care," Jackie snarled. She picked up the pint, looked at it, and set it back down. "I'm not going to end up in treatment because of her," she said, in a voice like barbed wire. "I'll do a lot, but not that!"

She went back into the living room. I followed, a little slower. Clare was huddled against Tom, who was trying to put on his jacket while being an unsteady rock for her to lean upon.

"Clare," Jackie said.

"Fuck off," Tom snarled. I stepped quickly over to the bookcase. Tom's voice no longer sounded shy and quiet, it sounded mean and drunk, and when I took a good look at him, I realized that that was exactly what he was. "Leave her the fuck alone. We were just fucking on your couch. What's the big fucking deal?" The man had an awesome vocabulary. "So we smashed up your coffee table, I'll buy you a fucking new one."

"I don't give a shit about the coffee table," Jackie said. "I want to know what you're doing here."

"What do you think I was doing? Until you interrupted us."

"*Tom*," Clare said urgently, raising her head from his shoulder. "Listen to me."

"No, you listen to me," he said, looking into her eyes. "Why do you let her order you around like that, huh? Her and that lesbian bitch in the corner? Have you told Jackie all about her? All about her and –"

"Shut up, please!" Clare wailed.

"Let him, Clare," Jackie said. "At least he's talking."

"What do you want to know?" he asked, cockily.

"I want to know who you are," Jackie said, as I sucked my breath in behind her. "Friend? Lover? Concerned citizen? A sworn officer of the law who might have committed murder?"

"Jackie," I hissed.

"You are fucking nuts," Tom said. "You think I killed the son of a bitch?"

"Somebody did."

"Yeah, they did. And you know who they killed?"

"Lewis Ford," Jackie said. I gasped.

"That's right, lady. You're not as stupid as she thinks you are." Clare was wriggling to get loose from Tom's arms, but so far wasn't having any luck. "Yeah, Lewis, her sugar-daddy, her big-time drug-dealing sugar-daddy was nothing but a faggot with AIDS. He'd had it over a year. He was so fucking scared that people'd find out he went to the doctor under another name. Gerald Lee. Real creative, huh?" Clare kicked him, hard, and he yelped as he reached for his shin. She broke free, but he reached out and grabbed her by her hair, so that she squealed with pain. "Quit that shit!"

"Let her go, you son of a bitch." Everyone stopped, mouths open, wide-eyed, and looked at me as I stood there, holding the shotgun. "You heard me," I said. "Let her go. Now."

Tom's eyes blinked once. "Okay," he said. "Fine. No problem. See?" He let go of Clare's hair.

"Good," I said. "Clare, get over here." Clare scurried over to our side of the room, next to Jackie.

Then I shot him.

It was loud, it was dirty, there was blood everywhere. The kick sent me back against the wall, which gave Jackie a chance to grab the shotgun. The barrel must have been hot, but she hung on to it, as if I was going to give her a fight. I wasn't. Clare was screaming, but I couldn't hear her. I was deaf from the blast. I didn't care. I kept my eyes on Tom. I was already telling myself to swear that I'd aimed for his feet, but the kick had knocked the gun up, and the shot hit him in the chest. I could suggest that maybe Jackie had grabbed the gun as I was shooting, changing the trajectory. Because the truth was… Oh, I didn't know what the fucking truth was anymore. I just kept my eyes on him. I don't know how long it took him to die. Probably only a few seconds, but it seemed like the blood pumped for a long time. When it stopped, when

I knew he was dead, I turned my head and looked around.

"I need a drink," I said.

"In the kitchen," Jackie said.

I walked by her. She didn't stop me, didn't touch me, didn't look at me.

"Karen –" Clare said. I walked by her, too. "What are we going to do about Tom?"

I kept walking. In the kitchen, I got a glass from the cupboard. I was shaking so badly I had to use both hands to pick it up and carry it over to the table. I had to use both hands to pour the bourbon into it. I had to use both hands to get the glass to my mouth and not spill it. Clare came in.

"Got a cigarette?" I asked.

"Jackie's calling the cops," Clare said.

"Of course she is," I said. I took another swallow, and it came right back up. I barely made it to the sink. When I finished retching, Clare ran the water. When the water was warm, she got a dish towel and soaked it and started to clean my face. I gave her a hard, cold look. She handed me the towel and backed off. I wiped myself off and sat back down. I was exhausted. "She called the police?" I finally asked.

Clare nodded. "Karen, we've got to do something."

"You don't have to do anything," I said. "I already shot him." I closed my eyes. "He's dead."

"You're not going to stop her?" I shook my head. "What are you going to say?"

"That I shot him," I said. "What else is there to say?" I opened my eyes and looked at my hands. They weren't shaking nearly as badly. "After all, two witnesses saw me do it."

"We could claim he was an intruder," Clare said. "He was threatening us all. We could hide the body. We're out in the middle of nowhere. We could get him out of here. We could clean the place up —"

"Oh my God! Clean the place up. What a mess. Jackie will never forgive me."

"Karen! This is serious!"

I looked at her again. "It's been serious for a long time, Clare. Ever since the first time we made love. Why didn't you tell me Lewis had AIDS?"

"He didn't want anyone to know."

"So of course you kept it a secret. God knows you're good at keeping secrets. I'd never have believed how good." I tried another sip of bourbon. It seemed like this time it was going to stay down.

"We were never lovers," Clare said.

"Yes, we were."

"I mean me and Lewis," she said. "You never believed it, but we weren't. He was gay. He didn't want anybody to know that, either. It wasn't good for his image. I was just a front."

"Gorgeous sexy blonde. Live-in girlfriend. Makes him look like a major stud. Which, of course, a drug dealer should be." I tried another sip.

"Karen, we've got to get out of here," Clare whispered.

"What do you mean, 'we'?"

"Like I said, Jackie's called the cops. If you stick around, you'll go to jail. To prison."

I waved my hand. "Maybe, maybe not." I managed a grim chuckle. "I know a lot of good lawyers."

"Karen – we can take Jackie's car, drive it to Fargo, ditch it there and get another one." She sounded serious. "I've got cash. A lot of cash on me –."

"What did you do, grab Lewis' stash on the way out?" Clare nodded, not blushing a bit. That's my girl.

"We don't have to worry about money. But we've got to get out of here."

"Let me get this straight," I said, sitting up. "You wouldn't come live with me, but now you'll go on the run with me? What kind of logic is that?"

"You wouldn't make it without me," Clare said. "You wouldn't know how to live on the run." She was probably right.

"You are nuts," I said. "I tried to kill you."

"I know," Clare said, soothingly. "But that was just because you were jealous."

I reached out and took Clare's face in my hands, burrowing my fingers deep in her hair. Blonde silk. She smelled like flowers. Her skin… I kissed her, and she gave it all back. It all made so much sense. Run away. With her. Us. Together. Oh, yes. It made perfect sense. Well, no, it didn't, but… Look, nothing made sense. But it sounded good. On the lam with Clare. Why not? We'd have a hell of a time for a little while at least. Maybe a long time. And Jackie —

That's what stopped me. I came up for air and asked, "What about Jackie?"

"Jackie'll cover for us," Clare said, close to me, almost whispering.

"No, she won't. We'd have to steal her car, for God's sake –"

"No, we wouldn't. She'd give us the car."

"No, we'd have to steal it. Listen to me, Clare. If we go off together, now, we'll lose Jackie forever."

"You mean you'll lose her." Clare pulled away. "That's what you're scared of. You've always wanted *me* to lose her. You've always hoped that I'd finally be out of the picture so you can have her all to yourself."

"Don't be ridiculous. She's married. To Steve," I said.

"So what? He doesn't count. Not to you. It's always been Jackie. That's what it's all about. Isn't it? Even when you made love to me. That's why you did it. You couldn't have Jackie, so you figured I'd be the next best thing." I couldn't believe it. She was crying. As if I mattered to her. As if I'd broken her heart.

"No, that's not true," I said, turning her face towards me. "I wanted you… But I'm not leaving Jackie with a corpse in her living room. And I'm not leaving because I'm guilty." I almost laughed. "I've killed two men in less than two weeks. I'm crazy, but I'm not a criminal. I never have been. I'm on the other side of the law of you and your friends and your lovers and all the rest of it. I always have been." I leaned into my hands. "I should have been a prosecutor, I really should. Defending criminals, it's just playing games… and I'm tired of that. I should have joined the prosecutor's office when I had the chance. Maybe then I wouldn't have… I don't know." I reached out and pulled her back to me. "I've damn near ruined my life over you. But not completely. Yet. But if I go off with you, I will. I don't want to be the person I'd have to become to survive the way you're talking about surviving. I don't want to be the person I am right now, even talking about it. So, when the cops come, I'm going with them." Clare looked at me, her eyes blurred. Or was it my eyes that were blurred? I kissed her, lightly, and said, "But you can bail me out if you want to. You said you had a lot of cash."

*****

It took half an hour for the police to arrive, and in all that time, Jackie never came into the kitchen. No, she didn't stay in the living room with Tom's drying body lying on the floor. She went to her bedroom, where she sat and smoked and waited.

*****

"Why didn't you come in and keep an eye on me?" I asked her, much later, over a telephone from behind a thick glass window.

"Oh, a bunch of reasons," she said. "One, I'd had about enough of both of you and I didn't want to say anything I'd regret later on. Two, I didn't want to drink, and I knew the bottle was in there. Three, I thought you and Clare probably needed a little time together to get your stories straight —"

"Like you'd let us get away with one."

"Okay, you two needed a little time together. Period."

"I might have killed her."

Jackie shook her head. "I had the shotgun with me."

"There are such things as knives."

"Not your style."

"She was trying to talk me into running away," I told her.

Jackie nodded. "I figured she would," she said. "In a way, I was hoping you would. Not that it would have solved anything."

"Where is Miss Harrison, anyway?"

"She called me from Houston," Jackie said. "I think she's going to move there. But she'll be back for the trial."

"Don't count on it."

Jackie shrugged. "Not my problem. Not yours, either."

"No, it's the prosecutor's."

And she's right. After all, without Clare, there's no motive for me to kill Lewis Ford, and even with her, there's no proof. And I haven't confessed to it. I think that one will be dropped. Just another unsolved drug-related homicide. As for Tom. Well, I've sworn it was self-defense, that he was drunk, belligerent, assaulting Clare. I think a plea bargain is in order, for manslaughter, but that's my lawyers' problem. I hired the best, and they're doing the best they can.

But you can see it in their eyes. One of their own, gone off the rails, killed one, maybe two men and for what? Well, they've never held Clare in their arms, looked in those sea-blue eyes, drowned in her scent.

No, I know, that's not a good enough reason. But it was all passion, and no reason. That's the point. And that's why you're never going to get rid of crime or violence or murder, not until the end of passion, not until the end of time.

Meanwhile, I've been making plans. Because when I get out, and I will, I'm going to have to make a new life for myself. And I've learned from this, I really have. I can't ever be a lawyer again, I'll be disbarred. So I'm going to go into counseling. I mean, I know how crazy it can get, right? I think I'll be perfect for the job. And I can probably stay up here, in the High Plains. Where I know I'll never see Clare again. But at least I'll be close to Jackie.

All that Glitters

Michael Wiley

Sam Kelson stood in Henry Dvorak's bedroom. The house was dark, silent except for the *tick, tick* of a dripping bathroom sink. Downstairs in the kitchen, Dvorak lay dead on the tile floor, his feet stretched under the open dishwasher door.

Kelson swept the beam of his phone flashlight over the bed. "A bunch of phonies," he said.

He held the flashlight beam on Dvorak's dresser. A wooden box the size of a pack of cigarettes lay on top.

Kelson checked the box. It was empty.

Then lights throughout the house flashed on. Blinded by the brilliance, he yelled. Then he was quiet until a new sound in the bathroom made him yell again.

*****

A week earlier, Dvorak had sat in Kelson's office on the north side of Chicago, the warm October sun shining through a window. Dvorak wore black leather motorcycle pants and a white T-shirt. His leather jacket, which matched his pants, was draped over the arm of the office chair. The bald middle of his head cut through his hairy fringes like a river.

"Mississippi," Kelson said.

"I'm sorry?"

Kelson shuddered. Since getting grazed by a bullet above his left eyebrow two years earlier, he'd suffered from disinhibition and would speak every thought that crossed his mind. But sometimes a shudder or a slap to the face kept him on track. "Tell me about the theft."

"The ruby was my mom's," Dvorak said. "The last thing I had of her. Sooner or later, you look around and all you have is the ghost of a person."

"What happened to her other stuff?"

"Half went to my sister," Dvorak said. "I Craigslisted the rest."

"Why keep the ruby?"

"My mom's grandpa worked at the Field Museum. He was a janitor, like a hundred years ago. He took it from an Ancient Mesopotamia exhibit."

"He stole it?"

"He claimed it fell out of a crown worn by Gilgamesh of Uruk. It was lying in the display case, and nobody else wanted it. That's what Mom said."

"That's just stupid," Kelson said.

"I know. I felt guilty. Last summer, I took the ruby to the museum. It belonged there, right? But the authentication guy laughed at me. It wasn't from a Mesopotamian crown. The story was a lie—my great-grandpa's, or my mom's. Still, sometimes a lie is all you have."

"Your sister didn't want it?"

"She got a painting of my dad. We've been through a rough couple of years, but I try to think about the good times."

"My philosophy." Kelson knew about making the best. Because of his disinhibition, clients often canceled contracts midway through an investigation. A couple of them had sued. He glanced at Dvorak's bald river, then his leather pants. "What do you do?"

"I work for the city as a compensation officer."

"By overcompensating?"

"I'm sorry?"

"It's all right. Me too. This ruby—is it big?"

"Like a ladybug. That's what Mom called it. The Ladybug."

"How much is it worth?"

"Well, it isn't real, is it?"

"I don't know..."

"Glass," Dvorak said. "Red as a maraschino cherry. It reminds me of Mom. Some things are worth more than money."

"You couldn't have misplaced it?"

Dvorak shook his head. "I kept it in a box in my underwear drawer."

"Do you have kids? Sometimes they get into things."

"No kids. Divorced."

"How do you get along with your ex and your sister?"

"My ex says she's moved on, and my sister and I aren't talking right now."

"Do they have keys to your house?"

"Sure, but the thief kicked in the front door."

"Who else knows about the ruby?"

"When I thought it was real, I would show it off to my neighbors after a couple beers."

"Would any of them break down your door?"

"Not Mrs. Alimov," Dvorak said. "She's honest as they come. Maybe Bill Mackay. Before my divorce, I caught him watching my house with binoculars—waiting for me to go out."

"Did he and your wife have a thing?"

"So did Steve Conti. He drives a Trans Am up and down the street day and night. Some guys never heard of mufflers."

"He gave your ex a ride?"

"She likes speed. I showed him and Mackay the ruby. I was trying to save my marriage and wanted them to see I had an edge."

Kelson pushed a pen and a pad of paper across the desk. "Give me their addresses. Your wife's and sister's too."

Dvorak wrote them down.

"Did the museum say where the ruby came from?" Kelson asked.

Dvorak looked up. "The authentication expert thought it might be costume jewelry."

"Uh-huh," Kelson said. "Now scribble out a check for me."

*****

When Dvorak left, Kelson Googled *Mesopotamian artifacts*. He saw few gemstones and no crowns, but he gazed for a while at something called the Warka Vase—alabaster, slender, curving gracefully inward. Like Dvorak's fake ruby, the vase had been stolen, but from the National Museum of Iraq, not an underwear drawer.

"The hell am I doing?" Kelson said, and closed the site.

*****

That evening, across the street from Dvorak's west-suburban two-story, Kelson rang Bill Mackay's doorbell. Autumn dark was settling hard over the neighborhood.

The front porch light flipped on, and the door opened.

"Mr. Mackay?" Kelson said.

"Uh-huh. Who are you?" The man looked about six feet tall, his thick chest sagging toward his belly. He wore jeans and a checkered flannel shirt.

Kelson showed him his ID, pointed a thumb over his shoulder at Dvorak's house, and said, "He hired me to recover his stolen property."

"That little red spitball?"

"Do you have it?" Kelson asked.

"*I* called in the burglary. I was coming home and saw his door knocked off its hinges. We watch out for each other in this neighborhood, keep an eye on each other's property."

"He says you spied on him and his ex-wife with binoculars."

"Prairie chicken," Mackay said.

"Huh?"

"Prairie chicken. I saw one on his roof." He put his hands on his hips, challenging Kelson. "I'm a birder."

"Mr. Dvorak says you had a fling with his ex."

"Cynthia?" He curled his lips as if he would rather kiss a prairie chicken. "Dvorak lives in a fantasy. Before she left, he accused half the guys in the neighborhood of fooling around with her."

"Steve Conti?"

"Well, maybe Steve Conti did. She rode around with him in his Trans Am. Scared the wrens and nuthatches."

*****

Ten minutes later and two houses down, Kelson stood on Conti's driveway.

Outside an open garage door, Conti was tinkering under the hood of his Trans Am. "Yeah?" He was small and wiry and wore a Chicago Bears hoodie.

"They say you try too hard," Kelson said. "Street racing against figments of your imagination—too much engine and too much gas."

Conti picked up a wrench. "What are you talking about?"

Kelson flashed his ID again. "What do you know about a ruby Henry Dvorak keeps in his dresser drawer?"

"That's no ruby? It's a piece of broken taillight."

"Did you steal it?"

"He's a whack job. I'd never touch anything of his."

"Not even his wife?"

Conti warmed. "That woman appreciates speed. But her marriage was already over."

"You gave her a ride?"

"Yeah, she sure likes to go fast."

"Any idea who might steal the fake ruby?"

"You might talk to Dvorak's girlfriend." Conti pointed at the house next door. "Jenni Alimov."

"The honest Mrs. Alimov?"

"He's there every night. The sounds from her bedroom window—someone should cite them for noise."

*****

When Kelson crossed the lawn and rang the bell, Jennie Alimov answered in a yellow sleeveless T-shirt, orange short shorts, and bright white cross-trainers.

"Candy corn," Kelson said.

"I'm sorry?" She'd been exercising, and her T-shirt collar was damp with sweat. So was her neck, which was slender, graceful, and as almondy white as alabaster.

"Warka," Kelson said.

"Excuse me?" She gave him a wide-mouthed frown.

"Great teeth," he said.

"Who are you, and what do you want?" she said.

Kelson showed his ID, saying, "From what Mr. Dvorak told me, I didn't expect *you*."

"Henry?" Her face softened. "What did he say?"

"He says you're honest."

"Henry and I have consoled each other," she said. "My husband divorced me, too. He's a dentist, and I'm a hygienist. He left me for a lab technician."

"I see." He stared at her neck. "I brush every day."

"Good for you."

"Twice. Three times if necessary. Clean as a whistle."

"Why are you here?" she asked.

"I'm looking into the theft of Henry's ruby."

She smiled. "He lives in a fantasy, doesn't he?"

"I'm getting that impression."

"That's why his wife left. He pretended their life was magic."

"You don't mind him, though?"

"We can all benefit from a little magic," she said.

"Did he ever show you the ruby?"

"It fooled me too. That glass must've come from an old church window."

"A beautiful lie?" Kelson said.

"A glittering one."

*****

The next morning, Kelson called the Field Museum and talked to an assistant curator named Suzanne Polanski. No, she said, she'd never heard of Henry Dvorak or his supposed ladybug ruby.

"Scarabs," she said.

"I'm sorry?" Kelson said.

"Scarabs. Dung beetles. The Mesopotamians worshipped them—other bugs too."

"Oh," Kelson said.

"Anyway, the Gilgamesh crown is missing two stones, not one."

"I was starting to wonder if the crown was real."

"Sure. It's ancient, though its connection to Gilgamesh is dubious. We think it was missing the gems when it came into our collection at the end of the nineteenth century. The early records are incomplete. There are other gems in it—a pair of diamonds, a pair of sapphires, and a pair of emeralds—but it's unlikely that the missing ones were rubies."

"Why's that?"

"Except in an amulet called the Ruby Eye, they don't appear in Mesopotamian regalia," she said. "If the crown originally had them, they would be nearly unique."

"Can I see it?"

"It's not on display right now. You would need to talk to our authentication expert, Richard Smethurst."

*****

At noon, Kelson rode an elevator into a subbasement at the museum.

In a narrow room, three men in white cotton gloves worked at a long table littered with pottery shards, metal scraps, and various cleansing agents and epoxies. Along one wall, there were six desks. Along another, a bank of file cabinets.

Tall and thin, Richard Smethurst was in his mid-fifties. Standing at the long table, he brushed dust from a hook-shaped chunk of metal big enough to land a tiger shark.

"Mr. Smethurst?" Kelson said.

The man set down the hook and twitched a smile. "*Doctor* Smethurst," he said.

"Ah, it's like that," Kelson said.

Smethurst's face creased. "Like what?"

Kelson tapped his forehead where the bullet had knocked out his ability to filter himself. "I see a doctor regularly. Her name is Dr. Prentiss. She has me call her Sheila. Real casual."

The crease became a scowl. "Suzanne Polanski said you were coming. But as you can see, I'm busy."

"A rush job on the meat hook?"

He turned the object over in his hand. "Khopesh."

"Gesundheit."

Smethurst narrowed his eyes. "This is the blade of a Khopesh. A brutal weapon." He laid it on the table. "Dr. Polanski says you have questions about the Gilgamesh crown?"

"Last summer you met with Henry Dvorak about—"

"Who?"

"Dvorak. Henry Dvorak."

"I don't know who that is."

"A fake ruby? A glass chip he thought belonged to the crown?"

Smethurst shook his head. "No…"

"A great-grandpa who supposedly stole it from a Mesopotamia exhibit?"

"Sounds like a story I would remember," Smethurst said.

"Dvorak never asked you to authenticate a ruby?"

"What ruby?" Smethurst went to the bank of file cabinets and removed a folder. He took out three photographs and laid them side by side on the table. They showed a golden crown, with diamonds, sapphires, emeralds, and two holes where gems could be set. "We assume the other stones were garnets or topaz. Rubies were rare in Sumerian Uruk." He eyed Kelson. "If this Dvorak had a ruby from the crown—or perhaps a pair of rubies—it, or *they*, would be of inestimable value."

"Historically?" Kelson said.

"Yes, or on the open market."

"How much is 'inestimable'?"

"There are Chinese and Saudi Arabian collectors—Americans too—who would pay a million or more for it. It's hard to know. If there were a pair, the potential would be mind-boggling."

"I understand boggled minds." Kelson eyed the man curiously. "But a pair *doesn't* exist—not that anyone knows of, right? There's just a glass chip—that's what you told Henry Dvorak."

"I don't recall such a conversation," Smethurst said.

"And you would, being an expert in the field."

"Certainly. But if he finds a second chip—if his great-grandfather claimed he found another ruby in the display case—I would be happy to examine it."

"Why would you do that?"

He gave Kelson an odd look. "Professional interest."

"You're a glass expert too?"

"The first glass was Mesopotamian, dating to 3,500 BCE, a millennium before Gilgamesh. So, yes, I'm an expert, and I would be happy to look at anything Mr. Dvorak has."

"If he has anything," Kelson said.

"Yes."

"Which he doesn't," Kelson said.

"Or so he says?"

"I see no reason he would make this up."

Smethurst gazed at him. "People are complicated."

*****

Late that afternoon, Kelson drove onto the car lot at North Avenue Nissan. A salesman in a starched white shirt and bright green tie charged from the showroom. Shaking his hand, Kelson asked if Dvorak's ex, Cynthia, was around.

Crestfallen, the man disappeared back inside, and a minute later a blond, round-faced woman came out. She had long fingernails, painted milky white. She pointed one of them at Kelson. "What do you say we get you some new wheels?"

"I like my current wheels," he said.

She frowned as if everything about him was flat, including his wheels. Then she brightened again. "Perks," she said. "Everybody likes perks."

"Sure," Kelson said. "What's not to like?"

"We can do floor mats," she said. "Rust protection. Extended warranties. Do you need financing?"

"I don't need a new car."

"Key protection? Leather seats? Mud flaps?"

"No."

She stared at him. "Chrome rims? Tinting? We have excellent terms."

"I'm sure you—"

"What *are* you looking for?"

"A fake ruby."

She screwed her lips. "Did Henry send you?"

Kelson introduced himself. "I'm making the rounds."

"I tried to get him to sell that little nugget when he still thought it was worth something. But he's a loser."

"Is that why you left him?"

"When we met, he had big dreams. He still talked a good game when we married. But sooner or later you need to get real. If I only fantasized, I would wake up in my own bed every morning, and suddenly I would be eighty years old."

"Lying next to a compensation officer."

"Exactly."

"So you hopped into Steve Conti's Trans Am and sped away."

She wagged a fingernail. "Why should I apologize?"

"You could fish termites from a mound with that thing," he said, then shook the image from his head.

She lowered her eyelids at him. "Henry's living a lie. He should apologize to me for misrepresenting himself."

"Who would want his fake ruby?"

She scowled. "Have you talked to that woman he's seeing?"

"Honest Jenni Alimov?"

"Slut."

"And I talked to Bill Mackay."

"Peeping Tom. I'll tell you who you should see. Henry's sister."

"She's next on my list."

"She's like a smart version of him. She knows what..." She stopped short, and her eyes widened as a white minivan drove onto the lot. The van pulled into a parking space next to Kelson's car. A thick-shouldered woman climbed from the driver's side, a short man in khakis from the passenger side.

Without saying goodbye, Cynthia Dvorak charged toward the new arrivals, extending a welcoming hand, smiling like list price, plus taxes and fees.

*****

Dvorak's sister, Ava, lived on the ninth floor of an apartment building facing Lake Michigan. Hanging from the wall opposite the front door, a larger-than-life portrait of a black-haired, heavy-jowled man greeted visitors.

"Whoa," Kelson said. "He looks like a bastard."

Seven years older than her brother, Ava wore her blond hair short. A half dozen hoops hung on her left ear, from the rim down to the lobe.

"My dad was strict," she said. "And like a lot of intolerant men, he was a hypocrite. He died of a heart attack in bed – not his bed and not with my mom."

"But you give him the place of honor in your apartment."

"I give him the place where he reminds me every day to never be like him."

"I guess that reminder is worth more than a glass ruby."

"Glass? When I was a kid, my dad paid a jeweler to appraise it. The jeweler said it was banged up but real. Dad might have whipped us for dishonesty, but he hid that ruby away."

"Henry thinks it's fake. He took it to the Field Museum. An expert said it was junk."

"Then the expert was messing with him—unless the jeweler messed with my dad, and I don't know why he would. He wanted to buy it."

"Does Henry know about the jeweler?"

"Maybe not. He was a baby when our dad went to the guy. From the time we were kids, Henry and I have lived in different worlds. I went to college before he finished elementary school. We never talked much even when we were still talking."

"What did the two of you fight about?"

"He dreams of fishing in Alaska, skiing the Alps, backpacking through Nepal, but he lives a small life. I told him so."

"Do you think the story about your great-grandfather stealing the ruby is true?"

"My mom always believed it. I grew up without questioning it."

"Did you ever hear about a second gem that matched it?" Kelson asked.

"Is that another of Henry's stories?"

*****

The next morning, Kelson sat at his desk and announced each thought as it crossed his mind. Then he turned on his computer and searched the people he'd talked with. Henry Dvorak's birdwatching neighbor, Bill Mackay. The Trans Am-driving philanderer, Steve Conti. Honest Jenni Alimov. The expert in all things Mesopotamian, Richard Smethurst. The speed-demon divorcee, Cynthia Dvorak. The level-headed sister, Ava. Scrolling down page after page, Kelson learned that Ava was a real estate agent and that Richard Smethurst had side hobbies in collecting rare coins and playing darts, but little else that he didn't already know. Then he Googled *Gilgamesh.* He read that Gilgamesh was the "semi-mythical" son of King Lugalbanda and a goddess named Ninsun.

"A goddess?" Kelson snorted.

He opened a new site. It said Gilgamesh was the "historical" fifth king of the Sumerian city of Uruk, ruling in the twenty-sixth century BCE. He built city walls on which archeologists had found inscriptions naming him.

"That's more like it," Kelson said.

He opened a third site. It said that, as a "demigod," Gilgamesh wrestled giant monsters and moved mountains.

"Mountains, my semi-mythical ass," Kelson said.

He got up and went to his window. Cars and trucks, inching past in the morning traffic, glinted under the October sun. A man stumbled down the sidewalk, spun to face the traffic, and screamed at a bus.

"We all have issues," Kelson said. He went back to his desk.

He Googled *Mesopotamian artifacts* again. He read about a gazelle-headed charm, an ornamental banquet plaque, and a mosaic of a striding lion. He studied pictures of winged monsters, serpent-necked tigers, and hyenas of all sorts.

"Where truth crashes into make-believe," he said.

Then he called Henry Dvorak and arranged to meet for lunch at a hot dog stand a block from city hall.

*****

Two hours later, over a chili dog with a side of fries and a root beer, Kelson told Dvorak what he wanted him to do.

Dvorak took a long drink of Coke and dialed the Field Museum.

"I have another one," he said to the phone. He listened, then said,

"The same but a bit bigger." He listened again. "Sure," he said. "Noon."

When he hung up, he told Kelson, "He's on. He wants to look at it tomorrow."

"If I'm right, he'll try to steal it tonight. He won't want anyone to see you at the museum."

Dvorak's eyes shone with excitement. "What do we do next?"

"You go home to welcome him when he breaks in. I wait outside and join the party once it starts."

Dvorak said, "What happens when he finds out there's no second ruby?"

"Unless he goes after you with a dust brush and a microscope, you should be fine. And I'll be right outside."

*****

At nine o'clock that night, across the street from Dvorak's house, Kelson hunched in the front seat of his car. He'd eaten half of a Giordano's deep-dish pizza, extra pepperoni, and the remainder lay in a box on the passenger seat. He eyed the box lovingly but said, "No," sharply, as if the pizza might grow legs and climb onto his lap. The pizza he'd already eaten lay in his belly, making him drowsy.

He talked to himself about the lousy game the Bears had played the past weekend and about the Bulls' chances for a respectable season. He talked about the difference between reality and imagination—and about situations when he could hardly distinguish between them. "We all fool ourselves," he said. "Why wouldn't we?" Aside from a dog walker, who paused and stared at him through the windshield, no one seemed to care that he was there or even to notice him. Between nine-thirty and ten, he turned on and off the radio three times, cycling through the channels.

"Fine," he said, and reached for the pizza box.

As he bit into a cold slice, the lights in all the houses up and down the block went out, tripped by a cut wire or shorted transformer.

"Huh," Kelson said. He chewed, scanning the dark yards for movement. He gazed at Dvorak's windows, which barely glistened in the moonlight. Then he rolled out of his car, drawing his Springfield pistol from a shoulder holster, and ran to Dvorak's front door.

It was open, though he'd insisted that Dvorak lock it, and it had been shut just before he reached for pizza.

He yelled into the house. "Mr. Dvorak?"

Silence.

"Dvorak!"

Nothing.

He stepped inside. The front hall was dark.

He fished his phone from his pocket and turned on its flashlight.

"Quiet now," he said—then mumbled, "Fat chance."

Sounds came from upstairs. Footsteps. The wood-against-wood of a drawer closing.

Kelson called out, "Dvorak?"

Again, nothing.

He shined the light up the stairs. "First thing... secure the..." He continued down the hall and shined the light into Dvorak's living room. Empty except for a sofa, a coffee table, and two armchairs. He said, "An ounce of prevention..." He shined the light into a dining room. A blond-wood table, four blond-wood chairs.

He went to the kitchen. He aimed the beam at the refrigerator and the oven. He aimed at the counters and sink. He aimed at the dishwasher next to the sink.

The dishwasher door was open. Dvorak's body stuck out from under it.

"Oh," Kelson said.

Dvorak's head was crushed, more or less in the spot where Kelson had taken the bullet two years earlier. "But with less fortunate results," Kelson said. On the floor, inches from Dvorak's head, a chunk of metal gleamed in the flashlight beam. It was bloody and shaped like a meat hook. "Khopesh," Kelson said.

Footsteps upstairs. Another drawer closing.

"Fine," Kelson said.

Aiming the flashlight with one hand and the pistol with the other, he went back through the hall and up the stairs.

Dvorak had converted a bedroom at the top of the stairs into a combination home office and exercise room. Kelson shined the light at a desk and chair, a bookshelf, a weight rack, and a stationary bike. Next he stepped into a hall bathroom. He jabbed the shower curtain with his pistol barrel. Then he went up the hall to another bedroom, furnished with Dvorak's bed, a steamer trunk at the foot of the bed, and a burgundy-red dresser. A half-closed door led to a master bathroom. Behind that door, a sink dripped. *Tick, tick.*

Kelson shined his phone light at the bathroom. In a dark house, shadows could play tricks. He shined the light on the dresser.

He went to it and peered into the wooden box on top.

Empty.

"What did I expect?" he said.

Then the lights in the bedroom, the bathroom, and the hallway outside the bedroom flashed on.

He yelled.

A shower door slammed in the bathroom.

He yelled again.

Smethurst burst into the bedroom. He wore black jeans, black tennis shoes, and a black turtleneck shirt, like a cartoon thief. He also wore his white cotton gloves from the museum.

"A thief, a murderer, *and* a mime," Kelson said.

Smethurst stared at him, wild eyed. He moved toward the bedroom door.

Kelson aimed his pistol at him. "Stop."

Smethurst kept going. Kelson raised the barrel and shot a round into the ceiling.

Smethurst froze.

"Sit down," Kelson said.

Smethurst did, on the trunk at the foot of the bed.

Kelson moved toward him, aiming at his nose. "The ruby is real?" he asked.

Smethurst stared at him contemptuously. "What ruby?"

"You have a dead man downstairs and phone records showing you talked with him today. Lying won't help."

"Are you sure?" Smethurst said.

*****

According to a *Tribune* article a week later, the ruby Dvorak had brought to Smethurst the previous summer was genuine. The police found it taped to the bottom of a coffeemaker in Smethurst's kitchen. They also found files on his computer indicating he'd hoped to sell it through a London antiquities dealer convicted twice in the past for trafficking stolen artifacts.

The *Tribune* said the gem was thought to be one of a pair, referred to in archeological literature as the Mesopotamian Ladybugs—the Sumerians having associated the insects, among other beetles, with good luck.

Although the ruby wouldn't be restored to the crown until after Smethurst's trial, the news of the theft and Dvorak's murder led the Field Museum to open a special exhibit, which they advertised as *Hot Rocks: The Reputed Gilgamesh Diadem*.

On an icy morning in December, Kelson went to see it. Sure enough, in a row of diamonds, sapphires, and emeralds, there were two spots where stones the size of ladybugs once had been set. A placard said the story about Gilgamesh wearing the crown was probably a fiction. Some experts thought the thing was a late-Mesopotamian forgery intended to legitimize a dynastic claim. But everyone agreed that its beauty transcended history. The gem stones seemed to smile through time.

"Except for the gap teeth," Kelson said to a woman standing next to him at the exhibit.

She frowned at him. "But what do *you* know?"

Kelson could have pointed to the paragraph following the description of the crown on the placard. It summarized the excitement involving Henry Dvorak and Richard Smethurst. There, at the end, was Kelson's name, credited with apprehending Smethurst. The placard described him as intrepid and called his efforts clever and courageous.

"Nothing." Kelson smiled at the woman with all of his teeth. "As it turns out, nothing at all."

A Long Dark Road

Joan Hall Hovey

Elsie Heming had spent the afternoon visiting with her oldest and dearest friend, Nora Rivers, who was recuperating from a gall bladder operation. Elsie had picked up several containers of Chinese food for dinner, Nora's favorite. Finished cleaning up, she was folding the red and white checked dish towel over the towel-holder by the stove, when a darkness descended over the kitchen, like a bad omen. When she glanced out Nora's kitchen window, she was surprised at how dark it had gotten. Thinking of the drive home, she felt a small rush of dread go through her. She hated night driving. The nights came so early now.

"I didn't realize it was so late, Nora, so I'm going to take off," she said," shrugging into her coat. "Will you be okay?"

"I'm pioneer stock, I'll be fine," she said, pushing back a few strands of hair that had escaped the thick braid coiled around her head. "I'm sorry, Elsie, I should have reminded you, I know how much you dislike driving at night."

Dislike was an understatement. Elsie wished her friend would move back to the city but Nora loved it out here in the boonies, unlike Elsie who liked the hustle and bustle of the city, the rumble of trucks, car horns, and people laughing and talking as they walked past her window. The pulse of life.

They'd been sitting at Nora's ancient scarred and battered wooden table all afternoon. As strong as the oak it was made of, it had been passed down through generations of the Rivers family. Elsie remembered it well, having spent a good deal of time at Nora's house when they were kids. Nora was a retired teacher, a widow like herself. Elsie had worked in the school office. So much water under the bridge. So many memories.

"I didn't plan to stay so long," Elsie said. "But you're such great company I never want to leave."

"We have lots to reminisce about, you and I. You do me good, my friend. Best I've felt in days. "I'd insist you stay the night, but I know you don't like to leave Molly alone." They both were cat ladies. They hugged like the old friends they were. Very different in many ways, yet connected at a deeper level. Nora had been her maid-of-honor when she and John were married. And was there for his funeral and Elsie's plunge into despair in the months following.

As Elsie draped her teal blue scarf about her neck, she admired the portrait propped on the sideboard. Nora followed her gaze. "And I really do love this painting, Nora. Wish I had your talent."

"I kind of like it myself," Nora smiled. "Ginger is a good subject, aren't you, sweet girl." The aptly named cat had awakened from her nap and was presently circling Nora's ankles, purring loudly. "It's a great pastime. And it makes me happy."

Elsie hitched her leather bag over her shoulder. "I know. And I'm glad. But don't overdo. Take care of yourself. Let your body heal."

"Don't worry about me," Nora said, walking her to the door. "I must say I like your hair. I wasn't sure when you said you were going to stop coloring it. But it looks great; pearl-white in that youthful cut. You remind me a little of Helen Mirren. Call me when you get home, okay?"

"I will. And thanks." Elsie felt a glow from Nora's compliment. The truth was the chemicals had been making her hair thin enough to see her scalp. "Glad you like it. Looks like a storm on the way," Elsie said as they stood in the open doorway gazing up at the roiling black clouds. A low rumble of thunder sounded, not far off. The leaves on the trees shivered.

Ginger added her own complaint and Nora scooped the cat up in her arms.

"It was nice out when I left home," Elsie said. "Didn't think to check the weather, not that it matters."

"If you didn't check the weather then you probably don't have an umbrella in the car."

"Oh, well, I don't think I'll need…"

"Take this one," she said before Elsie could protest further, retrieving it from the small closet. "I've got several. You'll still have to get from your parking spot to your building."

Settling into the driver's seat, Elsie gave Nora a departing wave and pulled out of the driveway, past Nora's jeep, taking a mental snapshot of her friend standing in the doorway lit by the night-light, cradling her beloved Ginger in her arms. That would have made a great painting, too, Elsie mused as she picked up speed and headed down the Old Post Road. She'd enjoyed the drive on the way up. The leaves had turned color and were glorious in their golds, copper, and scarlets. But now the woods were dark against an angry sky. She couldn't wait to get home to her apartment, get into her fuzzy white robe, then find a good thriller to watch on Netflix. Simple pleasures.

But she couldn't complain and mostly she was grateful. She was in good health and took care of herself, did her daily exercises, and walked the streets of her little city, always finding something to stir her interest, a historical building, a view of the bay. When the weather didn't cooperate she opted for her treadmill. Of course, she had her share of issues that aging brought to everyone, some neurological damage to her feet, arthritis, and so on. But nothing serious enough to slow her down and she mostly tried to ignore it. She wasn't *that* old. Seventy-three wasn't the seventy-three of her childhood. Several months back, she'd even taken some well-intended advice and dated a very nice-looking, pleasant man for a short time, but she didn't fit right in his arms. When she was with him she felt like she was cheating on John.

John would be gone five years this December. They'd been watching an old black and white noir movie on the Turner Channel. Something with Barbara Stanwick. He'd gone to make coffee and minutes later, she heard the thud of his falling and raced into the kitchen to find him on the floor. Just like that, he was gone. His eyes were open, though no longer seeing. There'd been no history of heart problems, no warning of a massive coronary. He'd had a full checkup only a couple of months earlier and received a good bill of health. Her life was changed forever.

For a long time after he died, she wandered around like the victim of a bomb blast. Cried till there were no tears left, and her eyes felt like they were scraped with sandpaper. Unconsciously, in the night, she would reach for him across the empty space in the bed. Sometimes a wall of grief would wash over her like a tidal wave, taking her breath, threatening to drown her. But we all suffer terrible losses during our lives. More so as we age. At some point, you just have to get on with it.

They'd had no children, though they tried. "Stop trying so hard and it will happen," the doctor said. But it never did, so they became everything to one another, and they'd been happy. She was kind of a happy camper by nature anyway, adaptable, John said. *You're the kind of woman who, if the door won't open, you'll carve out a new one.* She smiled at the memory and hoped she was that woman he described. But she missed him every day, his wry sense of humor, his touch. He was her safe place.

A light rain began to patter against the windshield and Elsie turned on the wipers. She tuned in to the station that played music of the forties and fifties: a little Glenn Miller at the moment, that sweet song. *Honeysuckle Rose. God, that was an old one.*

The Old Post Road was long, a narrow tunnel hemmed in by dark woods, and seemed even longer tonight. Most drivers used the new main highway now. She passed only a couple of cars along the way. Lulled by the rhythm of the wipers blended with the music, and the hum of the wheels on rough pavement, Elsie's heart leaped when the car dropped suddenly with a bone-jarring thump that reverberated through her body, followed by a jerky vibrating ride as the car took her further down the road. *Whump! whump! whump! She* eased off on the gas and brought the car to a crawling stop on the shoulder. Sat unmoving until her heartbeat settled down. *Oh, no, please not here. But it was* here; in the dark and the cold, and the rain. She had a flat, she was sure of it. Damn. She got out of the car long enough to feel the cold rain on her face and confirm that the flat was on the front passenger side.

Even as she dug the cellphone out of her bag to call Triple A, she knew with a sickening sureness that the thing would be dead. She'd purchased it for emergencies like this one and didn't miss the irony of that. She was always forgetting to charge it. John took care of mechanical issues or else she'd be fortunate enough to be near a service station if something went wrong with the car. Not this time.

Right again; the cellphone was dead. No pulse, zero, zip.

Hazard lights flashing, she sat and contemplated her situation. She seemed to recall seeing a spare tire in the trunk. After a moment, she got out of the car and hurried around to the front passenger side. A wet chill crept inside her coat collar and she turned it up, tucking the scarf inside her coat as a bolt of lightning flashed very low in the sky followed by a deafening crack of thunder.

She opened the trunk. The spare tire was there, but no jack, not that she'd know how to use it though she'd watched John change a tire often enough. She should have paid more attention. Her car was just a few months old, used but in excellent shape and she'd given the trunk only a cursory check.

Hearing a distant car motor, Elsie's spirits lifted. As the headlights grew brighter, she stood at the edge of the road waving her arms frantically, hoping to flag it down, but the car sped on by, leaving her to stare after it until the taillights disappeared around a bend in the road. *Thanks a lot.*

Someone else will come along, she told herself.

Forcing herself to remain calm, she remembered passing a store and small service station a few miles back; she could walk there if she had to. She was a good walker. She knew there was a flashlight in the glove compartment because she'd put it there herself. God knew, there was no place darker than a country road at night unless it was the grave. The lights were sparse along this road, but Elsie hadn't given it much thought since she'd expected to be home long before now. She clicked the button on the flashlight, and hope dimmed along with the faint, almost non-existent light. *When was the* last *time you changed the batteries?* she chastised herself. A further search in the glove compartment turned up no extras. *So what now?* The rain was coming down in earnest now, drumming on the roof. Well, nothing to be done for it.

Exiting the car again, she peered through the darkness and the driving rain hoping for a glimpse of headlights, willing them to appear. Standing there in the driving rain, she had never felt so alone or so stupid in her life. Might as well get back in the car. She'd be able to see any approaching headlights in the rearview mirror. She was cold now, wet and uncomfortable. Surely someone was bound to come along. The roar of the rain sounded faintly like applause in the dark confines of the front seat, as if mocking her.

She'd been sitting there for maybe ten minutes when she started at a sudden rapping on her driver's window, sending her heart into her throat. She turned to see a man smiling in at her, releasing a flood of relief through her. She lowered the window. He was a nice-looking man in a black raincoat with the hood drawn up. He held his flashlight off to the side. He was maybe in his mid-forties. The older she got the harder it was to tell people's ages. A policeman?

"Looks like you're having a problem, Ma'am," he said, almost shouting over the rain. *Where had he come from?* Glancing in the rearview mirror, she saw the van parked behind her car. She'd neither heard nor seen it drive up. She must have looked away from the rearview mirror for a moment.

"An understatement, to say the least. I've never been so happy to see anyone in my life. Thank you so much for stopping. I have a flat tire and nothing to change it with, not that I could anyway. There's a spare tire in the trunk but I wouldn't think of asking you to change it in this downpour. If you could just call Triple A for me that would be great. I'm afraid my cellphone is quite dead."

"I expect they're pretty busy on a night like this. Heaven knows when they'd get here and it's not safe for you alone on this road. But it's no problem changing the tire. It'll just take a few minutes. I've got a tarp in the van. Give me your keys and I'll get the tire out of the trunk. You just stay in the car so you don't get any wetter than you already are. Ma'am." Elsie handed him the keys and told him her name.

"Hi. Name's Ed. Ed Jones. I had a favorite aunt named Elsie."

Clutching the keys in his large hand, he smiled at her and

disappeared behind the car; a second later the trunk lid went up. Elsie watched in the rearview mirror as he lifted out the tire and laid it down beside the flat tire on her passenger side, then went back to the van to get the tarp, she assumed. Rain hammered on the roof. He's going to get drenched, she thought, despite the hooded raincoat.

She was surprised when the door of the van opened and two more men climbed out. Something in the way they moved seemed almost predatory. and Elsie's earlier sense of unease shot up a notch.

The dark rainy night and all. That's all it is. That, and your imagination. Trying to quell her nerves, she turned up the music on the radio and was about to withdraw her hand when the music was interrupted by a news bulletin: *"Police are on the hunt for three men who went on a crime spree earlier tonight robbing several businesses in Granville. One man was fatally shot and a young woman was rushed to hospital with life-threatening injuries from...."*

It was as if an anvil had dropped on her heart. Her hand trembled as she switched off the radio, her throat tightening. Had they heard the bulletin? Still looking in the rearview mirror, she thought they seemed nervous. What were they in deep conversation about? They couldn't have heard anything over the rain. Could they? Almost in sync, as if they'd read her thoughts, the two abandoned their discussion and looked in her direction. She looked away.

Elsie's heart raced, every cell in her body on alert. She could smell the rush of adrenaline that told us to fight or run. She wasn't much of a fighter. She would dare to drive away right now, flat or no flat, but she knew they'd be on her in a minute. And then she remembered that Ed Jones, if that was his real name which she now doubted, had her car keys, so driving away wasn't an option. He was clearly their leader. Her rescuer was no rescuer at all, but a con, a charmer. The other two were younger, rougher around the edges, and looked like what they were: criminals. Thugs.

Or was she jumping to conclusions? *Maybe they weren't the same men after all?* She knew she was grasping at straws. As if to confirm what she already knew, the taller and slighter of the two men grasped his arm, as if nursing a wound, his face twisted in pain. *He'd been injured.*

She might be forgetful but she wasn't stupid. She watched crime shows on TV, so knew exactly what was going on. These men weren't doing her any favors; they needed to switch vehicles, the only reason they'd stopped. They were desperate. They wanted her car. *You're in big trouble, Elsie Heming.* She had seen their faces; she could identify them. They had already battered at least one woman tonight and shot someone else; they wouldn't think twice about getting rid of her. You didn't need to be a genius to know how this would end for her. Elsie felt like the proverbial sitting duck.

"Get out! Run," she could almost hear John say. *"Run into the woods, my darling. Hide."*

Stricken with terror, but determined to fight for her life, she eased her door open an inch and waited. Remembering Nora's umbrella on the seat beside her, she gripped it in her hand. Not much of a weapon, but something.

Thunder rumbled and clapped and growled a short distance off. A steak of blue-white Lightning snaked across the black sky, turning night into day. *Once the tire is on, I will disappear. They will lose the van. And they would lose me.* She let out a long, shaky breath, counted in her head, visualizing a clean leap from the car. *One. Two. Three.*

NOW!

Elsie was out of the car and running down a brief stretch of road and into the woods, turning her ankle in a dip in the shoulder, not quite a ditch. The heels of her shoes sunk into the soft, wet earth, pain stabbing her ankle with every step. But she trudged on.

*****

The three turned in surprise. The one who'd introduced himself to Elsie as Ed Jones chuckled. "Fast for an old girl. Get her, Ham. Throw her in the van and ditch them both. Jake, grab the jack from the van. We need that wheel changing, fast as you can."

Ham, a bull of a man, short, with sheared hair, took off after her, guided by his flashlight, took off after her.

Jake watched Ham disappear into the woods, then set about changing the flat.

Less than ten minutes later he tightened the final lug nut, then slipped into the driver's seat. The wounded man climbed gingerly into the back seat and lay back. "I'm bleedin' bad, man."

"Quit bellyachin'. Make a tourniquet out of your tee-shirt, or something."

A short distance into the woods, Elsie ducked behind a tree and remained there, not moving, not daring to breathe as she watched the man run through the woods after her, thrashing and slipping as he went, once falling on all fours, cursing her in vile terms.

Elsie tried to make herself part of the tree, feeling the rough, wet bark against her cheek, aware of the sharp smell of pine and resin. Thunder boomed straight above her, and the rain came down with a new fury, pounding her bent head. Water ran from her hair, drenching her through her clothes within seconds and plastering her hair to her head like a tight cap. Close behind her, she heard his angry curses, his boots lurching through the woods as the circle of bright light darted here and there, seeking her out.

"Where are you, bitch?" came an angry bellow close by.

This could not be. She'd been chatting and sipping tea with her old friend just an eye-blink ago, it seemed, and now here she was; trapped in a nightmare, hiding in the woods from a madman who was intent on killing her.

She could see him now, a silhouette behind the flashlight he held and she clung to the tree like a second skin, quieting her gasps. The storm is your friend, she told herself, as she tried to relax her trembling body. Her sodden coat hung on her like a heavy blanket. She watched the circle of light dart here and there through the woods, spot-lighting patches of rain-battered trees, as in a stage setting. She could hear his stomping boots, his grumbling, and curses as he searched out his prey. Suddenly, the light flashed in her eyes and she blinked but didn't move. When he came at her, she drove the point of the umbrella into his throat with all the strength that was in her, and then she ran as fast as she could, hobbling on the ankle, hearing his howls behind her. Twigs and branches and twigs clawed her face, drawing blood that blended with the rain.

After a few minutes, she heard him say to himself, *"To hell with this,"* and the halo of light from the flashlight was moving away from her, gradually growing smaller, returning the night to darkness.

The rain was easing up. the storm calming, leaving the woods silent. Elsie remained still as a posed mannequin behind a different tree. But the tune of safety was a siren's song. She didn't trust it. Had he really left? Given up? It might be a trick. After what felt like an hour, she allowed herself to release her grip on the tree and let out a long, slow breath. She was soaked through, shivering uncontrollably against the cold that had burrowed into her aging bones. Her heart was fluttering wildly. Finally, she stepped out from the tree. She had taken one wobbly step when the blaze of light revealed the patch of woods before her and she realized he'd come up behind her. The flashlight arched through the darkness and in the instant before it came down, she heard the rumble of a motor starting up and visualized her bag with all her information, in the back seat. And then saw nothing at all as pain exploded inside her head, sending shards of lightning bolts through her skull. Elsie sagged to the ground, the thick blackness wrapping around her like a great shroud.

Far away, the faint wail of a siren sounded.

*****

"Mrs. Heming... Elsie... can you open your eyes?"

A woman's voice, soft, concerned.

Her lids fluttered open long enough to see a blurred vision of the nurse in white standing over her. White walls behind her. Medicinal smells under the stronger aroma of coffee permeated the air. Opening her eyes made her headache worse, so she closed them again. "My head hurts," she managed, her voice raspy. Her mouth felt dry as chalk and tasted of chemicals. The doctor came to see her and then the nurse brought her tea. She slept then and woke feeling much better.

It was a shock when she finally realised she'd been in a coma for four days. She learned she wouldn't be alive if not for Nora, who became concerned when Elsie didn't call her, as promised. "So I called you," Nora said. When I got no answer and knew you'd had plenty of time to get home, I grew worried. I turned on the radio just for the company while I paced and that's when I heard the news bulletin about the police trying to track three men in a van and called the police."

Elsie got the whole story piecemeal over the next couple of days, mainly from Nora. They'd found her leather bag in the ditch, relieved of a small amount of cash, and credit cards which the police had already reported stolen.

It wasn't until the next day when police spotted Elsie's car parked around the back of a rundown motel, that the three of them were rounded up and dragged off to jail in handcuffs. Two had to be taken to hospital, one with a bullet in his arm, the other with a puncture wound to the throat, serious but neither life-threatening. "I owe you a new umbrella," Elsie said.

"Oh, yes, I'm very concerned about that umbrella," Nora teased. "By the way, Molly says to tell you she misses you."

"Thanks for taking care of her."

"She's a joy. She and Ginger are already fast friends."

"Good. Why am I not surprised."

"When I think of what could have happened... you wouldn't have lasted the night out there with your injuries. Maybe even without them." She'd had some swelling, resulting from a brain bleed, along with severe hypothermia, various cuts, scrapes, and bruises. "It was pretty dicey for a while," Nora said. "You're no spring chicken, you know."

Elsie tried not to laugh. "I know."

"Anyway, I'm glad you're back."

"Me too." She saw out her window the enamel blue sky, not a cloud anywhere, the top of the church steeple. A seagull high up. "Well, maybe not entirely back," she said. I don't remember anything about what happened to me. The last thing I recall is seeing you standing in your doorway with Ginger in your arms."

Though that wasn't entirely true. She vaguely remembered the kindly face of a man with snow-white hair, and a deep, reassuring voice telling her that she'd be fine as she floated through the darkness to someplace warm and dry. The ambulance probably, she thought now. They'd no doubt removed her wet clothes and wrapped her in blankets.

"Your rescuer has been calling every day," the dark-eyed, very sweet nurse told her later that day. She was turning her pillows, straightening and smoothing her top sheet and blanket. "Those lovely roses are from him. Nice gentleman. Not hard on the eyes, either." She winked.

He arrived in the evening, during visiting hours. He was tall with thick, white hair as she remembered, dressed casually in jeans and a leather jacket. "Hello, Elsie. Ms. Heming."

"Elsie's fine. You must be George. The roses are lovely, thank you."

"You're welcome."

"I'm told you rescued me," she smiled. She wished she'd put on a little lipstick. At least the scratches and bruises were fading.

"Glad I was there. But one of them would have found you. Your shoe prints going into the woods were pretty clear. You're looking a whole lot better since the last time I saw you. Full name's George Watson," he said, drawing up a metal chair, the leg scraping lightly on the floor. His closeness gave off a hint of citrus and the outdoors, evidenced by his tan. After a brief shyness, they were chatting like old friends. He was a widower, with two grown boys, and almost grown grandchildren, he told her. Both families lived away, though visited quite often. Along with volunteering with the emergency team, where he'd spent most of his working life, he also taught an automotive class at the community college in the spring and fall

The nurse hadn't lied. He looked around her age, maybe a tad younger. Slate blue eyes, laugh lines fanning out from them. Two prominent lines bracketed his mouth, above a strong jaw line, if a little softer now. A face that had lived an interesting, if not an easy, life.

Over the next couple of weeks, George came to visit every day, always with a thoughtful treat. There was never a lack of something new to talk or laugh about. If someone else came to see her, or if he thought she looked tired, he would graciously take his leave.

"I'm going home tomorrow," she told him on the day her doctor signed the discharge form. "Nora is picking me up." She'd almost begun to regret going home. Almost. But the truth was, she couldn't wait to sleep in her own bed. And of course, see Molly.

He looked disappointed and she wondered if he might have wanted to drive her home.

"I'm glad for you. Please stay well, Elsie."

"Maybe I'll take your automotive class in the spring," she said impulsively, emboldened by the way he was looking at her. "Do you think you could teach me how to change a tire, George?" God, she was flirting like a teenager. It felt good.

"I'm quite sure of it," he said, grinning. "But I hope I don't have to wait until spring before I see you again, Elsie. "

Life can change on a dime, she thought. *John had simply gone out to the kitchen and never returned to her. This could have been her last chapter. And death lasts a very long time.*

"Call me," she said.

Deadly Sideshow

J. T. Seate

New Orleans, 1949

Kismet or karma? Destiny or divine providence? I could have asked myself such questions the night fate led me into a seedy carnival sideshow on the outskirts of Old New Orleans. Most cops have experienced car chases, armed gunmen, murder and mayhem, but crime can also involve the fairer sex. Occasionally you cross paths with a special breed of skirt. That's what happened on a late October night under a peepshow's tent.

While I watched the uniforms cuff Charity and place her in the back of a patrol car, I sensed a shimmering red blouse beside me. In it was a ravishing brunette.

"Excuse me," she said. Her voice low and husky. "Charity's a good kid. Give her a break."

I made her for pushing thirty, but not by much. For someone in her line of work, time had been kind. Her blouse revealed the tops of alabaster breasts stacked as nicely as feathered pillows. The rest of her was just as delectable, built like a Marvel comic book character come to life. Following the journey, I found her eyes and kept them riveted to mine. "And you are?"

The female observed me with green-eyed solemnity. "Sophie Barton. I'm the den mother around here."

"Head stripper, huh? Well, Sophie, it appears one of your cubs got careless and let a butcher knife slice through a midway barker's neck rather than a watermelon."

"The cad she's been living with? He's dead?"

"Charles Laskey. As dead as Rudy Valle's comeback."

Her bosoms swelled. "Serves the piece of garbage right. She's better off, but you're wrong about Charity, Mister. She's a rabbit. She'd run first."

It sounded like Sophie might've enjoyed watching the pathologist gut dear ole Charley. "This is New Orleans," I reminded this red-lipped doll. "Impulsive behavior is practically expected."

"Charity couldn't cut up anyone."

"We'll be taking your statement at a later time, Miss Barton."

"Would you ask Charity to call me the minute you finish working her over? She'll need a place to stay while your boys are playing with evidence in her apartment."

"Unless the boys downtown decide to book her tonight," I said, more interested in Sophie's shape than her words. "We'll let her make a phone call when we're through."

In a voice as stiff as starch, she said, "See that you do, Detective…?"

"Peters. Detective William Peters."

Sophie Barton shot me a look designed to drop charging elephants. She shrugged as if my name meant less than nothing, all business and sass, probably wondering who had cast this asshole for a part in her life. Then she turned on a dime and walked through the dusty earth beneath the protection of the canvas canopy with a swaggering wiggle that said, "I'm your wildest dream." Sticking a Camel between my lips, I thumbed open my Zippo, and leaned the cigarette into its flame. Sophie's sculpted torso probably drew more customers into the sideshow than a hole in a window screen draws flies. How many poor slobs had braced her over the years only to discover a cougar rather than kitten?

I followed the black and white in my unmarked car and thought about all the damsels who'd snapped due to some abusive piece of garbage, as Sophie had so delicately put it. I knew well the savagery of which humankind was capable, especially carnival types.

But my mind returned to the luscious form of Miss Barton. I wouldn't have minded getting jake with Sophie, her lips against mine, her body occupying the space between me and my mattress. She was the kind of dame who could make a man climb walls. Her appearance represented hopes and dreams. A fresh source of sustenance tantalized me, but she was undoubtedly all too familiar with coppers threatening to bust her and her tent full of Kewpie Dolls.

After spending most of the night grilling Lynn Dubois, a.k.a. Charity, and asking if she knew anyone who might benefit by turning the dearly departed Charley into a morgue job, we let her go on her own recognizance. Eliciting a confession would beat the hell out of questioning every sideshow and carnival employee who knew Laskey, but I knew she hadn't committed the crime. Most of these young women, naive girls from small southern towns, wouldn't see the evil in Jack the Ripper if you showed them the pictures of his six dead hookers.

A Packard Coupe picked Charity up and I went home to my small riverfront apartment which was sinking into the Mighty Mississippi. A breeze rippled through the trees carrying a whisper of death along with the scent of the river. It takes a tough egg to deal with both sides of the law. This time of year always conjured a long ago autumn when I was a rookie cop. My partner and I stumbled upon a backwater pigsty not far from the carnival grounds. It contained body parts of a Cajun male, the chunks left for the swine to root and dispose of. I chased away the memory and returned to the night at hand. It was Friday and Halloween began at midnight, a busy night for brawls. I wondered how many drunken Cajuns whose ancestors all married ugly would carve one another into 'gator bait' by Monday morning.

In my line of work, I've learned that humans will not take a straight diet of any one emotion. Happiness, fear, grief, even contentment all play into most personalities. I was no exception. I listened to a serenade by cicadas and bullfrogs along with the plaintive sound of an occasional lonely foghorn somewhere upriver, a searching signal issued in a mournful hope of reply. They were sounds which reminded me of twisted hopes and broken dreams, a longing for something which seemed just out of reach while hoping not to be dragged down into the black slime that waits just beneath the surface of everything. I fought the urge to dwell on the shapely Miss Barton, or the familiar tug of a dangerous thirst. Instead, I indulged in two of my three vices: Scotch and the Blues.

*****

The next morning I called Miss Barton and requested her presence at the station. I told the boys I wanted to interview her personally because she reminded me of a doll I had broken down once, due diligence and all that. Yeah, the line had whiskers, but I didn't care.

"The sisterly type, eh Peters," the Chief sneered, his mouth crowded with bad teeth and his belly, no doubt, full of Friday night gumbo.

Sophie Barton arrived late in the afternoon. I escorted her to a private room. She looked prim and proper compared to the night before, more like a society dame who'd just come from a Garden District soiree than the leader of a small time herd of strippers. Her pinned-up raven hair highlighted her long neck. The fading sunlight from a small window wrapped around her.

Through a swirl of blue smoke from our cigarettes, Sophie spent an hour and a half telling everything she knew. I injected an occasional "Uh-huh" as she spun her tale about Charity's whereabouts on previous evenings and what she knew of the deceased who currently resided on a slab in the morgue as cold as a dime's worth of baloney with a big smile carved into his neck, still as cement, a red tag tied around his big toe.

Her gaze was cool and detached. I made sure not to ask pointed questions and she seemed appreciative. The who, where, and whens fell from her mouth. Eventually, I stopped prodding her to go on.

"Thanks for not giving me the third degree," she said so pleasantly I almost believed her.

"You mean the spotlight and the rubber hose? We got rid of those a couple of months ago."

"I mean for taking me seriously. A refreshing quality for a cop. Most of you gumshoes take me for a high-class bimbo." Her eyes fell to her hands, folded in her lap as if in prayer. I wondered if her winding road might have begun as a good Catholic girl.

Another cigarette died and entombed in an ashtray. A thin trail of moisture glistened in Sophie's décolletage. I tried to keep my eyes trained on hers, but that little wet trickle got in the way. Even as she sat in the metal chair, Sophie Barton moved with the sensual promise of what could be, every inch of her shouting "Female."

She looked up, wondering why I hadn't responded. "So, are there any more questions, Detective Peter, or can I go home and take a hot bath?"

"That's Peters, Miss Barton." I had no other reason to hold her. "That's all for now, but please—"

"Don't leave town, like they say in the movies," she said.

"I was going to say, call me if you think of anything else that might help."

"Sure thing, Peters." She stubbed out her fifth butt, uncrossed her legs and stood, straitening her skirt. "I'll call the minute the real killer confesses."

There were enough bodies loitering around the station to cast a De Mille epic. I led her past the normal assemblage of cops, boozed-up rednecks, and hookers, through the heavy scents of sweat and musk to the double doors leading out of the station.

"Maybe we could have a drink some night you're off," I heard myself saying.

Sophie stared at me. A little frown line appeared between those pretty eyes that danced with frantic energy as if she could see into my soul. Then a wry smile softened her features. "In the carnival game there aren't any nights off except Sunday."

"Maybe Sunday then?"

She eyeballed me from underneath long, sooty lashes. "You know where to find me, Detective. But tonight's going to be crazy, being Halloween."

Sophie sashayed down the steps toward her Packard Coupe, the same vehicle that picked up Charity the night before. She was a knockout who could not only stop traffic but could make it go backward. Her smart-mouth had done little for me, but the way she walked sure as hell did.

The earthy tones from a distant saxophone floated on a chilly zephyr. In contrast, I listened to the staccato of Sophie's high heels attacking the sidewalk and grow faint with each deliberate step, mocking me. A burp of smoke curled from her Coupe's exhaust as I watched the vehicle disappear into the haze of twilight through the bloom of its tailpipe.

The day was dying. Night had fallen into shadows as quick as the closure of Venetian blinds. The moon was a golden glob of honey camouflaged in a cradle of cirrus clouds. The breeze off the river caressed my face like a woman's hands. I breathed deep and tasted the fragrance of the city not unlike the hard packed grounds of the carnival's Midway. It was a night made for, maybe not romance, but for contact.

The distant whine of a police siren brought me back to earth. *Damned fool asking her for a date.* I returned to my desk, sank into my chair, loosened my tie, and kneaded the back of my neck. For extra motivation, in lieu of Scotch, I decided on a little blast from a flask in the back of a drawer before doing the paperwork on Sophie's interview. The elixir spread its warmth from my gut to my extremities, but without relaxation, not with Miss Barton's firm and fully packed chassis stuck in my brain. While I sipped, I thought of seducing her. She might run girls through their paces under the canvas, but she was no tramp that would do a guy for postage stamps, or take her clothes off when she was down on her luck and then keep taking them off to pay for drugs, or booze, or support some carny yo-yo like Charity had done. Sophie was a sliver under my skin, like something stuck to my shoe, something I couldn't shake off, but I brought my attention back to the homicide case. If you let your mind drift too far, somebody will steal your wallet.

I loosened my collar further. My mother once told me people who were uncomfortable with anything tight around the neck must have hanged in a previous incarnation. She'd had a sack full of proverbs picked up from a voodoo nanny back in her youth, and some enticing tales surrounding Halloween. I credited my discomfort not to legends, but to the image of Sophie strutting down the street wearing nothing but her high heels.

With the help of the Irish penicillin I poured down my throat, I muddled through the bureaucratic paperwork. Then I slung my jacket over my arm, put on my snap-brimmed fedora and left the station. Although my stomach was getting sore at me, there was an uncomfortable undertow to my thoughts.

I drove by the carnival grounds wondering if I really wanted to see

Sophie's metamorphosis from her sweetheart street-wear into some Halloween getup that might include tasseled pasties. The backbeat of music and laughter emanated from the promenade—two earthy, fundamental sounds of New Orleans. I could almost smell warm bodies and cheap cologne.

Hanging another Camel from my lip, I reached for my lighter. The shiny object turned in my hand, my thumb rubbing against its smooth surfaces while I thought how Sophie's skin might feel. The lit tip on the fag flared red in the gloom as I inhaled, coughed, inhaled again letting the nicotine wander through my lungs. *Red—the color of danger.* I exhaled wishing the escaping smoke would expunge a few of my demons along with it.

My thoughts leapfrogged from Sophie to Charity, to the corpse lying in the morgue with the new mouth carved into his neck like a homemade Halloween mask, to the violent nature of the human species.

A couple stood in the sallow light of the midway's entrance hand in hand. Overwhelmed with emptiness, tortured by loneliness and an urgent hunger, I realized the laws of lust are as immutable as the laws of nature. Then I flipped the cigarette out the window, dropped the clutch and drove away, letting life move on for everyone else.

My abode was as empty as a broken promise. On the river, a lone horn wailed a single note, deep and mournful. It was a time when families would be telling one another goodnight, when men would be screwing their wives in both shacks and mansions. Thoughts of Sophie were destined to remain with me through the night, an unfinished mystery with the end yet to be written. And darker than the night were my thoughts, the tug of my third vice stronger than ever.

*****

The phone rang at 6AM cutting through the cottony layers of sleep like a cat's claw. I bolted upright in bed, rocked into wakefulness, tripping over a bad dream. My eyelids snapped open like a runaway shade. Their sandpapery feel told me I could have used more beddy-bye.

A call this early meant only one thing—somebody else had bought the farm. "What?" I said into the phone after the seventh ring with the voice of a mean-tempered zombie.

At 7AM, I was at the crime scene. A street cop started a rambling dialogue of the situation.

"Do me a favor, Sarge. Pretend I'm your wife and skip the foreplay," I told him.

"Here it is. Another slug took a slash to the throat last night, cut from ear to ear, just like the last one. This one ain't associated with the carnival though."

I nodded and entered the room where the fresh kill rested. The body lay splayed on the kitchen floor with a gaping, funhouse grin under his chin, a fly already investigating one of the dead man's eyes. His skin was the color of rain-soaked newspaper, his lifeblood spilled like oil through a blown gasket. "Trick or treat," I said to no one in particular. I revisited my list of those who had a connection to former homicides, providing my next opportunity to pursue Sophie Barton.

At 9AM, I parked my jalopy in front of a marble statue of a Confederate soldier covered with pigeon drippings and black and orange party streamers. The remnants of All Hallows Eve didn't lighten my mood nor put a melody in my heart as I got out and started to walk.

The canopy of overcast sky provided the usual high humidity, burning away the sordid dealings of the night. A covey of small children herded along by a gaunt nun passed on the sidewalk. She gave me a strained smile. Next came a group of kids with Halloween masks still perched on their heads providing a carnival-like atmosphere all its own. When they saw me, they quieted and parted to go around me like a stream around a boulder. It was more than subservience to an adult. I felt sure they sensed something better left undisturbed.

Next, I came upon a wino leaning against a storefront while the smell of simmering shrimp hung in the air along with the soulful rhythm of a bluesy song. On the far side of the street, a Creole woman was setting out her cheap souvenirs and trinkets beneath the overhang of a second story balcony, her pipe clenched between her teeth. An old black man was already tap-dancing for a group of tourists. A wisp of steam rose from wet pavement evoking things that wouldn't stay buried, taking on an unnerving quality.

An old city with a past, with its two-hundred year history of blood, sweat, and tears—with its fortress ramparts and its slave markets. New cities weren't good for hiding secrets. They were cheap imitations, towns without souls. This was a place shrouded with superstition and only as safe as the strength of its levies. But the soul of the city set in a swamp—*Vieux Carre*—had a strong, resilient heartbeat.

The whole scenario gave me pause. I reflected on the thin line between life and death, between these innocents and the scene I'd witnessed only hours before. It's a flimsy mask that divides beauty and ugliness, between innocence and a bloodbath. But this wasn't the time to dwell on how to penetrate the barrier. I had other fish to fry. I was on my way to find Sophie.

A wisp of steam rose from wet pavement with its portentous quality of something otherworldly, something carried on the breeze from its nooks and crannies, and the above-ground cemeteries. But there was something passionate too. Consider the woman I hadn't been able to get out of my mind—a woman who ran girls through their paces at night, but by day, resided behind a protective wall covered in creeping vines in a neighborhood that fostered pride.

I reached Sophie's address. Beyond a wrought iron gate nestled a courtyard draped with wisteria vines, dappled with shadows from an ancient live oak which dripped tattered banners of dusty Spanish moss. A wind-chime hung on a branch. It tinkled in a faint breeze. *Ghost music.* "A serenade for the dead," the superstitious contingent of the city would have said.

New Orleans was a strange and intoxicating place like the exotic mix of humanity which inhabited it. The elegant decadence of Halloween, Carnival, and *Mardi Gras* hung in the air like overripe fruit to accompany those feelings of otherworldliness and passion—all of it reminders of why I stayed in this mosquito-laden parish.

I climbed the balcony to Sophie's bungalow and found her China red door, the color of violent death and strong feelings. Both applied to the current case. I knocked on the door. *Not bad digs for the Madam of the*

Midway, I mused and was about to rap again when the metal peephole opened. A deep-set, greenish-gray eye the color of fine Burmese jade that could only belong to one of The Quarter's more exotic birds studied my face. I listened to locks disengage and a chain slide free.

When the door opened, Sophie looked at me with a lazy smile. My subconscious twitched from the smell the nicotine on her lips, which called like a naked lady riding a wild stallion.

"It *is* Sunday, Detective Peters, but couldn't you have called first?"

She was barefoot, her toenails painted bright red. Draped in an elegant, silver-blue silk robe which sculpted her body into an amazing thing, she was as sultry as the town we lived in, wrapped in a garment that could have said, "Danger: Handle with Care." Her business, after all, was to elicit from men the very response I was having.

I tried not to stare. "Are you alone?"

"Isn't everyone?"

"You look like a million bucks," I told her.

Small upturns lit the corners of her mouth. "In Confederate money maybe, this time of day."

A sense of humor. That was a plus.

"May I come in?"

Sophie stepped back with a rehearsed graciousness. She was wearing nothing beneath the sleek robe. She knew it. I knew it. She knew I knew it. With difficulty, I turned my head and took in her domicile. It was so clean it aggravated me a little. I wondered how she'd take to catfish sautéed with beer at my not-so-pristine joint along the river. Her place was clean, yes, but it dazzled with too many floral patterns for my tastes. A mahogany-encased radio sat in a corner of the bungalow's living room. Big band music for lovers was playing. It wasn't the Blues, but it wasn't bad.

Sophie turned the radio down, then said, "You know, detective, you could see more of me than this for a buck under the big top."

A soft silver ribbon held her hair back from her face. She looked more beautiful than the photo of the dead movie star that graced the cover of *Silver Screen* which lay on an end table. "Don't get me wrong, doll. I'm not looking to see you that way. I mean…"

"Relax. I guess I'd rather have you show up than a couple of thugs with bent noses and eyes like bloodhounds jamming through my doorway," Sophie said. "Sit down and I'll pour you a cup of coffee, unless you would prefer bourbon and branch water to soothe whatever ails you."

"No thanks. I'm basically a Scotch guy."

I sat on one end of the living room sofa. Sophie returned from the kitchen with two steaming cups of java and sat on the opposite end, a fresh fag lodged between her first and second fingers. The sight made me hunger for a Camel, but I merely took a sip from the cup and watched the languid smoke rise alongside her face in a long gray-white ribbon forming a hypnotic sway that pleaded for company.

"Can you tell me where Charity has been since you picked her up at the station?"

"Yes. She stayed with me that night, and then with a friend of mine last night. I told her not to come back to work for a few days and I called her several times to make sure she was all right. Why?"

"There was another homicide last night, not far from where Charity and her chum, Laskey, were shacked up. This guy's throat was slashed from ear to ear with a straight razor, same MO as Laskey. If your friend can confirm Charity's whereabouts, she might be in the clear."

Sophie appeared encouraged by this turn of events. "I'm sure Janie will say Charity and she were together the entire time. So this clears her?"

"Let's just say whoever did the deed last night got their cutting lessons at the same school."

She took a deep drag on her cigarette and exhaled seductively. "That is very good news. Not about another stiff, I mean the fact that it had nothing to do with Charity."

My eyes traced their way up Sophie's long neck to her deep icy pools that sparkled through a landscape of greenish-gray Lifesavers. "There *is* another connection. The type of character this stiff happened to be."

"What, you mean another loser, working over his old lady, someone who deserved what he got?"

"That's pretty close."

"The fewer like them, the better. I've seen many girls like Charity who end up with losers and worse yet, they wind up with a needle in their arm thanks to some pimp or Cracker. They deserve someone who will take care of them instead of the other way around, but it so seldom works out that way." She placed her smoke in an ashtray and scooted back on the sofa, raised her arms, liberated the ribbon and ran her hands through her hair as if to comb out whatever thoughts lodged in her pretty head.

"Let me tell you a story," Sophie said. "I had a cute little trick working for me a couple of years back. She was taken in by this sweet-talking customer. I told her he was no good. Told her she could do better, but she was headstrong, up from the bayous. Hadn't been around much. Can you guess what happened to her?"

"I have a pretty good idea."

"He ended up torturing and killing her. Left her battered body in the river." The demur Sophie was departing. She now seemed more like a volcano ready to blow. And still, she was beautiful. "Thanks to a magnificent job by your cronies at NOPD, they never caught him."

"Take it easy, Sophie. I sympathize."

Sophie observed me. "Sorry, flat fo…Bill. I guess that's a little harsh. Your job isn't easy, scraping victims off the walls and trying to find their killers. It's just that early on I decided I wouldn't take crap off anyone or become like so many women…. But what has your case got to do with Charity now?"

"Nothing. It has to do with *you*."

My final word hung in the air between us. Sophie's hands dropped from her dark brown mane. "Look. I don't know what your angle is, but I'm just a hardworking gal looking out for my girls," she said with an edge that could have cut a diamond. "Whatever you're trying to buy, Peters, I'm not selling. I'm not looking to cause problems or to get cozy with a cop. Get the picture?"

"In Technicolor, but I've been looking for *you*, Sophie, in the worst way. In fact, *you're* exactly the person *I've* been looking for."

"What makes me so special?"

I looked at the stubborn set of her jaw and dove straight to the heart of the matter. "Now get this news flash and hang on to it. I found something at the crime scene this morning. A tube of lipstick. I believe I could make a strong case about who it belongs to."

"That's ridiculous."

"There have been several murders around town in recent months. Some cut, some shot. There's been a similarity to all of them—men who abuse or otherwise take advantage of those weaker than themselves. Pretty, isn't it? Just the kind of man you profess to despise, guys who you'd as soon cut up as look at, bottom-feeders who deserve what they get."

Sophie jumped to her feet almost upending the coffee table. "Now wait a minute, buster, you can't play me for a sucker and hang this rap on me. I can find alibis a mile long and two miles wide concerning my whereabouts on almost any night you pick."

"Maybe, but I'm guessing your fingerprints are all over that little gold tube, and there's the cigarette butt with your brand of war paint."

Sophie's glorious cream complexion had turned ashen. "You really think I would kill because I have a low opinion of men who use women? If I wanted to do some joker in, I'd poison the SOB. You can't mean you'd let me take the fall…wait a minute." She dashed to the far side of the room and picked up her purse.

I stood and walked up behind her. I was sure she didn't carry a heater inside her bag, but you can never be absolutely sure of anything when dealing with a cornered female on the defensive.

"When did you take it?" she screamed. "When I used the powder room at the station or when you escorted me out? I wasn't carved out of a wet mouse turd yesterday, ya know."

I took her by the shoulders and turned her toward me. "Simmer down, doll face. Don't pop your cork."

"You were nice yesterday. Why the tough-guy act now?" She held her wrists out toward me. "Are you going to cuff me? I bet you like to play with handcuffs?"

"Don't worry, sister. I won't tell if you won't." I took her hands in mine. "I'm not planning to give the evidence to the lab boys."

"Did you pull that little stunt because you believe I'm a murderess?" Her tear ducts were on the verge of springing a leak.

"If I pulled a stunt, it's because I like the way you think. And, I like the way you look. We're not on opposite sides here." I moved closer. The front of her robe brushed against my jacket. "I admire your swagger, your shape, the cut of your jib, let's say."

"I don't understand. What about the murders?"

"That's where I come in. I think you will appreciate me all the more when I tell you last night's murder was necessary to give Charity an alibi."

Now Sophie looked at me with curiosity.

"Here's how it goes. I've established an alibi for one of your little chickens. Last night's execution should keep the NOPD from dropping on the peep show like a bunch of dive-bombing pelicans. And I'm not going to implicate you."

"I still don't get your angle. Why the phony evidence?"

"You're the woman who can replace one of my three vices with something more wholesome. I'm not someone who smacks females around. I hate those little punks as much as you do. The city doesn't need any more cockroaches, so I do something about them when I can. There are plenty of morgue material names on a list I keep in my noggin. I have a photographic memory, Sophie. That's an important thing to remember. Keep nothing that will tie you to a crime. Protecting you and your girls from further accusations isn't too high a price to pay, is it? Nobody knows I'm following up with you and nobody needs to. We're on the same team, you and me."

"So you swat away the bad guys like they were mosquitoes?"

"Like the scum they are."

"A rogue cop just looking out for my best interests as long as I play ball, huh? Use me like a puppet to achieve your own ends?"

"Looking out for *our* best interests. The only justice in this world is what you create yourself, *Cherie*."

"Maybe you expect me to take a knee and kiss your ring or something."

"Not exactly what I had in mind."

Sophie looked at me in a new light. "You're a very strange man."

"One of a kind. Aren't you the lucky one?"

"They say there's something in a man's eyes that always gives away his vices. I think I can see it now."

"My vices have rather large appetites."

She now knew the power I could wield. The truth is something I would share only with a woman worth having and holding on to. What we knew could land both of our butts in water hot enough to boil crawfish.

I studied her eyes looking for a hint of panic, or the twitch of a trapped bird looking for an escape. Neither was there. I should have known Sophie would be a tough cookie come hell or high water. But I wanted more than a lack of fear. I wanted her to feel the thrill of a new relationship enriched with an enticing secret.

The pad of my thumb brushed the corner of her mouth. "Relax. It'll be good, you'll see. We will be a rhapsody. Moonlight and magnolias."

Sophie's face reflected resignation as if realizing she'd struck a deal with the devil. Her green, unreadable eyes returned to me. Her voice deepened and took on the quality of a caress. "You get a window to open and then a person needs to crawl through before it closes. I get it."

"That's the ticket." I reached around and gave her bottom a squeeze. Then I lit two Camels with my trusty Zippo. I was glad I had her, but she had me also, not that anyone would believe her. She was quite a prize, but others would only see an uptown stripper who fell for a flat foot investigating a homicide.

Sophie's radio was playing Bennie Goodman's rendition of *Begin the Beguine*, much more pleasant than the calliope music from the midway. It seemed like the right song for the two of us to start a relationship on. I thought of women as various kinds of jam, each unique and flavorful. But Sophie was like rich honey spread on toast over creamy peanut butter, a voodoo priestess in silks and satin. While her mind would always be a work in progress, I could possess her body which might help on nights when she, a little Scotch, and Billie Holliday seemed too little to replace my urge to play a different rhapsody, to make the city a safer place for women.

That's all I've done, really. Not such a terrible vice, but perhaps the hours of pretending to investigate acts *I've* committed can be better spent with Sophie, willingly or unwillingly, in my arms.

I peeled open the robe of this Louisiana flower revealing the voluptuous body beneath. The opportunity to ogle her flesh hypnotized me. Only two irregularities—a small smooth burn mark along her left breast and a pencil-line white scar just above the knee. I couldn't have expected her not to have picked up a few nicks here and there. I had a few of those myself. Still, she was like a hot and spicy sauce poured over a thick piece of beef, capable of either heartburn or heaven. If she wasn't paradise, she would do until the real thing came along. The veil of cigarette smoke was thick in the air, forming an undulating cocoon around the two of us.

Different music played in my mind, the sultry, pulsating rhythm of a saxophone and a woman's seductive, sexy voice singing to my soul. I took another drag, admired Sophie from top to bottom and listened to the tender music in my head.

Sophie didn't bother to close her robe. I waited for a breathy retort, but she only closed her eyes. I took her smoke and set it aside along with mine. My fingers lost themselves within her raven tresses as I searched her face looking for acceptance or disgust, but found neither. The room seemed as small as a phone booth. The tip of my tongue grazed her earlobe. Her only visible reaction to my probing was a sigh of resignation.

She had nothing to say about my plans for her. A lot of talk always means lies. It goes along with the protective mask everyone wears, a freak show not limited to Halloween or *Mardi Gras* but year round, especially in the unreal world of sideshows, carnival barkers, and con men.

Sophie's eyes opened as if they were the counterbalanced lids belonging to a porcelain doll. It was a little spooky even for a man who had done the things I've done. An odd stillness came over her. Her breath puffed against my cheek. "I'll cook up a couple of steaks, Bill," she said, her words as silky as her garment. "I have a special spicy Cajun sauce I think you'll like."

Watching Over You

Madeleine McDonald

As I planned, Matt found me dead on Monday morning.

Even before the doctor shipped me off for autopsy, he called the police.

"Take your time, Mr. Jones," Inspector Capley told Matt. "If we could just go over it once again."

Matt fidgeted as he talked. The inspector had manoeuvred him into taking a hard chair facing the window, while the inspector occupied the leather sofa we had chosen together—one of Matt's rare contributions to our domestic finances, courtesy of an unexpected tax refund.

"You say you spent the weekend alone in a friend's holiday cottage." His voice was hard-edged with disbelief.

"I'm a songwriter." Matt paused, but the inspector said nothing. "I've got a big show coming up and I need my own space. I work better that way. Ask anyone who knows me."

It's true you needed space for your talent to flourish. You also craved attention. I know you inside out, Matt, right down to that instinctive pause when you disclosed your trade to the inspector. Even in a fraught situation, even with an uneasy conscience, you expected admiration. I know you. I watch over you still.

Your life was going nowhere until I stepped in. My guidance was gentle, but uncompromising. As I pointed out back then, all for one and one for all worked only if everyone in the band was equally talented. If it hadn't been for me, the four of you would still have been doing gigs in backstreet pubs for the price of a few beers. I rescued you.

Your old mates in the band weren't right for you. I did you a favour discouraging that connection, and they had the decency to keep away once you moved in with me. For a while life was the way I wanted it, just you and me together.

Your solo career took off in fits and starts, and it was while working as a session musician that you discovered your true métier, writing songs for other people. Sometimes you called me Melody, claiming I inspired you. When you were grouchy you called me Miss Moneybags.

At first it amused me that you couldn't get enough of your new friends, the fair-weather ones. I used to go through the wastepaper basket and examine the invitations you discarded, the ones from fledgling PR firms, or local radio stations beyond the M25. You bought a cork notice board to display the others, the ones to first night parties where you were certain to rub shoulders with chat show hosts and famous actors. Fickle, devious, disloyal Matt.

My Matt.

Sunlight laid a stripe across the carpet, just beyond the toes of Matt's trainers. "Ask the neighbours," he insisted. "The people in the brick cottages. I was on the piano all weekend, they must have heard me." A fly buzzed against the window. Matt gagged and made a sudden exit. "Sorry," he muttered when he returned. "It was the fly. There were flies when…when I found her."

The inspector opened the window and shed his jacket. "No need to upset yourself, Mr. Jones, we're making routine enquiries. Perhaps you could make us both a cup of tea." Balancing cup and notebook, he led Matt yet again through his movements over the weekend, hour by hour, until Monday morning.

"I needed to collect some stuff, and I thought Melanie would be at work."

The inspector pounced. "You wanted to avoid Miss Redburn. Why was that?"

"No." He tailed off. "I mean yes. The truth is that Melanie—Miss Redburn—had been difficult lately. You know what women are." He gave a man-to-man smirk.

"I wouldn't know, sir," said Inspector Capley. "Suppose you tell me."

Now, Matt, that was naughty. Difficult you called me. I had every right to be difficult. Eleven years we had together, eleven years of me making sure everything ran smoothly, and you were planning to dump me for some little trollop just out of stage school.

The theatre and media people took you up after you wrote the songs for a couple of shows, wanting their share of reflected glory. Whereas me, I wanted you from the start. The first time I saw you, fronting the band in the Red Lion, I knew you were my man. And to think that I only set foot in that pub because I had missed my train and needed the loo. I forgot about catching trains and stayed for three hours, watching you. The next night, and the next, and the night after, I was back.

Watching you. Watching over you.

Your new friends wondered aloud why you stayed with me, unaware I was listening behind the door. You took good care not to inform them it was me who paid the mortgage and the bills.

I was the one who had faith in you, Matt. It was me who allowed your talent to flourish.

"Well, Mr. Jones? In what way was Miss Redburn difficult?"

"She…" Matt swallowed, and confided in a rush. "She was jealous. She made wild accusations."

"Was there any truth in her accusations?" the inspector asked, his manner almost indifferent.

"We were finished. We both knew it." Matt hesitated. "But we needed time to sort things out. It's not that easy when you've been together for years."

"Were you seeing someone else?" The inspector was not going to let Matt off the hook.

"Sort of," Matt muttered. "But it's not serious." The man-to-man smirk re-appeared.

"Yet you still had a key to Miss Redburn's flat?"

Matt answered easily. "Melanie never asked me to return it. My new place is small, and I left some stuff here."

"Did anyone else have a key?"

"Her parents. Oh God! I haven't told them yet." He sank his head in his hands. "I'll have to do it, there's no-one else."

"Could one of her friends have had a key?"

"Melanie didn't have friends."

The inspector raised his eyebrows in silent query.

"I mean she didn't do company. I told her she couldn't expect me to live like a hermit even if she wanted to." Matt's tone held echoes of simmering grievance. "Don't get me wrong, I was fond of her, but she had her quirks."

"There wouldn't have been another man if that's what you mean," he added. "Melanie wasn't like that."

Thank you, Matt, for that one honest answer. I was a one-man woman and you knew it. Even as you prepared to eradicate me from your life, you were flattered that my existence revolved around you.

"Tell me, Mr. Jones, you say you moved out a couple of weeks ago. Did Miss Redburn throw you out?"

"It wasn't like that," Matt mumbled.

Matt hated scenes. He would go to any lengths to avoid them. So he denied his affair with Emma Adams.

"What's got into you tonight, Melanie?" He waved away my questions. "I can't avoid meeting the girl. For heaven's sake, there were fifty other people at that party, why pick on Emma?"

That was low cunning, Matt. You had a gift for wrong-footing me, for making your wants sound so reasonable. You told only part of the truth. You told me about the first-night party: you omitted to tell me about the candlelit dinners for two at that expensive riverside restaurant. You took her to our restaurant, the one where we celebrated our tenth anniversary.

Matt spent an uncomfortable couple of hours but in the end the inspector took his leave. The next time he was interviewed it was at the police station, under caution, in presence of a solicitor. In the meantime my flat had been searched, my colleagues interviewed, my bank accounts scrutinised. The findings were surprising.

"Well now, Mr. Jones," the inspector began, his face stern, "We have established that Miss Redburn applied for a loan of £100,000, using her flat as security. She received the money on the Thursday before her death. On Friday, she transferred the entire sum to your current account. What do you have to say?"

Matt sat stunned. "There must be some mistake. Melanie would never give me that much money."

"She lent you money before. Don't deny it."

"We were living together. Everybody accepts little loans from their partner."

"You call £200 a little loan? A month ago. And £500 two months before that?"

His protests cut little ice with the police, for Matt's affairs had also been investigated. The investigation revealed that he owed almost £50,000, mainly for expensive recording equipment for his new studio. Again they pressed him about his habit of borrowing small amounts from me.

Then Inspector Capley changed tack. "Well, Mr. Jones, if you can't tell us anything about the money, perhaps you recognise this?" He held out a sealed evidence bag containing a bottle of Drambuie, tilting it to show a small amount remaining at the bottom.

Matt looked, and shook his head. The solicitor reminded him he had the right to remain silent.

"Did you ever purchase a bottle of Drambuie?"

Matt answered readily. "Yes, sometimes. It's not my favourite tipple but Mel enjoyed a tot now and then."

"And the last time you bought a bottle?"

"Months ago." He paused to recollect. "I know, it was for Mel's birthday, but we finished that one, I remember us finishing it together when we were skint after Christmas and we had nothing else left to drink. I remember because she was in one of her moods and I thought it might cheer her up."

What Matt did not know was that I read his early emails to Emma in which he described me as a fixture in his life. "Darling Em, saying goodbye last night was torture. But I can't leave Melanie. Not yet. She's like a faithful, butt-wagging Labrador, always pleased to see me come home. I can't kick her in the teeth. I just can't. I couldn't bear to see the hurt in her eyes."

The night we finished the Drambuie, I sowed the seed in his guilty, befuddled mind. When he mentioned the possibility of a trial separation, I gave myself free rein. I stormed, begged and wept. The subject was dropped: his emails to Emma became frantic.

The one theatrical performance of my boring life and what a success I made of it!

"And you haven't bought a bottle since?"

"No. No, I'm sure."

"Then how do you explain the fact that the most recent fingerprints found on this bottle are yours and Miss Redburn's? How do you explain that the dregs contain a strong painkiller? We've checked with her doctor and Miss Redburn was never prescribed any kind of painkiller."

Despite his denials the noose closed round Matt. The tablets were the kind his mother used. The police had hard evidence, bank statements going back years. Unimpressed by his assurances that his next show would be a money spinner, all they saw was mounting debts.

"God knows how he thought he could get away with it." Inspector Capley commented to his colleagues when he reviewed the file.

"Might it have been suicide?" ventured one subordinate.

"Nonsense, she was under the thumb. Women like that never commit suicide; they botch the job so they can blackmail the man when they come round."

You had no reason to doubt the empty Drambuie bottle went in the bin. I saved it, later adding the contents of a miniature bottle, a size easy to conceal in my handbag. I stole the tablets from your Mum's bathroom. The longer you put off telling me about Emma, the longer I had to prepare my grand exit.

It was worth it. I am a one-man woman and loyalty deserves respect.

Which one of us will you think about in jail, Matt? Pretty little Emma or me, your faithful, butt-wagging Labrador?

I'll be there, watching. Watching over you, Matt, like I always have.

The Usual Unusual Suspects

Jim Guigli is a student of many interests: SCUBA diver, auto-mechanic, and gunsmith, served as an Army Security Agency Russian Voice Intercept Operator in Japan, studied Judo, played basketball, was a career mechanical designer for National Labs LBNL, SLAC, & LANL, trained at Gunsite with pistol & shotgun, designed and supervised firearms competitions, toured Quantico as an FBI Citizens Academy graduate, designed a 400 sq ft kitchen addition to his house, and earned BFA and MA degrees in Art/Photography. Jim is an active member of SMFS, PSWA, & Sacramento CWC.

Publishing History: Won 2006 Bulwer-Lytton Fiction Contest Grand Prize. The Grand Prize sentence and one other were published in *It Was a Dark and Stormy Night*, by Scott Rice, Friday Books, London, 2007. Self-published 2013 Kindle Bart Lasiter novelette, *Bad News for a Ghost*. Other Bart Lasiter appearances include *Looking for Mishka, (Rock and a Hard Place Magazine, Issue 7, Winter 2022)*, and *Cane Mutiny (May 2022 Pulp Modern Flash). Listen to the Gunsmith* appeared in the *July 2022 Guilty Crime Magazine*. Two new non-Bart pieces – *Ben Hurt* and *Not Funny* – are due to appear in *Guilty Crimes Magazine* during 2023.

Jim has written various articles for the *PSWA newsletter* and NorCal Chapter newsletters of MWA and SinC. Website: www.jimguigli.com

Glen Bush is a retired teacher who now lives in the Lake of the Ozarks, Missouri, USA. Since retiring, he has been writing crime noir short stories and urban fiction. While teaching, he published over thirty academic literary articles and book reviews. Bush has recently published several crime noir and mystery stories in the US and England in *Crimeucopia – Say What Now?, Retreats from Oblivion, Close to the Bone,* and *The Yard: Crime Blog.* Bush is also an active member of the

Short Mystery Fiction Society

Edward Lodi has written more than 30 books, both fiction and nonfiction, as well as a poetry chapbook. His short fiction and poetry have appeared in numerous magazines and journals, such as *Mystery Magazine*, and in anthologies published by *Cemetery Dance, Main Street Rag, Rock Village Publishing, Superior Shores Press*, and others. His story *Charnel House* was featured on *Night Terrors* Podcast. His *Death on a Pedestal* appears in *Crimeucopia – The I's Have It*.

Cate Moyle writes mystery stories; she's won numerous recognitions, including the latest as a Silver Falchion Award finalist. She is also an award-winning poet, having been published in literary journals from *The Southeast Review* to *Wicked Alice*. Moyle's latest writings appears in *Mystery Tribune* and is forthcoming in *Bowery Gothic*. You can find her on Twitter @CateMoyle.

John 'Jay' Andrew Connor has been writing and publishing under a menagerie of names and genres since the late 1970s – sometimes even professionally. He's worked at a variety of jobs, in a variety of locations, and has also published small press, and semi-pro magazines in the past. Sadly, even though he is now on medication, he's at it again. The second instalment of the Memindip 'saga' (*Memindip and the Persian Poet*) appears in *Criminal Intent – A Murderous Ink Press Sampler* (MIP 2020.)

Bob Richie wonders why author bios are always in the third person, and wonders why he cannot instead write the following: "I'm Bob Ritchie. Originally from California, I now live (and write) in Puerto Rico (Check out that sky!) My work has appeared in *Unlikely, Penumbric Speculative Fiction Magazine, Triangle Writers Magazine*, and others. I am a musician, as well, and have had the privilege of collaborating with Jon Anderson. Now, if I could just occupy a room containing a guitar, a piano, and a Paul McCartney, my life would surely be complete." He supposes we'll never know.

Michele Bazan Reed's short stories have appeared in *Woman's World* magazine and several anthologies, most recently *Detective Mysteries Short Stories, Mid-Century Murder, Malice Domestic 15: Mystery Most Theatrical, Masthead: Best New England Mysteries 2020, The Fish that Got Away, Crazy Christmas Capers* and *The Big Fang* (2022).
A member of Sisters in Crime and its Guppy Chapter, Private Eye Writers of America, and the Short Mystery Fiction Society, she won a 2017 Daphne Award in the unpublished mainstream mystery category. Michele's Crimeucopia appearances have been with *The Coveted Coverlet* (*Crimeucopia – The I's Have It*) and *Attempted Murder of Crows* (*Crimeucopia – Tales From The Back Porch*).

Eve Fisher has been writing since elementary school, and her mystery stories have appeared regularly in *Alfred Hitchcock Mystery Magazine* and other publications. She's part of the mystery writers' blog, *SleuthSayers,* at www.sleuthsayers.org (every 2nd Thursday!), and a fan in Shanghai is translating her work into Chinese. She's been volunteering at the local penitentiary with the Lifers' Group for over a decade, which gives her interesting acquaintances. A jack of all trades, she also writes historical articles, fantasy and science fiction. She lives in South Dakota with her husband and 5,000 books. Eve's previous Crimeucopia appearances have been with *Collateral Damage* (*Crimeucopia – We're All Animals Under The Skin*), *Truth & Turpitude* (*Crimeucopia – The Cosy Nostra*), and *Nude with Snow Geese* (*Crimeucopia – Say What Now?*)

Michael Wiley is the Shamus Award-winning writer of two series of PI novels – the *Joe Kozmarski and Sam Kelson* mysteries – and two other crime series – the *Daniel Turner* and *Franky Dast* novels. His short stories appear often in magazines and anthologies. Michael is also a frequent book reviewer and an occasional writer of journalism, critical books, and essays. He grew up in Chicago, where he sets his PI stories, and teaches creative writing and literature in North Florida. His kids accuse him of being as disinhibited as Sam Kelson.

Joan Hall Hovey is a Canadian author, living and writing in Saint John, New Brunswick. Her novels include *And Then He Was Gone, The Deepest Dark, Night Corridor. Nowhere To Hide, Chill Waters* and *The Abduction of Mary rose.* Available on Amazon and most online bookstores. Her short stories include *Dark Reunion* which appears in *Investigating Women*, published by Simon & Pierre, Canada.
Joan's *Freeing Henry* appears in *Crimeucopia – The Lady Thrillers*, and *When the Curtain Fell* appears in *Crimeucopia – The Cosy Nostra*.
To learn more about the author, check out her websites at http://amzn.to/M7mVAR and www.joanhallhovey.com.

J. T. Seate states that after reading a few early stories to his parents, they booted him out of the house. Undaunted, he continues to write everything from humor to the macabre, spanning a gulf between such publications as *Horror Novel Review's Best Short Fiction Award* to the *Chicken Soup for the Soul* series.

Madeleine McDonald finds inspiration walking on the chilly, windswept beach of her Yorkshire home. As a former precis-writer, she enjoys the challenge of writing flash fiction. Her short stories have been broadcast on BBC radio, and published in various anthologies and journals. Her latest novel, *A Shackled Inheritance*, is available from Amazon Kindle. Her most recent win is the *Press 53* contest for November2022, https://www.press53.com/53word-story-contest.

Karen Skinner - Hilary Davidson - Pauline Gostling -
Linda Kerr - Kate Miller - Tiffany Lindfield - Lena Ng -
Ginny Swart - Sandrine Bergèss – Michelle Ann King -
Amanda Steel - Kelly Lewis - Paulene Turner-
Claire Leng - Madeleine McDonald - Joan Hall Hovey

16 stories ranging from the 14th to the 21st Century,
all from women authors whose forte is crime.
Paperback Edition 9781909498198
eBook Edition 9781909498204

CRIMEUCOPIA

We're All Animals Under The Skin

Featuring: John Gerard Fagan, Nick Boldock,
Weldon Burge, Chris Phillips, Dan Meyers,
Jeff Dosser, Eve Fisher, Emilian Wojnowski,
Fabiyas M V, Lamont A. Turner, Edward Ahern,
Robert Petyo, Al Hagan, Caroline Tuohey,
Steve Carr, Bobby Mathews, Michael Bracken,
and June Lorraine Roberts

18 authors take time to look under the skin of the people who sometimes inhabit their heads, and put what they find down on paper.

Paperback Edition ISBN: 9781909498235
eBook Edition ISBN: 9781909498228

A Crimeucopia Family Gathering

17 writers take us on Cosy journeys - some more traditional,
while others are very much up to date.
Eve Fisher, Alexander Frew, Tom Johnstone, John M.Floyd,
Andrew Humphrey, Joan Leotta, Gary Thomson,
Eamonn Murphey, Matias Travieso-Diaz, Madeline McEwen,
Lyn Fraser, Ella Moon, Gina L. Grandi, Louise Taylor,
Judy Penz Sheluk, Joan Hall Hovey and Judy Upton.
Paperback Edition ISBN: 9781909498242
eBook Edition ISBN: 9781909498259

The five writers here have very respectable track records in the Western genre, and are old hands when it comes to telling compelling stories.

So join

John M. Floyd - Alexander Frew - Jim Doherty - Bruce Harris and Brandon Barrows

and let them take you back to a time of six-guns an' whiskey, an' wild, wild fiction.

Paperback Edition ISBN: 9781909498266
eBook Edition ISBN: 9781909498273

CRIMEUCOPIA

As In Funny Ha-Ha

Or Just Peculiar

Putting the Outré back into OMG are
Jesse Hilson, Gabriel Stevenson, Maddi Davidson,
Brandon Barrows, Robb T. White, Regina Clarke,
Martin Zeigler, K. G. Anderson, Andrew Hook,
Ed Nobody, Jody Smith, Michael Grimala,
W. T. Paterson, James Blakey, Emilian Wojnowski,
Andrew Darlington, Lawrence Allan, Ricky Sprague,
Bethany Maines, John M. Floyd and Julie Richards

Paperback Edition ISBN: 9781909498266
eBook Edition ISBN: 9781909498273

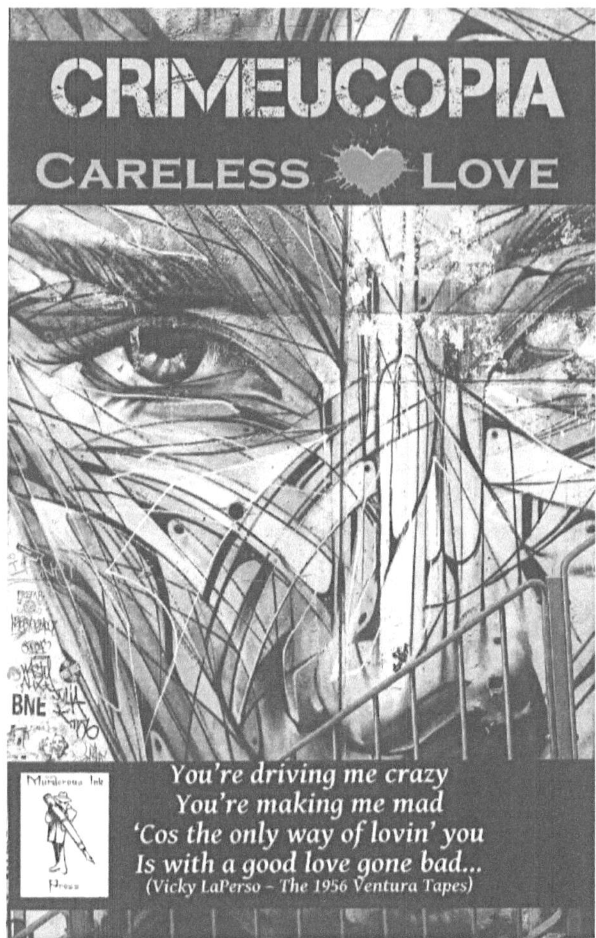

Fifteen writers tell us about affairs of the heart – some with humour, some with a darker intent, and others that are never quite exactly what they seem. Is it all about manipulation? Can there be more than one agenda? And does Love really conquer all, even when it's supposedly blind? Or maybe Love is just an old Devil, looking for mischief?

Steve Sneyd, Ange Morrissey, James Roth, Michael Wiley, Gustavo Bondoni, Matthew Wilson, Peter W. J. Hayes, Wil A. Emerson, Brandon Barrows, Bern Sy Moss, Michael Anthony Dioguardi, Russell Richardson, Robert Petyo, Sam Westcott, Bryn Fortey and *Vicky LaPerso* – all of whom take us on roller coaster rides through a fictional Tunnel of Love.

Paperback Edition ISBN: 9781909498303
eBook Edition ISBN: 9781909498310

Investigators and investigations are the mainstay of most Crime fiction sub-genres. Everything from the original *Golden Age* of country houses and the amateur sleuth, through to the high tech ultra-modern 21st Century – a place where the cyber investigators sometimes appear to be baffled by old-fashioned motivations of power and greed, and human foibles such as love and revenge.

So is there any real difference between the Private and the Public Sector investigators? Not much, if writers are to be believed, and the two can often be found straddling both sides of the 'what's legal procedure?' fence.

Of the twelve authors contained within, eleven are voices new to the world of Crimeucopia - and although the theme is *Investigators*, the material ranges from Cosy, through to not too Hardboiled - and most are touched with a vein of humour, be it light or dark. Rather like a box of chocolates…

Paperback ISBN: 9781909498327 eBook ISBN: 9781909498334

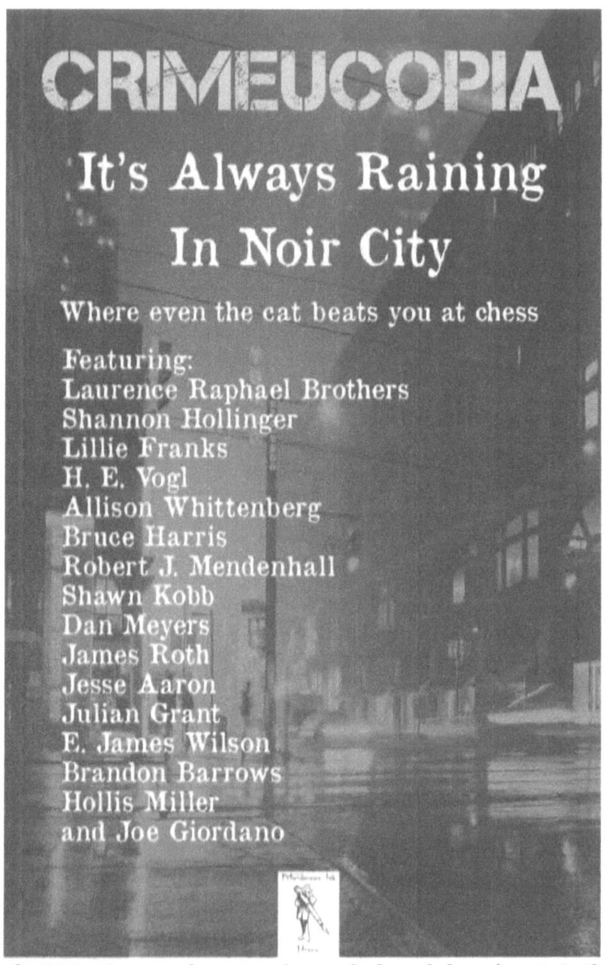

Is the Noir Crime sub-genre always dark and downbeat? Is there a time when Bad has a change of conscience, flips sides and takes on the Good role?

Noir is almost always a dish served up raw and bloody - Fiction bleu if you will. So maybe this is a chance to see if Noir can be served sunny side up - with the aid of these fifteen short order authors.

All fifteen give us dark tales from the stormy side of life - which is probably why it's *always* raining in Noir City....

Paperback Edition ISBN: 9781909498341
eBook Edition ISBN: 9781909498358

Small town, big city, watercooler or the back of that 1950s beat-up Chevy Bel Air with the leather back seat that your parents told you never to get familiar with. It doesn't matter where you hear it, gossip is 100% pure ear addiction – and knowledge is, after all, power when all's said and done.

So why don't you settle down, get yourself comfy, and pour yourself a drink – long and tall, or just short and nasty, the choice is yours – and let these 16 story tellers spin their tales as only they know how.

Paperback Edition ISBN: 9781909498365
eBook Edition ISBN: 9781909498372

CRIMEUCOPIA

When the theme is no theme at all, you've just got to ask the question

Say What Now?

Featuring:
Peter Ullian,
S. E. Bailey,
N. M. Cedeño,
Edward St Boniface,
Jan Glaz,
Eleanor Luke,
Momodou Bah,
Eve Fisher,
John M. Floyd,
Joan Leotta,
Glen Bush
and DL Shirey

Sometimes editors are forced to reject submissions through no fault of the author. It could be a wonderfully written manuscript, but if the editor cannot place it, then what do they do?

MIP has been lucky in its flexibility and its "Can we start a new project with this?" attitude. Some of the dozen authors contained within are seasoned professionals, having been published in the likes of Alfred Hitchcock's, Ellery Queen's, or other notable publications, while some are making their publishing debuts as Crimeucopians. And while the quality throughout remains exceedingly high, the subject spectrum is the widest we've published so far. But that's only fitting when you consider that the theme of this Crimeucopa is that of No Theme At All.

And in true Murderous Ink fashion, with a dozen authors to choose from, you're bound to find something you'll like, and something you didn't know you'd like until you've read it.

Paperback Edition ISBN: 9781909498389
eBook Edition ISBN: 9781909498396